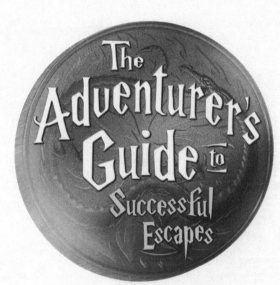

The Adventurer's Guide to Successful Escapes

WADE ALBERT WHITE

Illustrations by **MARIANO EPELBAUM**

LITTLE, BROWN AND COMPANY

NEW YORK BOSTON

Text copyright © 2016 by Wade Albert White
Illustrations copyright © 2016 by Mariano Epelbaum
Excerpt from *The Adventurer's Guide to Dragons (and Why They Keep Biting Me)* copyright © 2017 by Wade Albert White
Illustration in excerpt from *The Adventurer's Guide to Dragons (and Why They Keep Biting Me)* copyright © 2017 by Mariano Epelbaum

Cover art copyright © 2017 by Mariano Epelbaum. Cover design by Karina Granda. Cover copyright © 2017 by Hachette Book Group, Inc.

Little, Brown and Company
Hachette Book Group
1290 Avenue of the Americas, New York, NY 10104
Visit us at LBYR.com

Originally published in hardcover and ebook by
Little, Brown and Company in September 2016
First Trade Paperback Edition: August 2017

Little, Brown and Company is a division of Hachette Book Group, Inc.
The Little, Brown name and logo are trademarks of Hachette Book Group, Inc.

The publisher is not responsible for websites
(or their content) that are not owned by the publisher.

The Library of Congress has cataloged the hardcover edition as follows:
Names: White, Wade Albert, author.
Title: The adventurer's guide to successful escapes / Wade Albert White.
Description: First edition. | New York ; Boston : Little, Brown and Company, 2016. | Summary: "In a magickal world of floating tiers, mischievous dragons, and endless bureaucracy, Anne and her friends embark on a Rightful Heir Quest to claim her place in the Hierarchy and escape horrible consequences." —Provided by publisher.
Identifiers: LCCN 2015049764| ISBN 9780316305280 (hardback) | ISBN 9780316305273 (ebook) | ISBN 9780316391214 (library edition ebook)
Subjects: | CYAC: Fantasy. | BISAC: JUVENILE FICTION / Fantasy & Magic. | JUVENILE FICTION / Action & Adventure / General. | JUVENILE FICTION / Fairy Tales & Folklore / General.
Classification: LCC PZ7.1.W448 Adv 2016 | DDC [Fic]—dc23
LC record available at https://lccn.loc.gov/2015049764

ISBNs: 978-0-316-30526-6 (pbk.), 978-0-316-30527-3 (ebook)

Printed in the United States of America

LSC-C

10 9 8 7 6 5 4 3 2 1

To the squirrels

- CONTENTS -

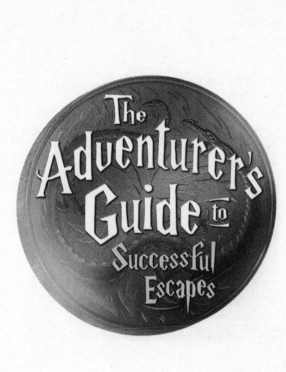

A Sort of Prologue

At Saint Lupin's Institute for Perpetually Wicked and Hideously Unattractive Children, every orphan is treated with the same amount of disdain and neglect. They are each provided with one set of threadbare pants and tunic, one pair of ill-fitting shoes, and one dusty and moth-eaten overcoat. They are also fed a steady diet of gruel and allowed to bathe exactly once per month—always just before their daily shift in the coal mine. This treatment, incidentally, is consistent with the advice given in the popular self-help guide *How to Raise Orphans and Make Money*.

Understandably, the orphans count the days until they can depart Saint Lupin's for good, and it is widely recognized that there are only three ways to leave:

1. Get adopted, perhaps by a nice family who will whisk you away to your long-dreamed-of castle on a hill, one surrounded by forests and glens, filled with interesting and friendly people, rich with history, and bright with promise and hope. (The Matron who runs Saint Lupin's is extremely pleased with her track record in this regard, for she has successfully managed to prevent any adoptions since taking charge.)

2. Reach the age of thirteen and be unceremoniously kicked out on your bottom.

3. Be selected for a quest. Although quests are heavily regulated (so they can then be heavily taxed), there are few restrictions regarding age or background, and thus almost anyone may apply. The most desired quests, however, are reserved for subjects of prophecies (also heavily taxed). At Saint Lupin's, both of these topics—that is, quests and prophecies—are considered particularly forbidden subjects of inquiry.

The Matron of Saint Lupin's

Anne was leaving Saint Lupin's.

At some point that day, a cargo ship would make its annual stop at the orphanage to drop off a year's supply of dehydrated gruel powder (*Just add water!*) and other provisions. Any orphan with a passenger ticket would then be allowed to board and leave with the departing ship. Since the government cut off its Orphan Tax Credit at age thirteen, the Matron was only too eager to get rid of children she could no longer exploit. The ship was scheduled to depart at exactly ten minutes past midnight, which was technically tomorrow, which was Anne's birthday, meaning she would be eligible to receive a ticket. So in less than a day, she would walk through Saint Lupin's gates for the last time. Or, in child labor terms, Anne was roughly twenty-three chores away from complete freedom.

There was only one problem: She had no place to go.

Or more accurately, she couldn't go to the one place she most wanted to go.

As the morning sun attempted, more or less unsuccessfully, to penetrate the grimy dormitory windows, Anne quietly walked down the hallway and slipped inside her tiny shared room. She closed the door equally as quietly and tiptoed the four steps to her bed, trying to avoid the floorboards that squeaked (which was especially difficult given that this included all of them). She took such care so as not to disturb the blanket-covered lump in the bed four steps in the other direction. The lump grunted loudly and mumbled but remained asleep.

Anne sat heavily on her bed, sending out a small puff of coal dust from her clothes. After a night spent working in the mines, her body ached for sleep, but there was no point even in lying down. Everyone was due in the front hallway in fifteen minutes. Besides, with the excitement of her birthday coupled with the unease of her coming departure from Saint Lupin's, her mind was anything but sleepy.

In an attempt to make herself presentable, she ran her hands through her thick, curly hair several times, but as usual, her hair had a will of its own. Then she tried to rub off some of the coal dust that seemed forever ingrained under her fingernails and in the pores of her dark brown skin, but she basically only managed to transfer dust from one place to another.

With a sigh, she moved on to packing (which is easy when you have next to nothing to pack). Anne reached under the thin mattress and pulled out her few meager possessions. The first was a homemade pocketknife she'd built from various odds and ends. The rest consisted of several dozen slips of paper. On one side of the papers was printed the rejections from all the quest academies to which she had applied. On the other side was the stated reason for the rejections:

(NO PROOF OF ORIGIN)

More than anything Anne wanted to go on adventures, and ultimately to find her real home. First, however, she had to obtain an official license. But no academy would enroll someone who couldn't prove where they came from. In defiance of this, she had filled the rejection slips with sketches of people. The faces were different sizes, shapes, and colors, yet she'd given all of them one shared feature: yellow eyes, just like her own. Anne had never actually met anyone else with yellow eyes, but she knew they must exist because she herself must have come from somewhere. That was her one and only clue.

To the knife and the papers Anne added a third item from her coat pocket: a small, thin book with a tattered red cover.

Every day after her shift in the mines, Anne would sneak into the boarded-up library, replace whatever book she'd taken the previous day, and unofficially "borrow" another one. She'd read hundreds of stories this way: tales of nobles, tales of pirates, tales of knights, and sometimes tales of noble pirate knights. One book had even contained a story about an accountant, which hadn't been very exciting, but it did help Anne understand how feeding orphans cheap food qualified as a charitable donation for Saint Lupin's.

"What are you doing?" asked a sleepy voice that came from the blanketed lump.

"New book," said Anne.

The lump rolled over and revealed itself to be a person—a pale, white-skinned girl (pores equally coal ingrained) with light blue eyes and tangles of dirty red hair. The girl's name was Penelope. She had already turned thirteen and was a full head taller than Anne. How anyone eating only gruel could still have such broad shoulders and thick, sturdy limbs was beyond Anne's comprehension. Penelope hadn't had any success getting into an academy, either, but for very different reasons.

She knew her place of origin. In fact, her parents had been famous—or rather, infamous. Tragically, they had died in a quest that ended in disaster when Penelope was only two years old, and the curse of their misfortune had followed her. No self-respecting academy wanted the child of notorious failures.

To make matters worse for both Anne and Penelope, any orphan leaving Saint Lupin's without an official destination would be sent to the Pit. There they would break rocks in a quarry until they could save enough money to buy passage elsewhere. The lucky ones made it out after only a few years of hard labor. Many were not so fortunate.

"What's this one about?" Penelope asked eagerly, staring at the book in Anne's hand. She loved fairy tales, especially those containing knights wielding swords and riding around on horses and stabbing things with them (that is, stabbing things with the swords, not with the horses, although she no doubt would have enjoyed those stories as well).

Anne read the title out loud: "*The Adventurer's Guide to Getting Your First Job.*"

"That's…a weird title for a story."

"Since we're leaving, I figured we could use something more in the way of practical advice. This sounded promising." Anne opened to the first page and frowned.

"What's wrong?" asked Penelope.

"There's only one sentence. It says, 'Keep in mind most entry-level positions for orphans involve a barn and a shovel.'" She flipped through the rest of the book, but all the other pages were blank. "That's all there is."

"Well, that advice stinks," said Penelope. "And forget entry level. I'm skipping the barns and shovels and going straight to rescuing some prince from a dragon and buying a castle with a tall tower."

Anne looked longingly at her stack of rejection slips. "I only wish we could."

"Never mind those snobby academies," said Penelope. "And don't worry about the Pit, either. We'll jump ship before we reach it, join up with some pirates, and go hunting for Old World treasure. All we need to do is find something really valuable, like the Fabled Slippers of Uz. Then we'll be rich and famous, and academies everywhere will beg to have us." Penelope leaned forward and spoke in a conspiratorial whisper. "Although I hear pirates make you pierce something before they accept you as part of their crew."

Anne grinned at her friend. Penelope could find the silver lining in a cloud that had just struck her with lightning.

Penelope clapped her hands together. "We could each do an ear! Or have matching nose rings!"

"Or pierced eyebrows," Anne suggested, playing along.

"I would look fantastic with a pierced eyebrow. And wielding a cutlass." Penelope jumped up, grabbed her pillow, and wielded it as a sword. "Aye aye, Captain! I'll take care of these scallywags for you and make them rue the day they crossed Penelope Shatterblade." She took a few good swings, and then tossed aside the pillow and jumped off her bed.

"Sorry about the book," said Anne. "I'll sneak back into the library and get us a proper story. One last good adventure before we board the ship."

While Penelope dressed hastily, Anne stuffed her drawings and the book into the deep pockets of her coat and slid the pocketknife into her sock. Then they headed downstairs together. All the younger children were already off to the kitchens for breakfast, but Anne and Penelope stood with the group of thirteen-year-olds waiting in the dormitory's front hallway. Many of the other orphans had received letters of acceptance from various academies and were talking excitedly about the grand adventures they hoped to go on once they were free of Saint Lupin's. Anne and Penelope said little, except for Penelope occasionally suggesting other suitable locations for a piercing. After several minutes of this, a hinge-rattling thump at the entrance silenced their chatter.

Anne wrung her hands in nervous anticipation. Even if the Pit was no better than Saint Lupin's, as long as she and Penelope stuck together, they would figure out the rest in due course.

A boy with coal-streaked blond hair opened the front door, and an eight-foot-tall hollow suit of armor tromped inside. It had a helmet with a ring of spikes around the bottom and an overly large torso that made it look like a barrel, albeit one with arms and legs and

12

bearing a longsword. Still, no one screamed or fled or fainted. If anything, there was an undercurrent of anticipation not typically reserved for well-armed barrels.

The orphans referred to the suit of armor as an "iron knight." The Matron employed three of them, primarily for heavy labor. The knights mostly ignored the orphans and went about their business, although if the small white stone in the center of their helmets glowed red, you knew you were in trouble. They were also prone to stepping on toes. Anne had spent years trying to figure out (without success) how the suits worked. She had finally decided it didn't matter as long as she could avoid them.

The iron knight didn't speak (which wasn't surprising, since to the best of Anne's recollection none of them ever had). In one hand it held a stack of papers. The passenger tickets. At the top of the stack was a message, which it handed to the boy who had opened the door. The boy read the message aloud:

To all the orphans who are scheduled to leave,

I wish I could say I have enjoyed the pleasure of your company, but I haven't. Not even a little bit. And in truth, I actually don't *wish I could say it. That part was a lie. Also, you still owe me one more day of chores, so stop standing around and get to work.*

> *Most sincerely NOT yours,*
> *The Matron*

P.S. Also, good riddance.

The iron knight handed the boy a second piece of paper, the year's roster, and the boy began calling out names in alphabetical order. As each person's name was called, they stepped forward to receive their ticket.

Anne sighed, knowing she would be last. In addition to not knowing where she came from, she didn't even have a surname, and so was always last. She and Penelope had once brainstormed possible last names to solve the problem, but the Matron had refused to submit the required application form to make her new name legal.

"Appleturner, Appollonia," the boy called out first, and a tall girl stepped forward. The knight handed her a ticket and she proceeded outside to begin her chores for the day.

"Barnacle, Rhoberte," the boy called next. This time a boy stepped forward and received his ticket as well. He followed the girl out the door.

The line shortened as each person received their ticket in turn: Iduardo Dribblenoodle, Mari Ficklefeather, Ebelleh Greatsword, Ty Queenflower.

"Shatterblade, Penelope," the boy called.

Penelope skipped to the knight to receive her ticket and kissed the piece of paper with a loud smack. "Princes of the world, here I come!"

Anne and the others laughed as Penelope danced out of the hallway, and everyone continued shuffling forward as yet more names were called. Soon there were only five orphans remaining. Then two. Then Anne was by herself.

"Anvil," the boy finally said.

Anne cringed at the sound of her full name, but she stepped forward with an impossible-to-contain smile nevertheless. Despite her uncertain future, there was still a sense of exhilaration. She held her breath, waiting for the iron knight to hand her a ticket.

Instead, it turned and exited the dormitory.

Anne stood frozen in shock. It made no sense. Granted, receiving a passenger ticket from an empty suit of armor didn't make a lot of sense in the first place, but in this particular instance, *not* receiving one made even less sense.

Penelope, who was now carrying a rake, stuck her head back through the doorway. "Are you coming? These leaves aren't going to pile themselves."

"I...I didn't get a ticket," said Anne.

"What?" Penelope looked from Anne to the departing knight and back again. "What are you going to do?"

Anne decided it must be a mistake and ran out after the knight. She skipped around in front of it and waved her hands. The knight stopped just short of stepping on her and looked down with its cold, empty gaze.

"S-sorry, but you didn't give me my ticket," said Anne.

The stone in the knight's helmet briefly flashed red. Had she angered it? She stood her ground, wavering between determination and fear, as the iron knight continued to stare. Finally, it simply sidestepped around her and continued on its way. Anne watched it go, a knot forming in the pit of her stomach. She didn't know why the knight hadn't given her a ticket, but she did know one thing: Without one, she couldn't leave Saint Lupin's.

Anne looked around. The other orphans had dispersed to begin their chores, but how could she work without resolving the issue of her ticket?

"I have to go see the Matron," said Anne.

Penelope paled visibly. "We're already behind. If you don't start your chores now, you'll end up with a double shift in the coal mine. She'll make you work right up until the last minute before the ship leaves."

Anne nodded. "As long as it leaves with me on it, I can live with that."

Before common sense could kick in, Anne left Penelope with the leaves and hurried across the yard to the Manor, a five-story building made of red brick in the center of the main compound. She ran up the front steps and entered through the large double doors. Several passages led off from the main entryway, and Anne took the one to the right of an antique longcase clock and navigated the twisting corridors until she came to the lengthy hallway that led to the Matron's office. The hallway was lined with the statues of former headmasters and headmistresses, each with lifelike glaring eyes that heightened the sense of walking to one's execution. Anne shivered as she passed.

The door to the office was open, but Anne stopped outside and knocked anyway. You didn't barge in on the Matron. When no reply came, she risked a peek inside.

The room was octagonal, with an ornately carved oak

desk, floor-to-ceiling shelves, and three tall stained-glass windows. Brightly colored sunlight filled the room, and every surface gleamed with polish, so that anywhere Anne looked she saw her own soot-streaked face reflected back. The only sign of life was the Matron's pet fire lizard, snoring quietly in a basket in the far corner. The fire lizard's name was Dog—or at least that's what it read on his collar. He was two feet long from snout to tail, with black scales, small black leather wings, and bright green eyes. He didn't so much fly as wobble a few inches off the ground and crash into things, like a bumblebee with zero depth perception. Anne liked the fire lizard and very much wished she could bring him along with her when she left.

"Ma'am?" she called out.

No response.

Anne knew she should leave. She was late for chores. But only the Matron could solve the problem of her missing ticket, so she decided to wait. Impulsively, she stepped over the threshold. Orphans were rarely permitted in the office unaccompanied, and the tiny act of defiance on this, her last day, gave Anne a thrill. The shelves were filled with thousands of glass domes of various sizes, with each dome containing a single unique medallion. Anne had spent many hours dusting and polishing them, always under close supervision, but now she twirled her way across the tile floor, enjoying a brief moment of exhilarating freedom. She stopped on the far side of the room in front of the dome that contained her favorite medallion: a small silver one that bore the image of a dragon. The dragon was carved in fine, intricate lines, marred only by a single deep scratch across the surface.

"And just what do you think you're doing?" asked a sharp voice.

Anne spun around, nearly losing her balance.

A tall, reedy woman stood in the doorway.

The Matron.

She strode across the room, her silver cane clanking on the stone tiles with every other step, and her mouth pursed in suspicion. She stopped in front of Anne. Inches away, the Matron's short-cropped white-gray hair stood out even more starkly against her brown skin. She was so close Anne could count the black threads on her finely tailored, high-collared tunic. So close Anne feared smudging the woman's brown woolen trousers with her own dirty coat or accidentally scuffing her fine leather boots. A crystal pendant hung from a gold chain around the Matron's neck and dangled in front of Anne's nose.

The Matron pointed to the glass dome with her

gloved right hand. "Well?" she said. "Explain yourself." She didn't raise her voice, but her coal-black eyes had a way of looking directly into a person's soul and making it shrivel.

Anne shriveled accordingly. "I—I didn't touch anything. I promise."

The Matron's eyes scanned the shelf, as though seeking even a hint of incriminating evidence, such as a stray fingerprint. "Then why are you in here?"

Anne took a deep breath. "I didn't receive a ticket for the supply ship."

"Residents receive a ticket when they turn thirteen. You are not thirteen yet."

"I know," said Anne. "I just thought, given the regulations about leaving, and what with the ship departing so soon after midnight tonight, that—"

"There's been a change in schedule. The ship is now leaving *before* midnight, which, as I'm sure even you can deduce, means you'll be staying a little longer than you expected."

Anne's heart beat faster. "Staying? Here? At Saint Lupin's?"

"Where else would I mean?" the Matron said, and she turned away, apparently satisfied that nothing had been tampered with, giving Anne space to breathe once again.

"But...the ship won't return again for a whole year." Anne's future flashed before her eyes: another year in the coal mines, another year polishing every nook and cranny of the orphanage, and all without her best friend to keep her company.

"And how is that my problem?" the Matron replied. Relying heavily on her cane, the Matron walked over to the desk and eased herself into the high-backed chair behind it. When her gloved hand touched the desktop, it made a distinct clunk.

Anne moved to the spot in front of the desk where a large X had been painted on the floor. There was a chair to the left of the X, but to the best of Anne's knowledge, no one had ever been invited to sit in it.

"But I'm scheduled to leave on this ship," said Anne. "My name is on the list. My birthday is tomorrow."

"Yes, and if the ship were still leaving tomorrow, you would most assuredly be on it. But as I said, there's been a change." The Matron leaned forward. "And just so there are no misunderstandings, you are not to go anywhere near that supply ship. I don't want you on the dock, or at the edge of the dock, or even standing in a place where you can see the dock. In fact, consider your-self restricted to the main compound until the ship has departed."

Tears welled up in Anne's eyes. "C-can't they wait just a few extra minutes?"

"No."

"Can Penelope stay here with me, then?"

"Certainly not," said the Matron in a tone that sug-gested further discussion was ill-advised. "If that is all, you may begin your chores."

Anne couldn't believe what she was hearing. She and Penelope would be separated—Anne wouldn't even be able to watch her leave. No adventures together. No pirates. They might never find each other again.

The Matron cleared her throat.

Anne looked up.

"Was there something else?" asked the Matron.

Anne decided then and there that she wasn't simply going to give up. "Actually, I just finished my shift in the mines," she said. "I'm only scheduled to help Penelope rake leaves and then go to bed."

"If you're awake enough to come in here and bother me, you're awake enough to work the full morning. And by work, I don't mean wasting time with your friend."

The Matron gestured to the basket in the corner where Dog was laying. "You may start by taking that wretched creature for his morning walk."

Anne suppressed a retort and shuffled to the corner. She removed a leash from the hook above the basket and attached it to Dog's collar. Dog snorted in protest but dragged himself out of the basket. Normally, two people were assigned to walk the fire lizard: One person held the leash, and another did the pushing and prodding and coaxing and begging required to get him moving. But lately he'd been obeying Anne without too much fuss.

"Remember," said the Matron, "no leaving the compound until after the supply ship has departed. I need not remind you of the consequences for disobeying orders."

Anne exited with Dog in tow. The eyes of the statues in the long hallway didn't bother her one bit this time. Instead, each step only strengthened her resolve. Anne didn't care what the Matron said. She wasn't going to be left behind. One way or another, she was leaving Saint Lupin's.

Even if she had to break every one of the Matron's rules to do it.

THE ADVENTURER'S GUIDE
TO SUCCESSFUL ESCAPES
OFFERS THE FOLLOWING TIPS:

1) Wait until after dark when everyone is asleep—unless, of course, the place from which you are trying to escape is patrolled by walking suits of armor that never sleep. If that's the case, sorry, but you're out of luck.

2) If you require a partner, choose someone quiet. Loud, talkative people who chatter on and on about pirates and castles they intend to buy are likely to get you caught.

3) Before you try to swim across the moat, check first to make sure it isn't infested with sharks.

2

Fire Lizards and Fireballs

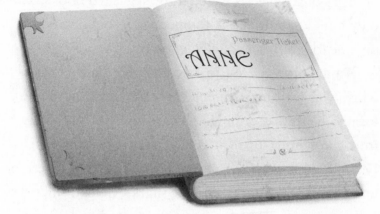

A fifteen-foot-high outer wall surrounded the main compound of the orphanage in a very haphazard fashion, and a lone iron knight walked along the top of it very haphazardly. Anne led Dog out of the Manor and along the wall, in the opposite direction from that of the patrolling knight. The fire lizard worked himself into a low, heel-dragging hover and only required the occasional nudge every now and again to correct his flight path. While Anne walked, her gaze drifted to the other buildings inside the walls. As she had with the orphans under her care, the Matron had turned a once-bustling estate into a shadow of its former self: The boarded-up bakery smelled only of mice and mold; the abandoned forge had a cold chimney and rusted tools; and the library's dusty shelves were full of neglected books. The only building outside the compound, an old observatory on a nearby hill, sat equally ignored.

Anne stopped Dog in front of the main entrance, which was little more than a curved archway in the wall located beneath a crumbling clock tower. A set of rusty iron gates hung open, dangling half off their hinges. Beyond the archway, a drawbridge extended over a moat filled with sharks (zombie sharks, in fact, since the Matron was far too cheap to pay for feeding live ones). In the middle of the moat, the drawbridge came to rest on the edge of a stone ramp. The ramp covered the rest of the distance to the opposite side. In a few hours, every thirteen-year-old orphan would cross the drawbridge, descend the ramp, and walk two miles down the sloping forest path to the dock. Anne hoped to be with them, but so far it wasn't looking good.

Penelope jogged over with a rake in hand. "There you are! Did you get a ticket?"

Anne shook her head.

"What!?" exclaimed Penelope.

Anne explained what she'd learned in the Matron's office: how the supply ship was now scheduled to leave before midnight, so Anne would have to stay at Saint Lupin's another year.

"That's completely unfair!" said Penelope, swinging her rake at a nearby pile of leaves and scattering them in all directions. "What are we going to do?"

"Well," said Anne, looking around to make sure they couldn't be overheard, "I was thinking I'd leave anyway, if you feel like helping."

"Yes!" said Penelope. "We'll storm the castle!"

"Er, I'm pretty sure you only storm a castle when you're trying to get into it. Technically, I'm trying to get out."

"Fine. We'll call storming it Plan B."

Since there were other orphans busy working around the grounds, they ducked beneath the archway and over to the edge of the drawbridge for more privacy as they plotted. The surface of the moat was calm, although every once in a while the rotting fin of a zombie shark crested the water, causing Dog to growl.

"You could try a disguise," suggested Penelope.

"I would still need a ticket," said Anne. "But maybe

I could stow away in one of the cargo crates after it's unpacked but before they return it to the ship."

Penelope shook her head. "They always check the empty crates. I'm sure I could throw you onto the ship from the dock, though."

Anne pointed to a scar on her elbow. "Are you forgetting the 'I'm sure I can toss Anne up into the oak tree' incident?"

Penelope grinned. "I was so close. And anyway, you healed up nicely, didn't you?"

"I'd like to avoid the *need* to heal this time."

"We should at least call it Plan C."

"You call it Plan C," said Anne. "I'm calling it Plan of Last Resort and Even Then Probably Not. Or at least not until I learn how to fly." She shuddered. "How about we make it simple? You board first, cause a commotion, and I'll sneak aboard while everyone is distracted."

"What sort of commotion?"

"I don't know. Start an argument with the first mate or something."

"Which one is he again?"

"Just a second. I think I have a sketch of him." Anne emptied her pocket to get her drawings. "Here, hold this for a minute." Anne handed the book with the red cover to Penelope.

"What book is this?" asked Penelope.

"It's the same one I had earlier. I haven't had a chance to exchange it for a new one yet."

"No it's not. This one is *The Adventurer's Guide to Clandestine Travel*."

Anne looked at the cover and frowned. "That's weird."

Penelope opened the book, and they both gasped. Printed on the first page, in crisp dark lines, was a passenger ticket. With Anne's name on it.

Anne took the book with shaking hands and stared at the ticket incredulously. "But...how?"

Penelope shrugged nonchalantly. "Eh, it's probably just magick or something."

Anne gaped at her friend. "*Just* magick?"

"Yeah. We read about magick stuff all the time in those books you get from the library."

"I know, Pen. But reading about it is one thing. This...this is incredible!"

Penelope laughed. "I know. I'm just kidding! This book is amazing! Quick, tear out the ticket before it disappears."

Anne clutched the open book tightly against her chest. "What!? We can't tear a magick book."

"Says who? It made the ticket for you, didn't it? Why would it do that if it didn't want you to take it?"

Anne glanced at the page again. "I suppose that makes sense, but...what if we break it or something?"

"Just tear it a little. If something goes wrong, we can always stop."

"What if 'something going wrong' means it explodes?"

"Then we'll definitely stop."

Typically, Anne preferred to think things through from all angles, but Penelope was right: She couldn't risk losing the ticket. She gripped the page as close to the spine of the book as possible and pulled until the smallest of tears formed. Nothing happened. She tore it a little more. Everything continued to remain fine. Anne kept tearing until the page separated completely from the book. The ticket was still clear and legible, and the rest of the book seemed otherwise unaffected. Anne sighed with relief.

Penelope clapped her on the shoulder. "Fantastic! I can practically smell the pirates."

"I think that might be the moat," said Anne.

As they stared at the ticket in wonderment, Dog

turned in the direction of the forest. His ears perked up and he sniffed the air.

Penelope pointed to the sky. "What's that?"

Anne shielded her eyes. "It looks like...a ball of fire...or something."

Indeed, a burning "something" arced across the sky— a bright green burning object—and dropped steadily until it disappeared into the forest. While they stood staring at the smoke trail, Dog shot forward, snapping the leash out of Anne's hand. The fire lizard rocketed across the drawbridge, down the stone ramp, and into the trees.

Oh no.

No, no, no, no, no.

Anne sprinted across the drawbridge but stopped short when she reached the ramp. She glanced back at the iron knight patrolling high up atop the wall. Had it seen the light in the sky? Or watched Dog run off? Would it notice if Anne left?

Penelope ran up beside her. "Are we going after him?"

Anne chewed her lip. The Matron had given her strict instructions not to leave the main grounds. Skipping out on chores might earn a double shift in the mines, but disobeying a direct order was worth a week scrubbing the dungeons—while being locked up in them. Then again, showing up without Dog wasn't likely to win her the orphan of the year award, either.

"Okay, I'll go," said Anne. "You stay here on look-out. Make some noise or something to warn me if the Matron or one of the knights shows up."

Penelope nodded.

Anne looked up again: The patrolling knight was heading away from them. There would never be a better opportunity. She shoved the book, ticket, and sketches back into her pocket, and then she raced down the ramp, across the path, and plunged into the undergrowth, hoping to find Dog just on the other side. Unfortunately, the fire lizard was already at the bottom of a long slope, and Anne watched as he disappeared into the thick of the forest. Heart thumping, Anne sped up.

After several minutes of running, Anne began encountering patches of scorched earth and blackened branches. She must be getting closer to the bright, burning object that had landed. As she hurried through drifting clouds of sparks and ash, her feet kicked up smoldering piles of leaves. Smoke stung her lungs and blurred her vision, becoming thicker the farther she went, until she was coughing and gasping for a fresh breath of air. There was no sign of Dog.

Anne was about to turn back when she stumbled past a dark opening on a hillside—a mine shaft entrance. It was Shaft Eleven, which had experienced a cave-in many years ago, around the time Anne herself was born. Various accounts had circulated among the orphans over the years as to exactly what had happened there, with some claiming it had been an army of tunneling coal worms and others making dubious reference to a firebrand and an angry canary. Regardless of the truth, everyone avoided it, since the Matron assigned extra chores to anyone who went near it. Anne ducked inside the mine's still-intact entrance and sucked in a lungful of cool, smokeless air. Several paces farther in there was a boarded-up door with the words STAY OUT (THIS MEANS YOU) painted across it.

While contemplating whether to press on or return to the compound, Anne heard a rustling noise from a nearby clump of trees. Thinking it must be Dog, Anne slipped quickly out of the mine entrance and went from tree to tree, hoping to sneak up on him by surprise. Just as she was about to jump through the undergrowth, Anne was stopped by a deep, teeth-rattling roar.

That wasn't Dog. It was something else entirely. Something big.

Perhaps that "something big" was friendly, and its roar was simply its way of saying "Hello, small person," but it was equally possible that the "something big" was hungry for a tender orphan snack. Rather than find out which, Anne retreated as quietly as possible, thinking she could hide back inside Shaft Eleven. Yet as she stepped around a rock, a twig snapped under her heel. This brought another tremendous roar, followed by a crash, which convinced Anne it was time to run, and she bolted straight for the mine entrance. However, she had to veer away suddenly when the tree in front of her exploded in green flames. To the best of Anne's knowledge, the only creatures who breathed fire were dragons, but she'd never met a dragon, and why one would come to Saint Lupin's and shoot fireballs at the trees, Anne had no idea.

Her heart pounding from the near miss, Anne kept her legs pumping. She was headed directly into the area where the falling object (or dragon?) must have landed, but she had no choice. She jumped over blackened stumps, skirted more piles of burning leaves, plunged blindly through a thick cloud of smoke—

—and ran straight off the end of the world.

Prologue Addendum

Technically, there is another way to leave Saint Lupin's:

4. Walk out the front door, proceed for roughly two miles in any direction, and fall off the end of the world.

This happens not nearly as infrequently as one might think.

THE UNCONTESTED AUTHORITY ON
DRAGONS IS THE THREE-VOLUME SET
ENTITLED *DRAGONS I HAVE KNOWN AND
WHY NOT TO POKE AT THEM WITH SHARP
OBJECTS* BY THE WELL-KNOWN WIZARD
AND HISTORIAN ONE-ARMED HENGEZ THE
OVERLY-TRUSTING.

THE INTRODUCTION TO THE FIRST VOLUME,
*THE INS AND OUTS OF BECOMING LIVE
DRAGON BAIT,* READS AS FOLLOWS:

Dragons are curious creatures, by which I mean people are curious about them and not that they are curious about people, except possibly when by "people" one means "lunch." Dragons can be identified by size, color, and class, and so the difference between, say, a large, green Three-Eyed Rhino dragon and a small, purple Slobbering Kiss-Me dragon should be readily apparent—although both should be given a wide berth. The careful observer will use these categories to quickly classify any dragon they meet and assess any potential threat. The less-than-careful observer should reread the part about people being lunch.

3

The End of the World

Anne lay on her back. She was no longer falling, which was good. Her body hurt in many places, which was not as good, but at least nothing felt broken.

Movement in the sky high above drew her attention. A colossal island of rock drifted slowly overhead, like an 800-quadrillion-ton cloud. That island and all the others, including Saint Lupin's, was known as a tier. Anne had learned in *Why the World Is a Bunch of Giant Floating Islands* that all the tiers (along with the sun, moon, and stars) orbited a big glowing field of magick that, due to either a sheer lack of imagination or just plain laziness, everyone called the "Big Glowing Field of Magick," or just BGFM. Together, the tiers and the BGFM were known as the Hierarchy, and somewhere out there was Anne's home, the tier on which she'd been born.

Anne sat up and discovered she had landed on a narrow ledge on the side, and some twenty feet below the top, of the Saint Lupin's tier. To her right were the ancient remains of a staircase carved into the rock; this must have once led to the surface, but it was too broken to climb anymore. To her left was a large gap where the ledge dropped away to the BGFM far below. Anne stood up. Neither direction offered an escape route, so she searched the cliff face for possible hand- and footholds to climb back up to the top. To her dismay, the stone was completely smooth. She considered calling for help, but she was too far from the orphanage for anyone to hear. Moreover, the dragon, if that's what the "something big" was, was still up there. Announcing her location probably wasn't such a great idea.

As she considered her options, she heard a faint noise.

O, o, o, o, o.

Was that Penelope searching for her? Or was it the "something big"? Anne strained to hear.

O, o, o, o, o.

"Hello?" she answered back, not daring to raise her voice much above a loud whisper.

Lo, lo, lo, lo, lo came back to her, a little stronger, a little closer.

"Hello? Hey! Hey, down here!" she called out, trying to find the right balance between keeping her voice low enough so as not to be heard by a roaming "something," yet loud enough to be heard by a person who might be able to help, yet again low enough so as not to draw the "something's" attention to that helpful person. Needless to say, it was a tricky balance.

A face appeared over the edge. It wasn't Penelope. It was a woman with dark brown skin and warm brown eyes and a head of voluminous, perfectly styled black hair.

"Excuse me, but are you the orphan with the identification number"—the woman read from a small slip of paper—"6-5-5-3-5?"

Anne blinked. "Um."

The woman checked the paper again. "Is your name Anvil?"

Anne grimaced. "I prefer Anne."

"Excellent. Anne it is, then." The woman leaned

farther over the edge. "I'm pleased to inform you that you are this year's completely random selection."

"I'm...what?"

"Otherwise known as the wild card, dear. I know, I know. It's all very exciting, and you're simply too shocked for words. No need to be embarrassed. It happens to everyone, especially those from lower tiers such as this. Have no fear, though. I'm sure you'll adjust in no time. Still, we should probably have a quick chat before getting under way."

"A chat?"

"To cover a few of the basics, so you're not completely overwhelmed."

Anne looked around. "You want to have a chat with me while I'm stuck down here on the side of the tier?"

"Actually, if it's not too much bother, I rather think up here would be best." The woman lowered one end of a rope.

Anne shied away. "But there's...there's something moving around up there."

The woman laughed. "Oh, that was probably me. My apologies if I caused any undue distress."

Anne remained wary. "Do you roar and shoot flames at people?"

"Only when I miss my midmorning tea." The woman chuckled again, but stopped when she saw Anne's guarded expression. "I'm kidding, dear, of course. But come, we mustn't dillydally."

The woman's warmth and self-assurance finally won Anne over. She grabbed hold of the rope and scrambled up the cliff and back onto level ground.

As Anne knelt at the edge of a small clearing, she got a better look at her rescuer. The woman wore dark trousers, shiny leather riding boots, and a rose-colored vest over a cream blouse. An ornate rapier handle stuck out from beneath a gray hooded cloak, and a richly embroidered bag hung from her shoulder. The ensemble presented a dashing appearance, but it was less the look of an actual adventurer than that of someone who had studied what adventurers looked like in great detail and who had done their best to mimic them.

The woman stood and brushed the dirt from her knees. "That's much better." She took Anne's hand and helped her to her feet. "Now, my dear, let's have a good look at you."

She stepped back several paces and studied Anne with a practiced eye. "Hmmm, I'm seeing some interesting choices. Orphan, obviously, but not outright vagabond. That's a smart pick this season. Vagabonds were completely overdone last year, and I'm simply sick to death of them. Nice solid shoes. Good. Good. I can't tell you how many times I've seen young women trying to manage it in heels. The Forest of Death is not a fashion runway, I always tell them."

"Er," said Anne.

The woman tapped her chin. "But the hair, dear, really, what are we trying to say? I'm seeing frayed. I'm seeing clumped. A little dirt. A little matting. It's too much. Far too much. You need to think about what message you're sending." She swept her hand in a wide arc, as though speaking to some invisible audience. "Yes, desperation, that's fine, we can work with that. But a quiet desperation, a reserved despondency, would be much better received, I think. It's your choice, of course. Completely your choice. I wouldn't presume to interfere. But I do urge you to give it some thought. I would hate to see you penalized for something so trivial."

"Er," said Anne again. She had only caught half of what the woman was saying, and she understood less than half of that.

The woman produced a lace handkerchief from one of her vest pockets and used it to dust a few flakes of ash from Anne's shoulder. "Still, all things considered,

I think you're off to a splendid start. Is there anything specific you'd like to ask before we get going?"

"Do I even know you?" asked Anne.

"Oh, of course. How rude of me. Introductions." The woman swept her cloak back in an elaborate bow. "I am Lady Jocelyn Abigayle Daisywheel the Third, student of the natural sciences, linguist, and most important for our immediate purposes, professor of mythological studies at the local quest academy."

That caught Anne's attention. "The local *what* academy?"

"Quest academy, dear. I teach all the courses in Old World mythology, and I offer the occasional evening class in rodent taxidermy. We make lovely dioramas."

"I didn't realize there was a local academy."

"I'm not surprised. We're an independent school, and not very large, but there are advantages to that, and I think you'll find that we take very good care of our students. We would love for you to join us."

Anne experienced a momentary glimmer of hope, which was quickly swept away by the crashing wave of reality. "I can't go," she said, hanging her head. "The other academies said I couldn't enroll because I don't know where I'm from. I guess it's a rule or something."

The woman—Jocelyn—smiled at her. "Well, if those other academies don't know how to bend the rules a little, that's simply their loss, then, isn't it? For starters, they could use one of these." Jocelyn dug into her pack, brought out a plain wooden box, and handed it to Anne.

Anne opened the lid. Inside, lying on a piece of crushed blue velvet, was a worn brown leather glove. The entire back side of the glove was covered in strips of overlapping metal that were riveted together, and it had a wide extended cuff that was also encased in metal. On the underside of the cuff was a circular inset.

Anne frowned. "An ugly glove?"

"Technically, dear, it's called a gauntlet," said Jocelyn. She motioned for Anne to pick it up.

Anne removed the gauntlet from the box, but she held it away from her body as though it were a dead fish—a really smelly one. "And, er, what am I supposed to do with it?"

"Why, wear it, of course." Jocelyn took the box and stuffed it back into her bag. "Surely you don't expect to begin your training without it?"

"My training?" Anne finally put the pieces together. "You're saying you're willing to train me? At your academy? To go on quests? Just as long as I wear this... gauntlet?"

"Precisely. With one of these, you don't need to know your place of origin. It's like having a free pass." Jocelyn pointed at the gauntlet. "Go on, then. Try it on."

With a sense of growing optimism, Anne slid her left hand into the gauntlet, pulling it snug. It fit her, for lack of a better expression, like a glove. In fact, it was almost as if the maker had measured her actual hand. A tingling sensation flowed through the fingers of her left hand and up her entire arm.

Anne held up the gauntlet and studied it. "So—so you're saying I can leave Saint Lupin's? No matter what?"

"Of course. You can't go if you don't leave."

"But what if the Matron tries to stop me?"

"Well, if this Matron of yours wishes, she can file a complaint with the Wizards' Council," Jocelyn said in a lecturing tone. "Although in that case, you would be well within your rights to contact a union representative and request arbitration. But in my experience things rarely come to that."

"And what about my friend, Penelope? I couldn't leave her behind."

"You'll need adventuring companions, so the more the merrier."

"That's wonderful." Anne faltered. "I should probably

mention that her family name currently has a ban on it, though. But she's really wonderful and works hard, and I know she would make a great adventurer if someone would just give her a chance."

"That's one of the advantages of being an independent school, dear. You don't have to follow everyone else's silly little rules. Your friend is more than welcome. And even if that weren't the case, a gauntlet-wearer may choose anyone she wishes for her adventuring party." Jocelyn closed her bag. "Well, are we set, then?"

"I think so. But where do we—"

Anne had been about to ask where she and Penelope should meet Jocelyn after they left Saint Lupin's, but she stopped midsentence as a large, shiny black shape burst from the undergrowth on the opposite side of the clearing. A twenty-foot-long serpent-like creature slunk along the ground on stumpy legs, its heavy scales sparkling like black diamonds in the sunlight. Anne opened her mouth to shout a warning, but before she could utter a sound, the creature reared up, its tiny leathery wings flapping madly, and spewed out a sizzling green ball of fire. The fireball struck Jocelyn and vaporized her instantly, leaving only a curling wisp of smoke on the ground where she had been standing.

The creature landed back on all fours with a

ground-shaking thump and turned to Anne, who dove behind a nearby tree at the edge of the clearing. The creature let out a low growl, as though Anne had cheated it out of its meal (which she was only too happy to do). She could hear the dragon—for she now saw that it was definitely a dragon—pacing back and forth, but it didn't come any closer.

She risked a peek.

The dragon glared at her with an unmistakable look of annoyance. Anne tried to recall anything useful she had ever read about dragons, but her brain was too occupied with being in the middle of a full-fledged panic attack. The dragon seemed to be waiting for something. If it was for Anne to simply step out and be voluntarily disintegrated, she wasn't about to accommodate it. Finally, the beast growled and started thumping across the clearing toward Anne's hiding place. She hastily calculated the number of steps it would take for her to reach the edge of the tier and jump down to the ledge below, but she felt fairly certain the answer was at least half a dozen steps past "burnt to a crisp."

Just before it reached the tree, however, the dragon stopped. It stared in the direction of the main compound, twitched its ears, sniffed, and without giving so much as a good-bye roar, turned and bounded over the edge of the tier and dropped out of sight.

Anne collapsed against the tree trunk and let out a shuddering sigh. That poor woman, Jocelyn—here one moment and gone the next, taken away in the blink of an eye. Or more accurately, torched away in the blink of an eye. Or even more accurately still, torched away in the crackling doom of a fireball. And along with Jocelyn had gone Anne's one chance of attending a quest academy. Her chance for adventure. Her chance to explore the world and maybe even locate her real home.

The whole thing made her ill.

Ill or not, Anne had to return to the orphanage before she got into deeper trouble, with or without Dog. In fact, in all likelihood the fire lizard had been reduced to ashes by the dragon as well. Anne took a calming breath, pushed away her bitter disappointment, stepped out from behind the tree—

—and walked straight into an iron knight.

Anne stumbled back. Next to the iron knight was the Matron, staring at her with a steady, chilling gaze.

"So, this is how you follow my instructions, is it?"

said the Matron. "I tell you to remain on the grounds, and you immediately run off? And what are you doing out here exactly? Trying to burn the forest down?"

"N-no, ma'am. There was a—"

The Matron's eyes widened. At first Anne feared the dragon had returned, but then she realized the Matron was staring at the gauntlet.

"What is that?" asked the Matron, her voice barely above a whisper.

Anne started to hide the gauntlet behind her back, but the Matron stepped forward and grabbed her arm.

"Where did you get this?" the Matron demanded.

"I—I didn't—"

"Where?" screamed the Matron.

Anne stood shaking. She had no idea how to respond.

The Matron stared at the gauntlet. Finally, her gaze flicked back to Anne, her eyes revealing a barely contained fury.

"Bring her," the Matron commanded.

The iron knight grabbed Anne by the collar and dragged her toward the compound. Anne didn't resist. She staggered along numbly, her head filled with images of green fire as all hope of ever leaving Saint Lupin's crumbled away.

———◄►———

TOTH'S GUIDE TO ALL THINGS DUNGEON RELATED SAYS THE FOLLOWING ABOUT DUNGEON DESIGN:

Use smooth stone for all surfaces (eliminates tunneling), a thick oak door with an iron bar (locks can be picked), shackles on the walls and ceiling (for variety), and the bones of at least one former occupant piled in the corner (for morale).

HOWEVER, IT ALSO ADDS:

Regardless of the design, never put an orphan in a dungeon. It's not worth the headache. The little rascals never stay put.

———◄►———

4

The Silver Medallion

...two hundred thirty-nine, two hundred forty, two hundred forty-one...

Faint vibrations.

Anne lay on the hard bunk, staring at the stars through the tiny, barred window high up near the ceiling. Like the Matron's office, the dungeon was immaculate to the point where a person could practically eat off the floor. In fact, knowing the Matron, one might be given no other choice. The Matron had thrown Anne in the cell without another word, but not before confiscating the gauntlet and everything in her coat pockets, including her drawings, the book, and the passenger ticket.

...*two hundred eighty-four, two hundred eighty-five, two hundred eighty-six*...

The vibrations increased and the bunk began to rattle.

Anne thought about the gauntlet. The mere sight of it had elicited such a bizarre response from the Matron. Anne had seen her angry many times, but never so livid as to be rendered speechless. Then Anne's thoughts shifted to Jocelyn. Anne pictured again the dragon rearing up, its glowing green eyes, and the green ball of flame. She shivered at the memory and shook her head to clear the images from her mind.

...*two hundred ninety-eight, two hundred ninety-nine, three hundred.*

An iron knight stomped past the little slot in the doorway.

Five minutes exactly. That was the length of its patrol. Anne had been keeping track, and it hadn't deviated once, not by a second. There had been little point in trying to sneak away during daylight hours, but now that night had fallen, Anne could make her way to the dock under the cover of darkness, hopefully in time to board the ship. That was presuming she could escape and avoid getting flamed to death or eaten by a roaming dragon.

As soon as the iron knight moved past the door, Anne rolled off the bunk. Fortunately, the Matron had been so furious she hadn't bothered to search Anne thoroughly, and the pocketknife was still tucked inside her sock. Anne took it out and moved to the door. It was solid oak, six inches thick, but Anne focused on its weak point: the lock. The pocketknife contained more than just a blade. Anne had attached other implements as well, including a thin probe perfect for lock-picking. She'd first created it to get into the library and had gotten plenty of practice with it over the years.

After only half a minute of careful work, Anne heard a satisfying click as the locking mechanism released. She pulled on the door handle, but the door didn't move. She braced her foot against the wall and pulled with her full weight, tugging repeatedly until she nearly hyperventilated, but it refused to budge. It must have been barred from the outside as well.

She let out a long breath and sank to the floor. "So much for Plan Whatever Letter of the Alphabet We're on Now."

A few minutes later the iron knight rumbled past again, shaking the cell, and Anne despaired of ever leaving.

Then she heard a knock on the door. Was that the iron knight? Since when did they knock?

"Pssst."

Anne jumped at the sound. She peeked through the slot in the door and saw a familiar redhead peeking back at her.

"Pen!" exclaimed Anne. Relief flooded over her. "How did—"

Penelope held a finger to her lips.

"How did you know I was here?" Anne asked in a quieter voice.

"I saw you return with the Matron and that iron knight, but I couldn't slip away until now."

"You're missing the ship!"

Penelope shook her head. "I double-checked the clock in the main entrance. There's still twenty-five minutes left. The ship isn't leaving until after midnight, just like it was supposed to all along. Anne, the Matron lied to you."

Anne felt a stir of anger. "Why would she do that?"

"I don't know, but I don't think we should wait

around to find out." She rattled the door handle. "The door's barred out here. I think I can lift it off, but I couldn't find the key."

Anne nodded. "Already taken care of."

Penelope ducked out of sight. Anne heard her grunt with exertion and then the clunk of something heavy hitting the floor. A moment later the latch clicked and the door swung open.

"How's that for a first-time prison break?" said Penelope. "This is going to look awesome on our pirate résumés."

After Anne and Penelope rebarred the door to cover their tracks, they snuck out of the dungeon, easily avoiding the patrolling iron knight. On the way, Anne gave a full account of everything that had happened, including Jocelyn, the gauntlet, and the dragon. Penelope gasped and cheered in all the right places.

"We got accepted into a quest academy?" exclaimed Penelope. "That's fantastic! When do we go? *How* do we go?"

"I have no idea," said Anne. "But I'm not sure we'd be welcome there anymore."

"Why not?"

"What would I say? 'Thanks for the invitation. Sorry

one of your instructors got flamed to death by a dragon when she came to get me.'"

Penelope frowned. "Okay, so that *could* be a little awkward."

They climbed the long, winding staircase up from the dungeons until they reached the main floor of the Manor. After checking that the coast was clear, Penelope started to move in the direction of the entrance, but Anne turned in the opposite direction.

"Where are you going?" asked Penelope. "The dock is this way."

"I need to go to the Matron's office first," said Anne.

"Are you serious?" squeaked Penelope.

"She has my stuff."

Penelope tugged at Anne's sleeve. "It's too big of a risk."

Anne placed her hand over Penelope's. "If I'm going to get away from here, at the very least I need that ticket to get aboard the ship. And Jocelyn said any academy could take me if I had that gauntlet. She also said I could take you with me. Maybe her academy won't want us anymore, but another one might. It's worth a try, isn't it? But you don't have to risk getting caught. I'll go alone. You head for the dock."

Penelope shook her head fiercely. "I'm not going without you. And we're nearly out of time."

"That's why we need to hurry."

"What if the Matron is in her office? Are you just going to march in and demand the ticket and the gauntlet?"

Anne shrugged. "I'll think of something. Maybe I can lure her out first."

"Leave that to me," said Penelope. "I'll make a distraction, like we talked about doing on the ship."

"No, Pen. I can't let you—"

Penelope crossed her arms. "I can be every bit as stubborn as you. I'll set off the alarm near the kitchens. It's the farthest place in the building from her office. That should give you plenty of time."

Anne sighed. "Okay. But after that, head straight for the ship."

Penelope nodded. They shared a quick hug and set off. Penelope ran toward the kitchens, and Anne once again made her way along the empty winding corridors. The statues in the hallway leading to the Matron's office created an eerie tunnel of horrors, and every creak of the floorboards made her jump. She crept along as quietly as possible. If the Matron caught her this time, she would drop Anne straight down Shaft Eleven and block up the entrance for good.

The door to the office stood wide open. Shadows played off the walls as someone paced back and forth. Anne could hear the Matron muttering to herself.

A wailing cry echoed down the corridor, and Anne nearly jumped out of her shoes.

The kitchen alarm.

Anne ducked behind the nearest statue. She had barely crouched out of sight when the Matron rushed from her office and hurried past. As soon as the Matron disappeared around the corner, Anne crept to the office door and glanced inside. Row upon row of glass domes gleamed in the moonlight, but the room was otherwise empty. Anne hurried over to the desk and began searching. Most of the drawers contained stacks of paper, but the large drawer at the bottom was locked. She crouched down and dug out her pocketknife again. This lock proved trickier than the door of the dungeon cell, but eventually she got it. She opened the drawer and a wave of relief washed over her. The gauntlet was inside, and underneath it was the book, still with the same title as before. Unfortunately, her drawings were nowhere to be found, and the loose page with the ticket was also missing (no doubt the Matron had destroyed it). Amazingly, though, when Anne opened the cover of the book, there was another ticket, identical to the first one, printed on what was now the first page. She shoved the book into her pocket, confident this time that the ticket would remain until she needed it, but the gauntlet was too bulky. It would be easier to wear than to carry, so she pulled it onto her left hand.

Then the alarm cut off.

Anne knew she had to leave the office before the Matron returned, but as she stood she noticed something: On the desk was the dome containing the silver medallion with the scarred dragon image. What had the Matron been doing with it?

Another faint sound rang out.

The clock in the entrance was chiming midnight.

Anne panicked. The ship would soon be leaving. She ran for the door and was halfway across the room when the twelfth chime struck.

Anne's hand twitched inside the gauntlet.

She stopped and stared at it, unsure what had just happened.

It twitched again.

She tugged at the gauntlet, but it wouldn't come off.

It began to grow warm. Anne tried to wrench it from her hand, as it soon was so hot it burned. She suppressed a scream while waving her left arm wildly in the hopes of shaking it off.

Then the whole room started rattling, and despite her pain, Anne froze in terror. All the medallions vibrated against the glass of their domes, including the silver medallion on the desk. The rattling intensified as the gauntlet became even hotter, until suddenly the glass dome on the desk shattered and the silver medallion flew directly at Anne. She raised her arms to shield her face, and the medallion struck the gauntlet. The force of the impact knocked her backward into a shelf, and she tumbled to the floor.

A tiny rainbow-colored sparrow appeared above the medallion in a burst of light. It swooped around Anne three times, its wings brushing against her hair as it passed, but then it fell back into the medallion, almost as if it had been pulled back, and disappeared in another splash of light.

For a long time, Anne just sat, rocking back and forth, tears streaming down her cheeks, as both the gauntlet's heat and her pain gradually subsided. When she opened her eyes again, she saw that the medallion had fixed itself to the circular inset in the gauntlet cuff. Whatever had just happened, Anne suspected it was about to create more problems for her than it would solve.

Something clanked in the doorway. The Matron stood at the threshold along with a single iron knight.

The Matron held out her hand. "Give me the medallion."

While the gauntlet belonged to Anne, the medallion admittedly did not. Thinking she might appease the Matron by cooperating, Anne tried to remove the silver disk, but like the gauntlet itself, the medallion refused to budge.

"It won't come off," she said breathlessly.

"Then give me the gauntlet."

Anne hugged the gauntlet to herself. "It's mine," she said defiantly. "Besides, it's stuck on, too."

The Matron clenched and unclenched her jaw. Finally, she turned to the iron knight. "Remove it for her," she said.

"But—but how can it remove the gauntlet when I can't?" asked Anne.

In answer, the iron knight stepped forward.

And drew its sword.

---

*Getting your hand cut off
is less fun than you might think it is.*

—A quote from some guy who got his hand cut off and
discovered it was less fun than he thought it would be

5

Flight from Saint Lupin's

As the iron knight reached for Anne, she instinctively held up her arms to protect herself, prepared for the worst.

Several seconds passed.

Nothing happened.

The iron knight stood before her, its hand outstretched, quivering slightly but otherwise frozen in place. Anne gripped the edge of the shelf and pulled herself to her feet. As soon as she lowered the gauntlet, the iron knight lurched forward and clutched at the empty space on the floor where she had been sitting.

The iron knight regained its balance and grabbed for her a second time. Again, Anne raised her arms. Again, the iron knight stopped.

Anne lowered the gauntlet.

The iron knight began to move.

She raised the gauntlet.

The iron knight froze.

"Well, what are you waiting for?" barked the Matron.

Anne ran behind the desk. As she expected, the iron knight surged forward, grasping at the spot where she had just been standing. Undeterred, the iron knight tromped around the desk after her. Anne clambered up onto the sill of an open window and braced herself against the frame. The lawn lay ten feet below. She held the gauntlet out toward the advancing knight, forcing it to stop.

"Wait!" said the Matron, rushing around the other side of the desk. "You could damage the medallion."

"Stay back, then," said Anne, leaning farther out.

The Matron halted. "Come down from there. We'll figure something out."

"Figure what out? You ordered that iron knight to cut off my hand."

"An overreaction. We can search for a way to remove it safely, but your life is in peril. That gauntlet is dangerous, especially when combined with that medallion."

"Why should I believe anything you say?" asked Anne.

The Matron held up her right hand and, one finger at a time, removed her glove. Anne held her breath. She had never seen the Matron without her glove on. With a final tug, the Matron whisked it off. Underneath was a hand unlike any Anne had ever seen. It appeared to be made of some sort of gray metal and contained lots of tiny moving parts. It wasn't a gauntlet, but it definitely wasn't flesh and blood, either. Anne couldn't begin to guess how it worked or even how it was attached to the Matron's arm. Was it magick, too, like the book?

"This is nothing you're prepared to deal with," said the Matron. "Now step down, and I promise no harm will come to you."

Anne shook her head. "I don't trust you."

The Matron glared at her. "Very well. Back to the hard way, then."

She raised her metal hand toward the iron knight, who slowly began to move forward even though Anne's gauntlet was still raised. Whatever power the gauntlet had over the iron knight, the Matron's metal hand had more. As the iron knight reached her, Anne summoned her courage and leapt. For a heart-stopping moment it felt like she might fall forever. Then she landed and tumbled down the short slope. She jumped to her feet and glanced back up at the open window, expecting to see the Matron standing there shaking her fist. But the window was empty.

Anne wasted no time and immediately set off running alongside the building toward the main courtyard. At the corner, she crashed headlong into Penelope and nearly jumped out of her own skin.

"What are you still doing here?" said Anne, picking herself up off the ground.

"I was busy avoiding an iron knight," said Penelope. "What took *you* so long?"

Anne held up the gauntlet and showed Penelope the medallion.

Penelope gasped. "You stole from the Matron?"

"No," said Anne. "The medallion attached itself to the gauntlet on its own. Painfully. And now it won't come off."

Anne checked the central yard for any signs of

activity, but the coast was clear all the way to the main entrance with its looming clock tower. Anne could see the drawbridge just beyond—their best chance of escape.

"Ready?" asked Anne.

"Ready," said Penelope.

"Go!"

They dashed across the courtyard.

They were only steps from the archway when the gears of the drawbridge began to grind. Anne's eyes shot up to the top of the tower and her stomach flip-flopped. An iron knight stood silhouetted against the clock, winding the winch that raised the bridge. Their feet hit the planks of the rising deck, and they redoubled their efforts, pounding their way up the ever-steeper slope. The giant gears groaned. When they reached the end, Anne planted a firm foot and leapt for the opposite side, Penelope right beside her.

In the terrifying moment that they hung in the air, Anne realized their mistake. The drawbridge had risen too high. If they landed on the stone ramp from this height, they might break their legs or worse. Anne willed herself to drop straight down like a rock instead. As she fell, however, she saw that Penelope had propelled herself closer to the other side—but not quite far enough.

Penelope's head hit the edge of the ramp with a sickening thunk, and she fell into the moat.

A split second later Anne smacked into the icy water, the impact momentarily knocking the wind out of her. She struggled to the surface, gasping and gagging. Nearby, Penelope floated faceup—thankfully—and Anne grabbed her friend's coat. The moat was only fifty feet wide, and they had landed halfway across. Anne held on to her unconscious companion as best she could using the gauntlet and started paddling for shore with her other hand.

Anne was making achingly slow progress when something brushed against her thigh. She kicked out but didn't make contact. She knew what it must be, but she pushed the thought from her mind and paddled more frantically.

Less than ten feet from shore, she spotted it out of the corner of her eye: a large rotting fin, circling back toward them. Anne stroked harder, but her arms were tired and her breath was coming in short, sputtering gasps. She maneuvered herself between Penelope and the oncoming shark, which disappeared beneath them. Anne felt a tug, but no bite. It had Penelope! Her friend jerked again and was pulled under the water. Anne held on and went with her. She struggled to pull Penelope back up, but the shark was too powerful. It dragged them down into the reeds at the bottom.

With her lungs bursting and the cold quickly leeching away her strength, Anne pulled out her pocketknife, opened the blade using her teeth, and then swam past Penelope and stabbed desperately at the shark.

Contact.

The shark released Penelope, swimming away erratically, the knife lodged in its eye. Anne grabbed Penelope's coat with both hands and kicked furiously, desperate for air. They surfaced at the edge of the moat. Penelope started to come around, and Anne helped her as they crawled onto the bank. As Penelope coughed out a lungful of sour moat water, Anne checked her over for signs of injury. Luckily, other than a lump on her forehead from where it made contact with the ramp, she was fine. A pattern of tears in her coat showed that the shark had only gotten hold of her clothing. Anne flopped onto her back, exhausted.

"Let's...call that one...Plan Really Bad Idea," mumbled Penelope.

The drawbridge gears started grinding again. Their pursuers were lowering the bridge.

"Come on," said Anne.

Penelope had trouble rising on her own, so Anne put a steadying arm around her and helped her up, which was no small task given how much larger Penelope was than Anne. They started down the path leading to the dock, but paused when they noticed the swinging lanterns of an airship in the distant sky, slowly sailing away from the Saint Lupin's tier.

They were too late.

Anne's heart sank.

She dug the soggy book out of her coat pocket and looked down at the cover. The title had changed again. It now read *The Adventurer's Guide to Running Far Far Away*. Wondering what that could possibly mean, she turned to the first page. The second ticket had disappeared, and in its place was a single word:

Hide.

Anne steered Penelope into the trees in the same direction she'd gone that morning. She figured they could take cover in the forest or in the entrance to Shaft Eleven and plan their next steps from there. Jutting roots and fallen branches threatened to send them sprawling, but Anne kept the pace steady and continued to support Penelope as best she could. After several frightening minutes of stumbling through the darkness, they broke into a clearing—the same clearing where Anne had fallen off the tier and onto the ledge earlier. She cursed their luck. They must have passed the mine in the dark.

"Look at the pretty light," said Penelope, sounding dazed. She pointed.

Anne scanned the night sky, where one twinkling star caught her attention. It was growing bigger and bigger, which was unusual behavior for a star. Then again, it had been that sort of a day. In fact, the star seemed to be traveling right at them, and it was accompanied by an increasingly loud whooshing sound, giving the distinct impression that it was in fact another ball of fire (which is technically what a falling star is, except whereas one holds the promise of wonder and the fulfillment of wishes, the other promises instant crispification).

Just before impact, Anne hauled Penelope behind a tree. The fireball exploded in the middle of the clearing and sent a cloud of smoke and dust rolling past them. Anne snatched a knobby stick off the ground and held it in her gauntlet-hand; any weapon was better protection than none. A woman stepped forth from the thick smoke, spotted Anne, and walked over.

Anne blinked, disbelieving she was really seeing what her eyes told her she was seeing.

"Wherever have you been, my dear?" said Jocelyn, sounding somewhat annoyed. "This delay has put everything behind schedule." She flipped open a small notebook. "We've missed the opening ceremonies, the Getting to Know You luncheon, the academy tour, everything."

Anne needed two or three tries before she was able to speak actual words. "Y-you're alive."

Jocelyn frowned. "That's a rather odd thing to say."

Anne shook her head. "But—but this morning. That dragon torched you with a fireball."

Jocelyn laughed. "Well, of course she did. I believe you've been referring to her as Dog, yes? Nana, come out now, don't be shy. Come and say hello."

Anne looked around. "You found Dog?"

A black form emerged from the smoke—a large black "something" that was all too familiar.

"Dragon!" yelled Anne, throwing her stick with all her might. It soared through the air in a perfect arc, struck the dragon's thick scales, and bounced harmlessly away over the edge of the tier.

The dragon lowered its head until its large reptilian eyes stared directly into Anne's. "You're new at this," it rumbled in a deep, gravelly voice, "so I'm going to overlook that."

"Wow," said Penelope. "Dog got real big."

Anne shook her head vigorously. "You can't be Dog. That's impossible."

"Nana is a Phantom dragon," Jocelyn explained. "They can change their size and appearance. She only disguised herself as your fire lizard so she could assess the situation prior to my arrival."

"You—you were *spying* on us?"

"Assessing, dear. Nana is the academy's dragon. She's here to help."

Anne stepped back, not taking her eyes off the dragon. "But she attacked me with a fireball."

"And you'd be a lot easier to hit if you stood still," grumbled Nana. "It's hard to mount a rescue when you run away like that."

"That was a rescue?"

"Naturally. You want to leave the orphanage, don't you?"

"But you nearly incinerated me!"

"Nonsense," said Nana. "At most you would have gotten a little singed around the edges. Or maybe a nice tan."

"Fireballs are a common form of transportation," Jocelyn explained. "Green ones, that is. Not the red."

"What's wrong with red fireballs?" asked Anne.

"Red means dead," said Nana.

"It's the best way to reach these more outlying areas without it taking forever," said Jocelyn. "Saint Lupin's is not exactly on the central tiers, you know. Still, personally I only use them when absolutely necessary. It takes me *days* to clean the sulfur smell out of my clothes. No offense," she added to Nana.

"None taken," growled Nana. "I make them smell that way on purpose. Consider it payback for forcing me to wear a dog collar."

"But if you're not Dog, then where is he?" asked Anne. "You...you didn't eat him, did you?"

Nana grinned, and her giant teeth glistened in the moonlight. "Maybe I did. Goodness knows I get paid little enough for everything I do around here. A tasty fire lizard steak would really hit the spot."

Anne gasped.

"Now stop that," Jocelyn scolded Nana. "I assure

you, Anne, your fire lizard is perfectly safe back at the academy. We'll return him as soon as possible."

A distant crashing echoed through the forest, accompanied by the sound of approaching footsteps. Very heavy footsteps.

"Were you expecting company?" asked Jocelyn.

Anne gripped Penelope's arm. "It must be the Matron and her iron knights. We're, ah, sort of in the middle of escaping."

"Understood," said Jocelyn. She turned to Nana. "Three fireballs, if you please."

"Wait a minute," said Anne, "by fireballs do you mean—"

But it was too late. Nana reared back, opened her mouth wide, and belched flame.

While the concept of traveling by fireball understandably raises a lot of eyebrows (or at least those that haven't been scorched off), it has been certified by Fireball Travel Incorporated as being "absolutely safe." The fact that Fireball Travel Incorporated also has a monopoly on the dictionary industry and has redefined the word *safe* to mean "extremely dangerous and in fact likely to cause grievous and lasting bodily harm" should in no way be considered a conflict of interest (*conflict of interest* having been redefined to mean "giant potato").

6

Welcome to Death Mountain

Anne couldn't be certain whether she screamed the entire trip. Granted, it is extremely difficult to hear anything above the deafening roar inside a fireball, even the sound of your own voice shrieking in horror.

The last flames dissipated, and Anne found herself staring at a mountain—staring *down* at a mountain, that is, which is an unsettling feeling even if you haven't just traveled an unknown distance inside a blazing sphere of destruction. Dozens of buildings dotted the mountain-side, connected via winding paths and steep staircases, all sitting in the shadow of a large shelf of overhanging rock at the mountain peak. When Anne examined her immediate surroundings, she discovered she was standing atop a small floating island roughly a hundred feet in diameter. At the center of this island, a giant metal ring stuck out of the ground with a giant metal chain attached to it. The chain extended over the side and disappeared into the mists below, presumably tethering the tiny tier in place.

Two more fireballs landed next to Anne, depositing Penelope and Jocelyn.

Penelope pumped her fist in the air. "That. Was. Awesome!"

Anne touched the spot on Penelope's forehead where she had struck the bridge. There wasn't even so much as a bruise showing. "How are you feeling?" she asked.

"Great," said Penelope. "Although I don't know how. A moment ago I was still seeing two of everything."

"Fireballs have healing properties," said Nana behind them.

Anne jumped in surprise. She hadn't seen Nana arrive. "How did you get here?"

"I flew here right after I sent you on your way. Eight hours ago."

"Eight hours?" For the first time Anne took note of the early-morning sun; they had left Saint Lupin's not long after midnight. "But it only felt like a minute or two."

"That's due to the time-compression feature," said Jocelyn. "Because honestly, who wants to experience that amount of time inside a fireball? Premium fireballs are nearly instantaneous, of course, and dragons themselves can travel at supersonic speeds, but the travel time for all regular fireballs is set at eight hours."

"*All* fireballs?" said Penelope. "That seems a bit arbitrary."

"Oh, it is. Completely. It's even in the dragons' contract under the section titled All the Arbitrary Things Dragons Get to Do That Annoy People."

Nana yawned. "As interesting as all of this isn't, I'm long overdue for a break. So if you'll pardon me, not that I would care if you didn't, I'm off to eat a herd of sheep and nap for a month. Enjoy your studies." With that, she dropped off the edge of the tethered tier and swooped away.

Penelope looked at Anne and grinned. "Well, we made it."

Anne took a big breath and exhaled. It was true. Despite the perilous circumstances of their escape, they were finally free of Saint Lupin's and of the Matron as well. Not only had they avoided the Pit, but they had made it to an honest-to-goodness academy. She could go on adventures. She could search for home. A wide grin spread across her face.

Jocelyn gestured to the mountain with a sweep of her arm. "Welcome to the Death Mountain Quest Academy."

"Thank you," said Anne. "But, erm, it's called Death Mountain?"

"Oh, did I not mention that?" Jocelyn gave an embarrassed cough. "It's a tradition of sorts. Each academy is named after the nearest landmark of note. It could be worse, though. Before it moved here it was the Stinky Gas Swamp Academy. In any case, after some breakfast, I'll give you the grand tour. This small tier we're currently standing on, incidentally, is the designated fireball landing zone."

As she took it all in, Anne held up her arm to shield her eyes from the morning sun. It was strange and intriguing and beautiful all at once.

Jocelyn gasped. "What's that?"

"What's what?" asked Anne, looking around.

"That light on your gauntlet."

Anne lowered her arm. The medallion was pulsing. "That's weird. It wasn't doing that before."

Jocelyn grabbed the gauntlet and yanked it forward, nearly pulling Anne off her feet. "But where...where did you...how did you get this medallion?"

"Th-the gauntlet took it," said Anne.

Jocelyn shook the gauntlet. "Took it? I don't understand."

"In the Matron's office. When the clock struck midnight. All the medallions started vibrating and then this one attached itself."

"You mean you picked up this medallion and inserted it into the slot?"

"No, it flew across the room on its own."

Jocelyn released Anne's arm and began pacing while muttering to herself. "Unbelievable...never heard of... who leaves one out in the open like that anyway...need to consult with..."

"I'm sorry if I've caused any trouble," said Anne. "I didn't know that would happen."

Jocelyn shook her head. "It's not your fault, dear. It's mine. I never should have left you unsupervised with that gauntlet." She stopped pacing. "What has the GPS told you so far?"

Anne raised an eyebrow. "Er, GPS?"

"It stands for General Pathfinder Sparrow," Jocelyn explained.

"I did see a little rainbow sparrow, just for a few seconds," said Anne, recalling the brightly colored bird.

"Yes, that's it. Each gauntlet contains a sparrow who interprets the prophecy medallions."

Anne stared at the medallion. "Did you say *prophecy*?"

"Of course. Anyone may go on a run-of-the-mill quest," said Jocelyn. "All you need is a one-year Adventurer's Certificate. But only a gauntlet-wearer can trigger a prophecy quest."

"Wait. Are you saying this medallion might have triggered something?" said Anne.

"That's what we're trying to determine. Now, please try the sparrow. Just say 'Activate GPS.'"

Anne held up her gauntlet-hand. "Activate GPS."

Nothing happened.

"Activate GPS," Anne said again, this time a little louder.

Still nothing.

Jocelyn shook her head. "I'm not sure what the problem is. If the quest has been activated, the sparrow should appear. But I'm not going to attempt repairs here, and in any case, medallion maintenance is hardly my area of expertise. Follow me."

A narrow suspension bridge hung precariously between the tiny tethered tier and the mountain. The bridge consisted of two thick ropes holding up a bunch of planks and other smaller ropes all knotted together and pretending to be a real bridge and not the inevitable death trap it looked like. Each end was anchored to a pair of rectangular stone pillars. Jocelyn led the girls quickly down the bridge (granted, given the steep angle, there was really no way to go down other than quickly), and once the group reached solid ground again, they hurried past a large warehouse-looking structure and descended the steep winding paths and twisting staircases of the academy. Most of the buildings were single story, each with a gently curving peaked roof that extended over a veranda.

As they passed one of the few two-story buildings, Jocelyn said, "This is the main administration building. Typically, all newcomers to the academy are brought here first to register, but given your special circumstances we'll head straight for—"

"Professor Daisywheel."

The man who spoke stood in the doorway of the

administration building. His dark, wavy hair contained a hint of gray at the sideburns, his white skin was evenly tanned, and he had just the right amount of freckles. He wore crisp gray trousers, a charcoal tunic, and a midnight black cape, which was slung over one shoulder. Curiously, a crow was perched on the other shoulder. The crow stared at Anne without blinking.

"Oh dear," Jocelyn murmured. She ushered Anne and Penelope back over to stand before the man. "Minister, such an unexpected pleasure to see you," she said with forced cheerfulness.

The man smiled the smile of someone who didn't much care for smiling, felt smiling generally to be a nuisance, and whose facial muscles were so out of practice they seemed to have forgotten most of the required movements.

"I've been waiting here for over an hour, Professor," he said. "I do have other matters that require my attention, you know."

"My apologies. I had no idea you were coming in person." She turned to Anne and Penelope. "This is Lord Greystone from the Wizards' Council. He's the current Minister of Questing and oversees everything related to academies and quests." Jocelyn turned back to Greystone. "Speaking of which, Minister, please meet Anne, our newest Keeper."

Greystone gave a startled look. "Keeper? Your note only mentioned new students. Who gives a gauntlet to an untrained child?"

"She's thirteen, which is hardly a child. And in any case, you know full well there is no age restriction. She was the first to wear the gauntlet, meaning it has now bonded itself to her, which makes her a Keeper. On that point, the rules are extremely clear."

"What's a Keeper?" asked Penelope.

"That's what we call anyone who wears one of the gauntlets, dear," Jocelyn explained. "Anne is a Keeper of the Sparrow now."

Greystone's expression darkened as he tried to come up with an argument against this but failed. "I presume you have the paperwork?" he said finally through gritted teeth.

"Right this way," said Jocelyn, pointing inside.

Greystone turned on his heel and entered, but Jocelyn momentarily held back Anne and Penelope. "Say nothing unless spoken to," she whispered. "And no matter what, do not allow that medallion to be seen."

"How?" asked Anne. "It's still blinking."

Instead of answering, Jocelyn merely held a finger to

her lips and continued into the building without another word, leaving Anne confused. Why were they hiding the medallion from the one person who would likely most want to see it? Wouldn't a Minister of Questing want to know about a potential quest? Nevertheless, Anne did as Jocelyn had instructed and pressed the gauntlet to her side to hide the pulsing light. They proceeded through a sliding door, down a short corridor, and into a large room where several tables were covered in stacks of paper.

Jocelyn retrieved a small pile of documents and handed them to Greystone.

He examined the top page. "It doesn't list her official status."

"She's an orphan," said Jocelyn.

Another flicker of irritation crossed his face. "Yes, but from which preparatory school?"

"None. She's been a resident of Saint Lupin's Institute almost since birth. The parents and place of origin are unknown. She's a genuine orphan."

Greystone gave a look of triumph. "If she cannot provide proof of her home tier, she cannot enroll."

Jocelyn pointed to the gauntlet. "She can if she has

that, along with the permission of the head of an academy willing to take her. Which she most certainly does."

Greystone scowled and went back to flipping through the documents, pausing every now and then to study a page more closely.

"I assure you, everything is in order," said Jocelyn.

"What about the gauntlet?" he asked without looking up.

Jocelyn motioned for Anne to step forward. "Place the gauntlet here, dear," she said, indicating a spot on the table. Anne placed her gauntlet-hand palm-down so as to hide the medallion from view, but she couldn't prevent a faint glow from reflecting off the surface of the table. The crow hopped down and peered curiously at the flickering light. Anne wanted to shoo it away, but she couldn't do so without attracting attention.

Greystone stared at the gauntlet with an expression of shock. "Dear gods above and below, where did you find that antique?"

"It's a castoff," said Jocelyn. "From one of your new council-run academies, no doubt. The paperwork for it is there in the documents I gave you."

Greystone sniffed, as though the gauntlet were

omitting a bad odor. "Well, no wonder they got rid of it. It's not even fit for a museum."

"Yes, pieces of it will probably begin dropping off before she makes it through her first year," said Jocelyn. "I'm afraid it's the best we could do under the circumstances."

Anne's eyes widened, and she opened her mouth to speak, but Jocelyn clamped her hand firmly over it. "Yes, dear, I know. It's deeply upsetting."

"This is precisely why I wish to see all the quest academies brought under the direct oversight of the Wizards' Council," Greystone said. "We could standardize testing, provide access to proper, well-maintained equipment, and ensure a minimum level of quality control. You do your students a disservice by equipping them so poorly."

"I expect we have somewhat differing views on what counts as a disservice to our students," said Jocelyn.

Greystone grunted.

"Very well." He laid down a piece of parchment. "Place your signature here," Greystone said to Anne as he pointed to a blank line at the bottom of the page. "And also here…and here…and here and here." As he spoke, he added several more pages to the pile.

The papers were out of reach, but Anne didn't dare move her arm. "What are those for?"

"Oh, just the usual hero stuff," said Jocelyn, drawing the papers over and shoving a quill pen into Anne's right hand.

"Hero?" said Anne.

"Exactly." Jocelyn counted off on her fingers. "Things like fulfillment of contract, completion of all quest-related tasks, person-of-unspecified-gender in distress contingencies, injury clauses—"

"Injury?" said Anne.

"—insurance against fire-breathing creatures, insurance against non-fire-breathing creatures, beneficiaries in the event of death—"

"*Death!*"

"—disposal of remains not incinerated, next of kin, et cetera, et cetera. You know, the usual. Ms. Shatterblade, you'll need to sign some of these papers as well."

Penelope was only too eager to sign up for adventure and moved quickly over to the table.

"Shatterblade?" said Greystone. "This is their daughter? Are you seriously proposing to enroll this girl after that business her parents were involved in? After every other academy in the Hierarchy has vowed to strike their family's name from the records?"

Penelope's cheeks grew as flame red as her hair.

If possible, Jocelyn stood even straighter than usual. "Yes, that's exactly what I'm proposing to do. And all Keepers are free to choose whomever they wish for party members."

Anne didn't comment, as per Jocelyn's instructions, but she did do her best to convey through her posture and expression that in no uncertain terms she and Penelope were a team.

Greystone fumed and ground his teeth together, and Anne thought for sure one of the blood vessels in his forehead would burst. Then a gleam appeared in his eye.

"You can't have an adventuring group with only two members," he said. "The minimum requirement is three. If you are unable to provide another recruit, the council has the authority to assign—"

At that moment one of the side doors slid open, and a boy with a dour expression stepped into the room. He had light beige skin and brown eyes and appeared to be the same age as Anne and Penelope. His long dark green coat was buttoned down to the knees, and a long colorful scarf was wound loosely around his neck and under his long, straight black hair, which was pulled back into a ponytail. He walked over and stood stiffly next to Jocelyn.

"I saw you arrive and thought it best to come and find you," the boy said to her.

"Excellent timing, dear," Jocelyn murmured to him, and then she turned her attention back to Greystone. "Your offer to supply a third party member is very generous, Minister, but as you can see, that won't be necessary." She handed some additional documents to Greystone. "This is Hiro Darkflame. He studied at Cloverfield."

Greystone perused the papers and raised an eyebrow. "Cloverfield? That's a top preparatory school. How did you manage to acquire a student from there?"

Jocelyn smiled confidently. "I have my connections."

If possible, Greystone scrutinized the new student's papers even more closely than he had Anne's. Apparently finding nothing to complain about (and being visibly annoyed by that fact), he handed the documents back. Anne finished signing the papers in front of her, and both Penelope and Hiro signed next. While Greystone watched them, Anne swiftly lifted her arm away and pressed the gauntlet against her side. The crow seemed disappointed that the light had gone away.

Once everyone finished, Greystone gave one set of copies to Jocelyn and stuffed the second set into his leather satchel.

"And what about the Bag of Chance?" he asked.

Jocelyn produced a small pouch. "Each party member requires an official role," she explained to Anne and Penelope. "By tradition they are assigned randomly. Simply draw a token from the bag."

She held the pouch out to Penelope first. Penelope stuck her hand in and drew out a tiny wooden token.

"Yes. Fighter," said Penelope, looking pleased. She showed it to Anne. It had a picture of a sword with the word *fighter* written in plain script underneath.

Jocelyn next held the pouch out to Hiro.

"Wizard," he read from his token, but he didn't show it to anyone other than Jocelyn.

Anne was last. There were dozens of tokens in the bag, and she dug around until her fingers closed on one that felt especially cool to the touch. She took it out. It had a picture of a hammer on it.

"Blacksmith?" she read.

Greystone frowned. "The standard beginning party is supposed to be fighter, wizard, and thief."

"Well, as I'm sure you'll agree, this group is anything but standard," said Jocelyn. "And it *is* called the Bag of Chance, after all." Greystone raised an eyebrow, but

Jocelyn quickly continued. "Splendid, everyone. Well done. I'm sure you'll all settle into your new roles in no time. Was there anything else, Minister?"

Greystone handed Anne a pamphlet. "This is your copy of the Wizards' Council's official *Rules for Quests*. It should answer all your Keeper-related questions."

"What if it doesn't?" asked Anne, weighing the thinness of the pamphlet against the multitude of thoughts buzzing around inside her head.

"Then you're obviously asking the wrong questions," he said coldly.

"Well, don't let us keep you," said Jocelyn. "I know what a busy individual you are."

Greystone gathered his satchel. "Come, Neeva," he commanded, and the crow perched on his shoulder once again. With that, he brushed past the group with a swish of his cape and exited the building.

"Is it me, or is that guy a little intense?" said Penelope.

Jocelyn smiled at Anne. "That was excellent work, my dear. You're a natural, if I do say so myself."

Anne blushed, unused to praise of any sort from an adult. "Why didn't you want the minister to see the medallion?"

"Because while there is very little he can do about the gauntlet itself, it is highly illegal to possess an active prophecy medallion without a permit."

Hiro's eyes widened. "She has an active medallion?"

"Not now, Mr. Darkflame," said Jocelyn, and she led them back outside. "I work very hard not to give the council any reason to stick its nose into our business, and it's an open secret that Lord Greystone despises the current academy system."

"What's the current system?" asked Penelope.

"The Wizards' Council oversees everything related to magick, quests, and prophecies. The academies have to adhere to their regulations and file the required paperwork, but otherwise the council has little say in how each individual academy is actually run. Greystone wants to change that. He's been trying to abolish the independent academies one by one and bring them all under the direct control of the council. Some say he's even sabotaging them, ensuring recruits either transfer out or flunk out. Dozens have closed already."

Penelope looked around. "Say, where are the other students, anyway?"

"That's my point," said Jocelyn. "You three are this academy's only remaining students. We once had hundreds of aspiring adventurers and dozens of professors, but now there's just a handful of us left. That's why we're so glad you're here. If you fail, this academy will be forced to shut its doors forever."

Anne's chest tightened. The last twenty-four hours had been a whirlwind, with one revelation after another, but knowing that the fate of Jocelyn's academy depended on her as well made Anne more anxious than ever.

"Well, we won't fail, then," said Penelope. "We'll study like crazy and pass any test Lord Stonehead wants to throw at us."

Jocelyn smiled. "That's a lovely sentiment, dear, but I'm afraid it's not that simple." She stopped them at the base of a five-story tower. "Keepers typically don't go on a prophecy quest until they've had three years of intense study. If you've activated one now, you'll have to undertake it with no training whatsoever. And if you fail the quest, you fail the academy."

"We might fail?" squeaked Hiro.

"Not now, Mr. Darkflame," said Jocelyn.

Anne swallowed. "So where are we going?"

"To the one place where we can hopefully get some answers," said Jocelyn, pointing to the top of the tower. "I'm taking you to see the cat."

The Death Mountain Quest Academy has had many nonhuman headmasters and headmistresses over the course of its existence. Dozens of dwarves and elves have served in the top position, along with gnomes and ogres and at least three sentient trees. Then there was the famous Equestrian Council, a group of five horses who served as co-heads until it became clear they couldn't get anything done. Every time one of them tabled a motion, the others always voted "neigh."

There was also one summer afternoon when for three-quarters of an hour everyone believed the current headmaster had transformed into a cherry pie. It turned out he'd merely snuck off for a nap and left his lunch on his chair.

Only once in all of its history, however, has the academy ever been led by a cat.

7

The Cat and the Quest

Anne, Penelope, and Hiro followed Jocelyn to the top of the tower, where there was a large oak door with a plaque over it that read HEAD OFFICE. Sitting behind a small desk next to the door was a short, burly, ruddy-cheeked man with a thick, unkempt beard. He wore a rusty breastplate and a dented helm, and he carried enough weapons to put the armory of most small villages to shame, which gave him the overall appearance of a receptionist who took no prisoners.

"Everyone, this is Captain Yngvi Copperhelm," said Jocelyn.

Copperhelm grunted, which Anne took for "hello."

Jocelyn pointed to the door. "We're here to see the headmistress."

"It's her morning naptime," said Copperhelm.

"Well, her nap will just have to be interrupted, I'm afraid. We're here on a matter of great urgency."

Copperhelm surveyed the group. "Let me guess. Someone received their gauntlet, and the first thing they did was go and stick a prophecy medallion in it."

Anne's cheeks grew warm. "It's not my—that's not how it happened." She placed a hand over the medallion, which was flashing even faster now.

"Actually, we're not certain yet that the medallion is active," said Jocelyn.

Copperhelm slid out of his chair and walked around to the front of the desk, mumbling as he went. "Crazy recruits...no common sense...probably blow the place up...and look at me...used to lead troops into battle... now I'm secretary to a cat...hardest part of my day is digging lost toys out from behind the shelf and cleaning the litter box."

He stopped in front of Anne, the top of his head

barely level with her shoulders. From one of his many belt pouches he produced two items: a small tube of stiff leather with a curved piece of glass at both ends, and a dinner fork with a bent prong.

"Let's have a look at it, then," he said.

Anne held out her gauntlet-hand. Copperhelm held one end of the tube in front of his eye, leaned close to the gauntlet, and probed the medallion with the bent prong of the fork.

"Well?" said Jocelyn.

"It's active, all right," said Copperhelm. He prodded the medallion several more times. "Looks like the sparrow got caught in a loop trying to read the medallion. Not surprising given that scratch across the top. Should be a quick fix, though. Presuming it doesn't explode first."

"They explode?" said Anne.

"He's joking, dear," said Jocelyn. "Mostly." She turned to Hiro. "I need to consult with the captain for a moment. Mr. Darkflame, would you please introduce Anne and Ms. Shatterblade to our headmistress? Also, you may try the level stones, if you wish. They're in the desk. Top drawer on the right-hand side. We'll join you shortly."

Hiro nodded and turned to Anne and Penelope. "Follow me," he said in what Anne considered an unnecessarily officious tone given that they had all heard Jocelyn's instructions. He opened the large door and led Anne and Penelope into the head office.

The bright morning sun streamed in through seven large windows. Between the windows, shelves were stuffed with ancient tomes, scrolls, and dozens of balls of yarn. The inner wall of the office was covered with paintings, both portraits and landscapes. The "headmistress" in question was curled up on a richly embroidered cushion lying on the desk in the center of the room. She had orange fur except for a white belly and paws, and in every way possible resembled a typical alley cat. The cat yawned, but otherwise seemed disinclined to move or in any way acknowledge their presence.

Hiro walked over to the desk and cleared his throat. "Please allow me to introduce the current headmistress of the Death Mountain Quest Academy, Her Royal Highness Princess Fluffington Whiskers of the Mouse-trapper Clan." As if the title wasn't pompous enough on its own, Hiro enunciated the words as though he were speaking them inside some royal palace.

"Nice to meet you, Fluffy," said Penelope.

The cat hissed at her.

"She prefers to be addressed as *Princess Whiskers*," said Hiro. Penelope rolled her eyes at both him and the cat.

Anne fidgeted with the sleeve of her coat, searching for the right words. "But…it's a cat."

"It's a bit unorthodox," said Hiro, sounding less like a fellow student and more like a tour guide. He even began pacing. "The academy was in serious debt a few years ago, and a wealthy donor offered to help it out on the condition that, after the donor's death, her beloved cat be appointed as the next headmistress."

"And the academy agreed to that?" said Anne.

Hiro blushed slightly. "I think they were counting on the donor living a lot longer. If it helps any, from what I hear, she attended a very prestigious post-secondary school."

"Let me guess. Yours?" said Penelope.

Hiro sniffed. "Blackbriar College, actually. The donor funded it as well."

Anne tilted her head and studied the cat from a different angle. "So, is she, like, magickal or something?"

Hiro shook his head. "No, nothing like that. She's an ordinary domestic shorthair breed, just one who happens to have an advanced degree in educational theory and practice."

He opened the top drawer on the right side of the desk and took out a cloth pouch. Holding it carefully in his hand, he moved to the other end of the desk and slowly dumped the contents onto the table. Twelve small polished blue stones tumbled out, numbered one through twelve.

"These are level stones," he explained as he lined them up in order. "Each one vibrates at a different magickal frequency, corresponding to the different quest levels. Twelve in all. When you match the correct stone to the medallion, it glows." He picked up the closest stone, the one with the number twelve etched into it, and held it against the medallion. "Like that," he said.

The stone remained unchanged.

"I hate to point this out to you, but nothing is happening," said Penelope.

Hiro placed the stone back at the end of the line. "That's actually a good thing. Few adventurers ever attain the skills necessary to tackle a Level Twelve quest." Somehow when he said "few adventurers," he made it sound very much like he was referring only to Anne and Penelope and not himself. "Hopefully your medallion is a Level One quest, or at worst a Level Tw—"

Something flew across the desk and scattered the stones.

Princess Whiskers.

"Hey, cut that out!" said Hiro while Penelope suppressed a smirk.

But the cat kept batting the stones, even flinging some of them off the desk. Hiro managed to snatch away the number one stone before she could get to it, and he held it against the medallion. As with the number twelve stone, there was no change.

"Hmmm, so not a Level One, either," he said, this time with a genuine hint of concern in his voice. "But I'm sure it will turn out to be a Level Two at most. From everything I've read, which includes some of the top researchers in quest theory, that would be considered quite advanced for beginners, but with extra classes I'm sure you'd be fine." Again, Anne noted that he didn't seem to include himself among the "beginners."

"*Extra* classes?" Penelope whispered to Anne. "Who is this guy?"

Hiro scanned the desk and the floor. "Now where did the number two stone get to?"

Hiro and Penelope knelt on the floor and began searching. Anne was about to join them when she noticed that Princess Whiskers had nudged two of the stones remaining on the desk closer together, the number three and the number ten. The cat sat hunched on the desk, staring at them intently. Anne picked up the number three stone and hesitantly set it on the medallion.

To her relief, it, too, elicited no reaction.

Anne placed the stone back on the desk next to the number ten, but as the gauntlet passed over them, a flash of light erupted from the two stones. Curious, she moved the gauntlet back and held it in place. Both stones began to glow steadily.

"Found it!" exclaimed Penelope from under the desk. She crawled out and stood, holding the number two stone triumphantly in her raised fist before handing it smugly over to Hiro.

"Um," said Anne, pointing to the table. "I think you might want to have a look at this."

Hiro looked at the two glowing stones and gasped.

"Doesn't three plus ten equal thirteen?" asked Penelope.

"But—but there's no such thing as a Level Thirteen quest," said Hiro.

"For which you should be thankful," said Copperhelm,

marching into the room alongside Jocelyn. They joined Anne, Penelope, and Hiro (and the cat) at the desk. "In fact, at this stage in your careers, anything above even a Level Three or Four quest would chew you up and spit out the pieces. And that's assuming there would be any pieces left to spit out. Which there probably wouldn't be."

"Who threw level stones all over the floor?" asked Jocelyn.

Penelope pointed at Princess Whiskers.

Jocelyn shook a finger at the cat. "Is this the example you feel the headmistress of a quest academy should be setting? You're being a very bad professor."

The cat hissed at her, too.

Copperhelm studied the glowing stones. "What made you place them together like that?"

Anne shook her head. "It wasn't me. Princess Whiskers did that, too."

Copperhelm took hold of Anne's gauntlet and gently moved it away. The stones stopped glowing. He moved it back. They glowed again. This time the light of the medallion pulsed even faster until it became a steady glow itself.

"What do you think it means?" asked Anne.

"Personally, I think it means you're all doomed,"

said Copperhelm. "But that could just be me. Try the sparrow now."

Anne held up her gauntlet-hand. "Activate GPS."

As soon as the words left her mouth, a rainbow-colored streak shot out of the gauntlet. It bounced around the office, off walls, off shelves, and even off the cat, sending her howling behind a shelf.

"Er, is that the sparrow?" asked Anne, trying to follow the blur around the room.

Jocelyn pressed her fingers against her temple. "They can be somewhat overenergetic, especially at the beginning of a quest."

The sparrow finally stopped moving, alighted on the desk, and began chewing on a scroll. "Now, stop that," Jocelyn said.

"I'm sorry. Was this yours?" said the sparrow. Since its mouth was full of scroll, this sounded more like "Em srbi. Wezzis urs?"

Copperhelm yanked the scroll out of the sparrow's mouth. The bottom half had already been completely shredded.

Jocelyn sighed. "They also have a serious appetite for information, so you have to watch them constantly around books, scrolls, pamphlets, and pretty much anything with writing on it."

The sparrow smacked its beak. "Needs more salt," it chirped in a squeaky voice.

"You eat books?" asked Anne.

"It's the best way to read them." It hopped over to Anne. "You must by my Keeper. The name's Jeffery." He held out a tiny wing and Anne shook it. When she touched his feathers, she experienced a mild tingling sensation.

"Hi, Jeffery," said Anne. "I'm glad you're finally unstuck. We were hoping you could tell us about this medallion."

"Sure," said Jeffery. "It contains a Rightful Heir quest."

Anne frowned. "A rightful what?"

"Obviously that's a quest to become the heir to a kingdom," Hiro interjected. "They're not overly common these days, but they used to be popular a few centuries ago. If you finish the quest, you become the ruler of a tier, typically whatever tier you originated from. They can be very lucrative quests, too, although they do tend to be high level, from what I've read."

"An excellent summary, Mr. Darkflame," said Jocelyn.

Anne was momentarily stunned. "Wait. Are you saying that if I go on this quest, I'll become the ruler of the tier I came from?"

"Sure," said Jeffery. "I mean, where else would you be the heir of?"

"But what if I don't know where I came from?"

"Not a problem. In fact, the quest is designed to help you figure that out."

Home, Anne thought. She might actually find home. As much as she had dreamed of the possibility, she knew it might take years, and she also knew she might never discover where she came from. But less than a day after leaving Saint Lupin's, she was being presented with an opportunity to actually find it. Anne didn't know whether to smile or laugh or cry or do all of them at once. Penelope gave her a huge hug that lifted her clear off her feet.

"Yes, yes, it's all very exciting," said Jocelyn. "But let's stick to the issue at hand. Jeffery, what level is it exactly?"

"Thirteen," he chirped.

Jocelyn put her hands on her hips. "Now, Jeffery, we all know there's no such thing as a Level Thirteen quest."

Jeffery flapped his wings. "Hey, tell it to the medallion. I just work here."

"Fine. We'll come back to that part. Can you at least give us the quest riddle?"

Jeffery gave a tiny salute with his wing. "Yes, ma'am."

He hopped back up onto the gauntlet, cleared his throat, opened his beak, and started singing in a clear, high voice:

> *Climb the tower with no door.*
> *Ask the knight who never lived.*
> *Take the key you cannot hold.*
> *Claim the throne without a crown.*

Anne waited for him to continue, but that was all he said.

"That's it?" she asked.

"Yep," said Jeffery. "I mean, unless the medallion is holding back on me. Sometimes they do that." He gave the medallion a kick.

"But it didn't rhyme," said Hiro.

"Indeed," said Jocelyn. "And there's a poetry category on your evaluation form, so I'm afraid that's going to affect your mark."

"Wow, tough crowd," said Jeffery.

Penelope scratched her head. "But it doesn't make

any sense. How can you climb a tower that doesn't have a door? Or talk to someone who never lived? And what good is a key you can't pick up? And how can you claim a throne if you can't also claim the crown?"

"It's a puzzle," said Hiro. "We need to figure out the meaning of each line and follow the clues."

"We'll focus some of your classes specifically toward deciphering riddles and codebreaking," said Jocelyn.

"We still have to attend classes?" said Anne.

"Not to worry. We can adjust your course load throughout the year as needed, and you might even be able to earn some extra credit. We'll put together a schedule. Jeffery, how much time is there to complete the quest?"

"Four days," chirped Jeffery.

There was a collective gasp throughout the room.

"I'm sorry, but did you say four *days*?" asked Anne.

"Whoops," said Jeffery. "Nope. Sorry. That's wrong. I miscalculated."

Jocelyn nodded. "I should think so."

"What I should have said was, you *had* four days at the moment you activated the medallion at precisely midnight last night. Now you have three days and fourteen and a half hours."

THE ADVENTURER'S GUIDE TO PROPHECY
SAYS THE FOLLOWING:

Before the implementation of medallions, the traditional manner of communicating prophecies was through dancing two-headed goats. Before that there were prophets. And before that there simply were no prophecies. Life was a lot less complicated then.

The best-known prophet in the entire history of the Hierarchy was Hoppert the Impeccably Accurate. Everyone hated him. Not because his prophecies came true (which they always did), but because they came late. Hoppert received his visions only moments before something catastrophic was about to happen, and therefore they never arrived in time to do anything more than help pick up the pieces. He even foretold his own death, which involved slamming into the bottom of a ravine. Unfortunately for Hoppert, the prophecy didn't come to him until two seconds after the local villagers pitched him over the edge.

8

Not-So-Basic Training

So far, escaping from Saint Lupin's hadn't turned out exactly the way Anne had anticipated. Since yesterday morning, she'd been threatened, imprisoned, shot at with fireballs, chased by iron knights, and attacked by zombie sharks and a dragon. She'd fallen off a tier, been burned by a magickal gauntlet (which, incidentally, was now stuck on her hand with a silver prophecy medallion stuck to it), and narrowly escaped an arm-chopping headmistress. Now she had a chance to find her true home—but only if she could complete an impossible quest against impossible odds in an impossible amount of time.

"How much time do you usually get for a prophecy quest?" asked Anne.

"A year," said Hiro. "Sometimes more. Whoever heard of a four-day quest?"

"Maybe someone was trying to keep their long weekend free," said Jeffery.

Jocelyn began pacing. "Quests are supposed to be grand and epic and allow you time to grow and develop as a person. Visit an exotic locale. Explore ancient ruins. Discover your mysterious origins. Four days is utterly ridiculous. Captain, do you have anything to say about this?"

"Sure," said Copperhelm. He pointed at Anne, Penelope, and Hiro. "You're all going to die horrible, agonizing deaths."

"Captain! That is no way to encourage the students."

He shrugged. "I wasn't trying to encourage them."

"Don't listen to him," said Jocelyn. "You won't die. Or at least probably not."

"*Probably* not?" said Anne.

"What *is* the penalty if we don't finish the quest?" asked Hiro.

"Lifelong imprisonment as traitors to the state," chirped Jeffery. "But that includes a great health plan."

"What!?" said Anne and Penelope at the same time.

Hiro turned pale and sank onto a nearby chair. "I signed my life away."

Jocelyn pulled out her notebook and began making a list. "You'll require the standard adventuring outfits. Weapons. Possibly a magick item or two if we can spare them. And while we're doing that, we can provide you with some basic training."

"Training?" said Copperhelm. "They're supposed to receive three years of strategic combat and tactical warfare before going anywhere near a prophecy quest."

"Can you condense that into a one-hour session?"

Copperhelm glared at her. "You know what, I'll do even better than that. I'll do it in under ten seconds." He unsheathed one of his short swords. "This is the handle. That's where you hold it. Up here is the pointy end. Don't stab yourself with it. Class dismissed."

Jocelyn frowned. "You know, with that kind of attitude, you're in serious danger of getting yourself kicked off the Welcoming Committee."

"Gee, that'll be a heartbreaker," he said, crossing his arms. Jocelyn glared daggers at him until he relented.

"Look," he said, "the truth is, we don't have time for lessons. About all I can teach them is how not to impale themselves or each other."

Jocelyn sighed. "Fine, but we are still required to equip them."

"Yeah, best of luck with that, too. You-know-who has locked himself in the warehouse again."

"Well, we'll just see about that, now won't we," said Jocelyn with a look of determination. "Follow me, everyone."

Jeffery disappeared back into the gauntlet (after Anne gave a "Deactivate GPS" command), and Jocelyn led the entire group (minus Princess Whiskers, who seemed happy to return to her nap) back up to the warehouse near the rope bridge. It was a two-story stone structure with large sliding doors in front and a regular-sized door on the side with a covered slit at eye level.

Jocelyn knocked on the side door.

The slit opened. "Password," said a creaky voice.

"It's me, Sassy. Open the—"

The slit closed, cutting her off.

Jocelyn knocked again.

The slit opened. "Password."

"We have three new students who need immediate—"

The slit clicked shut.

Jocelyn took a calming breath and knocked a third time.

The slit opened. "Password."

"Sassafras, you know perfectly well there's no password required for gaining entry into the warehouse," said Jocelyn in a rush.

"That's exactly the type of trick someone who doesn't know the password would try."

The slit snapped shut yet again.

Copperhelm stepped forward. "Let me try." He pounded his fist on the door. The slit opened, but before the voice behind the door could say anything, Copperhelm spoke. "You're going to open this door right now, you ninny, or I'm going to chop it down with my axe and make you eat your own hat."

"That's fine," said the voice. "I honestly don't remember the password anyway."

The door unlocked with a click and then opened. A brittle-looking old man stood just inside the warehouse. He was slightly hunchbacked, and his light brown skin had what appeared to be a subtle wood-grain pattern. He wore a faded brown cloak over an equally faded yellow robe, both of which did little to disguise his wiry frame. A small pointed cap sat atop a tangle of white hair, and a pair of bent spectacles perched uneasily at the end of his long, thin nose. There was also a peculiar glint in his eye that Anne felt might be indicative of some impending madness—minus the impending part.

"This is Professor Sassafras," said Jocelyn. "Wizard extraordinaire, master of the magickal arts, diviner of the dark forces of the universe. He's also one-sixteenth dryad on his mother's side and just celebrated his one thousand and first birthday. He currently teaches all of our courses on magick."

Sassafras extended an unsteady arm. Anne reached out, but instead of the wizened hand she had been expecting, a rubbery, beak-like snout poked out of the old man's sleeve. She jumped back.

"What is that?" said Anne.

Sassafras swung his head from side to side. "What is what?"

"That thing. On your arm."

"Oh, that," he said. "It's a duck-billed platypus." And indeed, a platypus gurgled happily from his sleeve.

"But…it's alive," said Anne.

Sassafras looked perplexed. "You would prefer it dead?"

"No. I just mean, it's attached to you. Where an arm should be."

"I still have half an arm." He rolled back his sleeve to show that the platypus ended several inches before his elbow. "Some spells are trickier than others." The platypus playfully nipped at his ear. "In any case, it's nothing a little platypusectomy won't eventually cure."

Penelope scrunched up her nose and whispered to Anne. "I think that's the most disturbing word I've ever heard."

"The really disturbing part is, I hear this isn't the first occasion he's had to use it," Hiro whispered to both of them.

Jocelyn waved everyone forward. "Sassy, the long and short of it is, these students have an active prophecy medallion and require whatever equipment we can spare. I'm also going to need you to provide them with an accelerated course of study in magick."

"How many weeks should I schedule?" asked Sassafras.

"You have fifteen minutes."

"Oh. Well, in that case, I should probably cancel the field trip."

Sassafras ushered them over to three stools in the corner. While Anne and the others took their seats, the wizard hobbled back and forth unsteadily in front of them, looking as though he might tip over at any moment.

"So then," croaked Sassafras. "Welcome to Magick 101—and also apparently 201, 301, and 401. Since almost anyone can learn to use magick, it's beneficial for everyone to study at least the basics. Given our limited time, however, I will restrict my comments to the three most essential things you need to know about magick. The first, and this is very important, is that magick always has a cost. The cost is unique to each user and can be almost anything. One person might lose a single hair every time they cast a spell. Another might get the hiccups. In my case, with every spell I cast, I also conjure an animal." Sassafras stopped and held up his platypus-arm.

Anne swallowed.

"Now I'm doubly glad I drew the fighter token," said Penelope.

Hiro said nothing, but he looked more despondent than ever.

Sassafras resumed pacing. "The second thing to know about magick is that you require a license. A wizard token usually suffices."

"What happens if you cast a spell without a license?" asked Anne.

"They feed you to a dragon."

Everyone's eyes went wide.

Sassafras chuckled. "Just kidding. You pay a small fine. But the dragons might still eat you anyway," he added with a shiver.

"Finally," he said, "in order to cast a spell, you require a spell book." He shuffled over to a nearby shelf and began rummaging. "Somewhere here I have the unabridged edition of *Magick Spells for Nearly All Occasions*. It's an older text, but still serviceable. Ah, here we are." He handed a slim volume to Jocelyn.

"Sassy, this is a Wizards' Council Special Order Spell Catalog," said Jocelyn.

He adjusted his spectacles and studied the cover. "Oh yes. Quite right. I remember now. My last copy of *Magick Spells* got eaten by a flying goat. Well, the catalog has a few sample spells in the back. Those should be enough to get you through. If nothing else, you might find the Minor Exploding Spell useful."

Jocelyn passed the catalog over to Hiro. "Mr. Darkflame drew the wizard token, so obviously it should go to him. He received top marks in all his pre-magick theory classes at his former school, and I expect he has the makings of a great wizard."

Hiro looked as though he was about to say something, but he pocketed the catalog without speaking. Anne wasn't quite sure what to make of this. Hiro seemed to alternate between showing off his knowledge at every opportunity or else total silence, especially when the topic of wizards or magick came up.

"And that about covers it," said Sassafras. "Now to a more important topic: Has anyone seen my slippers?"

With that, Sassafras and the platypus both promptly fell asleep where they were standing, and the group proceeded across the warehouse. As they walked past rows of shelves, Anne noticed a stack of metal crates along the wall that were rocking slightly, with random flashes of light seeping through the cracks.

"What's in these?" she asked.

"Backup fireballs," said Jocelyn. "Nana left them here, for when we don't have a dragon handy."

"Is that safe?"

"Reasonably so, as long as you don't accidentally drop one and send yourself someplace random. Some years back we had a professor of literature who did that. We haven't seen him since."

When they reached the far side of the warehouse, Copperhelm opened a door and led them through. The room beyond was dim. One side was filled with empty weapon racks. The other side was lined with empty shelves. Copperhelm walked over to a bin filled with broken swords and shields and searched through it.

"This room contains the outfits and weapons," said Jocelyn. "As you can see, we're currently a little low on supplies."

"It looks more like zero supplies," said Penelope.

Anne bumped into something. She turned to look and stumbled back. A suit of armor that reminded her very much of an iron knight stood in the center of the room. It was smaller than the knights at Saint Lupin's but had the same small white stone in the center of its helmet.

"Is there a problem?" asked Jocelyn.

Anne pointed at the armor. "What is that doing here?"

"We have a first-rate collection of antique Keeper's armor. Unfortunately, this one is missing some pieces. The better exhibits are on display around the campus."

"You put them on display?"

"Of course. They add to the overall aesthetic."

"But—but—what if they come to life?" said Anne.

Jocelyn laughed. "Come to life? It's a harmless suit of armor, my dear. They don't just get up and walk around

123

on their own." She rapped a knuckle on the breastplate and it echoed dully. "See. Completely hollow."

"If you say so," said Anne, but she stayed well away from it.

Jocelyn handed each of them a dull yellow cloak. "Remove your dirty old coats and put these on instead."

Anne held up her cloak. On the back in bold black letters were the words:

The three of them donned their cloaks. As Anne transferred the contents of her pockets to her new cloak, she noticed the cover of her book now read *The Adventurer's Guide to Fashionable Adventure Wear*. Flipping it open, she discovered it contained several pages of ads for dashing outfits and matching weapons. She tucked the book away in the inner pocket of her cloak as Copperhelm returned carrying several items.

"We have one usable sword," said Copperhelm, holding up a worn leather sheath with a plain-looking hilt sticking out of the end. "And one dagger," he finished, holding out a small blade.

"Isn't that a letter opener?" asked Hiro.

Copperhelm handed it to him. "Congratulations for correctly identifying it. That makes it yours. May all unopened letters tremble in fear before you. And who gets the sword?" he asked, turning to Anne and Penelope.

"I guess that should go to our fighter," said Anne. Penelope squealed with delight, snatched the sword from Copperhelm, and immediately unsheathed it. Anne suddenly realized that with her pocketknife now lost in the Saint Lupin's moat, she was the only one without a weapon.

"Hey, what gives?" said Penelope. "This thing has a wooden blade."

"It's a practice sword," said Copperhelm. "That's standard issue for a first-year student with no training."

Jocelyn handed them each a small pack filled with a few rations of crackers and cheese and a canteen of water. Then she had them stand together in a group: Anne with her gauntlet, Penelope holding the wooden sword, and Hiro holding the Special Order Spell Catalog. Hiro had tucked his letter opener into his boot.

Jocelyn stood back and dabbed the corner of her eye with a handkerchief. "Oh, what a lovely group you all make. You know, it reminds me of my first quest—"

Copperhelm leaned over. "If she starts reminiscing, run for your lives."

"Not necessary, Captain. I'm well aware the clock is ticking." Jocelyn clapped her hands together. "So, you're all equipped and ready to go. Now comes the best part of any quest."

"Breakfast?" said Penelope hopefully.

"No, dear. Research."

"Research?" said Penelope. "But when do we get to fight something?" She took a swing at the suit of armor but lost her grip. The sword flew out of her hand and, despite being only a practice sword, nevertheless embedded itself a full three inches into the doorframe between Copperhelm and Jocelyn.

Copperhelm looked across the blade to Jocelyn. "Still convinced this is a good idea?"

Anne awoke with a start.

They were in the library, a spacious three-story building packed with bookshelves, various artifacts, and at least a dozen suits of armor on display. Despite Jocelyn's assurances that the armor was not alive, Anne had picked a spot at the table farthest from them. She'd fallen asleep on top of an open book, and her face had stuck to a page with her own drool. She peeled herself off and wiped her cheek on her sleeve.

Jeffery appeared in a burst of light. "Just so you know, that's really gross. Also, your nose whistles when you sleep."

"Thanks for letting me know," said Anne. "But how did you appear? I didn't summon you."

"Yeah, I know. Usually I can only appear when my Keeper activates me, but I was just thinking about how great it would be to come out, and voilà, here I am. I think that scratch in the medallion might have wedged open the door, so to speak. Which is great, because now I can come out whenever I want. Like if I want to complain about something completely arbitrary. Or if I'm just really restless, like now. Honestly, have you figured out the riddle yet? Because even my boredom is getting bored."

"Not yet."

Although Jocelyn had claimed research was the best part of a quest, Anne had found it to be equal parts excruciating and frustrating. Except for a couple of hastily eaten meals in the dining hall, they'd spent the entire rest of the day in the library and had yet to turn up any information about a tower with no door. They'd read about a tower made of all doors, and a tower with no windows, and even a tower in a wealthy kingdom with no doorman, which had apparently caused some sort of national scandal. The book Anne had fallen asleep on was entitled *Towers of the Hierarchy and the Vegetables They Most Resemble*. It had proven especially worthless and had left her with an unexplained craving for radishes.

Penelope was curled up in a large armchair, snoring loudly. Hiro sat at the other end of the table surrounded by stacks of books and piles of scrolls. He was currently skimming through a thick reference book. The instructors weren't in the library. Hours earlier, Copperhelm had excused himself to attend to the cat, and Jocelyn had gone to help Sassafras find his fuzzy slippers. But shouldn't they have returned by now?

"What time is it?" asked Anne.

"Nearly midnight," said Jeffery. "You're almost down one whole day."

Anne slumped back in her chair. "We're going to waste all of our time in here just trying to figure out where to go."

Tired of digging through ancient tomes written in languages she couldn't understand, Anne pulled the red-covered book out of the inner pocket of her new cloak on the off chance it had anything useful to offer. Unfortunately, the cover was blank, as were the pages.

"Oh, a new book?" said Jeffery.

Anne held it away. "No eating," she said.

"Aw, shucks." He looked up at her. "What's it about?"

Anne gave the book a shake. "Nothing at the moment. It's kind of been helping me, but I guess it doesn't know anything about a tower with no door, either."

"Helping you?"

"It's given us some advice, and even a passenger ticket when I needed one, although I never did get to use it."

Jeffery stared wide-eyed at the book. "You have a copy of *The Adventurer's Guide*?"

Anne shrugged. "Which one? It keeps changing titles."

Jeffery hopped over and sniffed the book. "It is the guide! Wow, I thought they'd gone extinct. Adventurers relied on these all the time to help them with quests, but for some reason the publisher stopped making them. They can be super useful, though. They're filled with all kinds of information."

"Well, it's not offering anything right now."

Jeffery sniffed the book again. "Hmmm. This one's pretty old. That might explain why it's not working quite right. Let me try giving it a little boost." He laid a wing on the cover and his feathers pulsed briefly with light, but rather than simply fade away, the light seemed to get sucked into the book. After a moment, a title appeared: *The Adventurer's Guide to Towers of the Hierarchy.*

Anne hastily flipped the book open and squealed. There on the first page, drawn in fine, delicate lines, was a map with a large oblong shape in the exact center with a picture of a dragon over it. She jumped out of her chair and ran down the length of the table to Hiro.

"Take a look at this," she said, plopping the book in front of him.

Hiro examined it. "That definitely looks like a tower. I think these other markings are some sort of ancient runes. When Jocelyn gets back, she might be able to decipher them. And this dragon symbol here is—"

"—the exact same as the image on the medallion," said Anne. "I know."

Hiro snapped his fingers and dug out another book from one of his piles. "I found the symbol in here, too, while you were asleep. It's actually not very common. In fact, as far as I can tell, it's never been used on a quest medallion before. It's called the Sign of Zarala."

"Who's Zarala?"

Hiro shrugged. "I haven't been able to find anything more."

Penelope stirred in her chair. "Why are people being loud?" she mumbled.

"*The Adventurer's Guide* has a map in it," said Anne.

"That's great. What's *The Adventurer's Guide*?"

"The book, Pen. This wonderful book." For the first time since they'd learned about the quest, Anne felt a glimmer of hope. "I'll go find Jocelyn and let her know we found a map."

"I'll go. I'm a lot faster," said Jeffery, and he leapt off the table and flew out through an open window.

Penelope sprang out of her chair and over to the table. "Excellent! The book strikes again."

"Again?" asked Hiro.

"It's done this before," said Anne. "It's from the Saint Lupin's library."

Hiro's eyes widened. "Wait, you're saying you *stole* this?" He eyed it as though it might burst into flame.

Penelope shrugged. "She is the thief of the party."

"No, I'm the blacksmith, remember? And I only

131

borrowed it," said Anne. "Er, although possibly indefinitely. Look, I think it really wants to help us. It gave me a ticket, and now it's showing us this map."

Hiro flipped through the pages. "There's no mention of the author."

"So?"

"So we're not permitted to use a magick item unless we know it's been approved," he said in a lecturing tone.

Anne didn't want to begin their quest by breaking rules, but the book contained the only clue they'd been able to dig up so far, and the quest clock was ticking. Hiro might know more about quests and academies and official guidelines, but Anne knew all too well from experience that sometimes you simply had to make do with whatever you had on hand.

Penelope snatched the guide out of his hand. "It's Anne's quest, so it's her call."

Hiro snatched it back. "It's against the rules."

"What is it with you and rules?" said Penelope. "The book belongs to Anne."

"Actually," said a cold voice behind them, "I believe the book belongs to me."

Anne's heart nearly stopped.

In the doorway of the library stood the Matron.

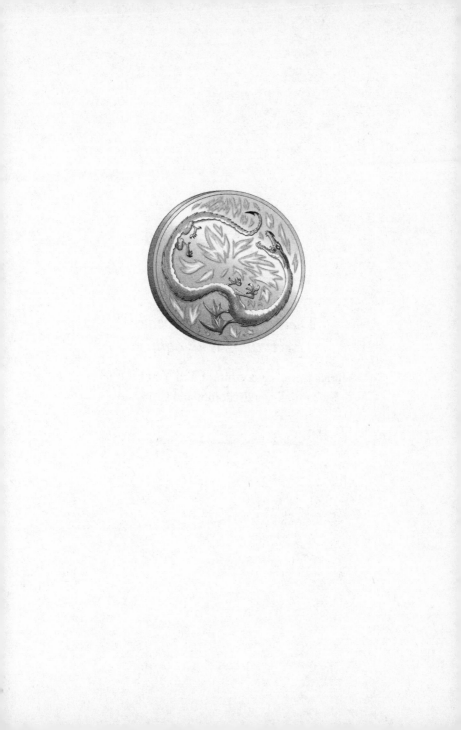

There's no reason to panic.
Everything is all right.

—lyrics from "Everything I Tell You Is a Lie"
by bardic legends Pompf and Company

The Official Antagonist

No one moved.

Anne glanced past the Matron, hoping desperately to see one of the instructors returning, but the corridor was empty. She willed Jeffery to deliver his message quickly.

"Who are you?" asked Hiro before either Anne or Penelope could stop him.

The Matron strode into the room, her cane clicking with every other step. "I'm the person who's come to reclaim what belongs to her. Starting with that book you're holding."

Hiro hastily dropped *The Adventurer's Guide* onto the table. "Anne was just explaining how she had borrowed it."

The Matron smiled. "Was she now? And did she also happen to mention 'borrowing' one of my prophecy medallions?"

"She might have left that part out," said Hiro, his voice cracking slightly.

Anne snatched the guide from the table. "The book wanted to come."

The Matron raised an eyebrow.

"Or, well, it's been helping us," Anne elaborated. "The medallion chose me, too."

"That prophecy belongs to me."

"Well... well, you're too late. The quest has already been activated."

"Oh, I'm well aware," said the Matron, reaching into her vest pocket and drawing out a small card. She placed the card on the table and slid it across.

Hiro picked it up and read it. "This says she's the Official Antagonist for the quest."

"The what?" asked Penelope.

"It means she's the bad guy," said Anne.

"No, it means I'm your opponent," countered the Matron. "Which of us is truly the 'bad guy' is yet to be seen. I'm not the one who broke the rules of an institution that provided her with food and shelter for thirteen years, who refused to accept discipline for her actions, who robbed a poor woman of her rightful property, and who attacked an innocent marine animal."

"But...that's...that's ridiculous," Anne protested. "You locked me in a dungeon. And that zombie shark tried to eat us! And how did you become the Official Antagonist, anyway?"

"Simple. I applied for the position. Now all I need to do is defeat you, and then the gauntlet and the medallion will be mine once and for all, without question."

"This seems highly unusual. I—I think we should ask one of the instructors about this," said Hiro.

"Oh, no," said the Matron. She held out her cane, and it flattened itself into a thin blade. "You're not getting away from me this time."

"Oh, I rather think she might," Jocelyn said from the doorway. She was holding a rapier in her hand in a manner that very much suggested she knew how to use it.

Anne let out a huge breath.

Jeffery flew over and landed on the gauntlet. "Mission accomplished," he chirped, and disappeared in a flash of light.

The Matron lunged at Jocelyn with her blade, but Jocelyn parried her strike. Both Jocelyn and the Matron retreated, weapons at the ready, as Jocelyn circled around next to Anne and the others.

"Get out of my way," said the Matron. "I'm here on official business."

"So I heard," said Jocelyn.

"You would dare to interfere with a quest?"

"Of course not. But as I'm sure you know, academies are neutral ground. If you attack a Keeper here, you risk incurring a serious penalty. And we are permitted to offer our assistance." As if to emphasize this, she adopted a new defensive stance.

"I don't care about penalties," said the Matron. "I. Want. That. Medallion."

Jocelyn laughed. "And you expect her to simply hand it over? I say, did you complete your villain's diploma by correspondence? If you want it, you'll have to follow the rules like everyone else."

The Matron lunged a second time, but Jocelyn blocked her again.

"You can't stop me forever," said the Matron.

Captain Copperhelm and Sassafras appeared in the doorway.

"Actually, I don't think I'm your biggest concern at the moment," said Jocelyn.

The Matron lifted her metal hand and made several intricate gestures. Throughout the library, the suits of armor sprang to life. The small white stones in the center of their helmets glowed red, and they stepped heavily from their pedestals and drew their swords.

"And I don't think I'm yours," countered the Matron, springing to the side out of the way.

One of the suits of armor surged forward, and Copperhelm rushed in to meet it. He blocked its swing with his axe and countered with a sweeping cut, lopping off one of its legs. The armor tumbled back into the two suits behind it. Sassafras leapt spryly onto the table and sent out a weaving cluster of tiny balls of light. They converged on one of the suits and exploded, blowing it to pieces. With each light, a hummingbird appeared, and these immediately flocked together and attacked another suit of armor.

Keeping her rapier pointed at the Matron, Jocelyn stepped close to Anne and lowered her voice. "Jeffery said you found something."

"A map," Anne whispered back. "We think it leads to the tower."

Jocelyn nodded. "Then go. There's an exit at the back. Follow the main path down into the valley and locate Nana. Her lair is in a cave near the bottom. She can send you wherever you need to go."

"But—"

"I'm sorry we couldn't offer you more, but know that I have every confidence in you and that I believe you're going to make a wonderful Keeper." She gave Anne a warm smile. "Now be off. Quickly. You don't have a lot of time."

Anne ducked under the sweeping cut of one of the suits of armor. Jocelyn ran her rapier through its helmet and beheaded it with a flick of her wrist. Then she charged forward and reengaged the Matron.

Another suit of armor ran at Anne. She raised her gauntlet and the armor froze, but a second suit of armor came stomping around the other side of the table. She couldn't freeze them both. As the suit reached for her, the bookcase next to it toppled over and knocked it to the floor. Penelope and Hiro were standing on the other side of the bookcase.

"Come on!" shouted Penelope, moving toward the main entrance.

"No, follow me," said Anne.

She led the others full speed toward the back of the library. As they threw open the door and charged out into the night, the Matron yelled.

"Stop them!"

They raced along the side of the building, but just as they reached the corner Penelope grabbed hold of Anne's collar and yanked her back. An axe blade swished through the air in front of them and embedded itself in the ground. The suits of armor inside the library weren't the only ones under the Matron's control. Penelope shoulder-charged the armor, knocking it off balance and toppling it over. When it hit the ground, it fell to pieces.

"This way!" yelled Anne.

They headed along the main path, but when a suit of armor appeared up ahead, they were forced to duck into a small alley between buildings. They tried another route, but they encountered another suit of armor. For ten minutes they dodged attackers and tried different paths, until finally they ducked into a small alcove so everyone could catch their breath.

"Where...are...we?" asked Penelope between wheezes.

Anne looked around. They had zigzagged completely at random. Anne had seen only a small part of the academy grounds, and she didn't recognize any of the buildings. "I have no idea. I was just trying to avoid another fight."

Penelope nodded. "I approve of that plan."

"This is the indoor archery range," said Hiro, tapping the wall of the building. "The next one over is the medical hut. The one past that is storage shed twenty-two. It stores mostly spare arrows and bandages."

Penelope frowned. "What did you do, memorize the entire layout or something?"

"Of course," said Hiro. "Didn't you read the 'Tips and Tricks' section of *Rules for Quests*?"

"I only received my copy this morning," said Anne.

"Well, it says to take every opportunity to study your surroundings, because you never know when you might need to make use of that knowledge."

"That's…actually a pretty good tip," admitted Penelope.

"Hiro," said Anne, "do you know the layout well enough to guide us down to the lowest part of the academy without using the main pathway?"

"I suppose so," said Hiro. "But maybe we should wait until things have settled down and one of the instructors can tell us what to do."

"I hate to agree, Anne, but I don't think we're going to get past those suits of armor," said Penelope. "They seemed to be getting thicker the farther down we go."

Anne shook her head. "We only have three days left to complete the quest, and now the Matron is officially trying to stop us. If we stick around, we're going to get captured, and then we'll fail our quest. That means the academy gets closed down, I miss my chance of finding home, and we all spend the rest of our lives in a dungeon. So we need to find Nana and get moving."

Jeffery appeared in a flash of light, causing everyone to jump. "Why not bring Nana to you?" he said.

"What do you mean?" asked Anne.

"I come equipped with one emergency signal per quest. I can use it and have her meet us at the fireball landing zone."

"Why not have her meet us right here?" asked Penelope.

Jeffery shook his head. "It works better in the zones, especially if she has to do it quickly. Something to do with dragon math."

"Are you sure?" asked Anne.

"Sure I'm sure. I wouldn't be much of a GPS if I couldn't find you transportation."

Anne nodded. "Okay, do it."

"Sure thing. I'll include the map information in the signal, too. That way she can work on her calculations before she gets here."

Jeffery's eyes glowed momentarily, and then two small orbs of light shot out from them. The orbs rose high into the sky toward the place where the tiny tethered tier floated. A second later, a giant dragon made of light appeared overhead.

"As long as we keep it subtle," Penelope said dryly.

"Nana should be there shortly," said Jeffery, and he disappeared into the medallion.

Anne looked over at Hiro. He nodded and took the lead. Anne and Penelope followed him through the back alleys of the academy, over stone walls, and up behind the warehouse near the top of the mountain. From there they had a good view of the rope bridge. Anne's heart was pounding, but she couldn't tell if it was from all the physical exertion or the prospect of leading a group on a quest with little preparation and almost no idea what she was doing.

"Look," said Hiro as they peeked around the corner of the warehouse.

A suit of armor stood between the two support pillars that held up the bridge.

"I guess they saw the signal, too," said Penelope. "Now what do we do?"

"These can't be the only two ways off the mountain," said Hiro. "Maybe there's a third path that isn't marked on the map. Something that leads around to the other side."

Anne shook her head. "You might be right, but who knows how long that could take. You two wait here. I'll deal with the armor."

Every fiber of Anne's being screamed at her to stay hidden, but she stepped out from behind the warehouse and headed straight for the suit of armor. She could handle one, she told herself. One was no problem. The suit soon spotted her, but before it could take even a single step, she raised her gauntlet and froze it in place. Holding it there, she motioned for Penelope and Hiro. They dashed from their hiding place and joined her.

Anne looked across the suspension bridge. The way was clear. All they needed was Nana, and they could make their escape.

"Heads up," said Penelope.

Two more suits of armor clanked up the pathway. Anne, Penelope, and Hiro all crouched behind one of the stone pillars, with Anne keeping the gauntlet aimed at the frozen suit of armor.

"This isn't going to work if we don't have a dragon," said Penelope.

"Don't remind me," said Anne.

The two suits of armor stopped well back, in front of the warehouse. They hadn't noticed their frozen companion. Yet. Anne knew that once they did, there was no way she could control all three.

Penelope pointed to the tethered tier. "So how are we going to make it up there without getting noticed?"

"I don't think we can," said Anne. She looked at Hiro. "Do you have the magick catalog?"

Hiro nodded.

"Sneak out onto the bridge and see if you can hit them with that Minor Exploding Spell Sassafras mentioned."

"Y-you want *me* to stop them?" said Hiro, sounding strangely hesitant. This only confirmed further Anne's observation that talk of magick seemed to unnerve him.

"I won't be able to control all three," said Anne. "Besides, you're the wizard, right? You're our best chance."

Hiro nodded reluctantly.

Anne checked to make sure the suits weren't looking in their direction, and then she signaled for him to go. He crept out onto the bridge.

"Do you think he can pull it off?" asked Penelope, watching him go.

"We better hope so," said Anne, "because here they come."

The two suits of armor had started moving again and were walking directly toward them. Perhaps they had finally noticed their immobile companion and were coming to investigate. There wasn't much time before they would see what was really going on.

Hiro started chanting behind them.

The two suits drew closer.

The chanting grew louder.

The suits finally spotted them and began to run.

Hiro yelled out a final word and then fell silent.

A boom like thunder reverberated through the air, and the two suits exploded midstep. Or, more accurately, were obliterated. As in, where once there had been two suits of armor, now there was nothing but a giant hole in the ground. Penelope pulled Anne back behind the stone pillar as the shockwave blasted the first suit of armor—the one Anne had been holding in place—over the side of the mountain. The shockwave also punched into the warehouse, setting off a massive secondary explosion. The backup fireballs! The warehouse roof disappeared in a pillar of green fire that rocketed up the side of the mountain. Flaming debris rained down all across the academy, setting some of the other roofs aflame.

Anne's jaw dropped.

"Whoa," said Penelope. "Do you think we lose points for blowing up the academy?"

Before Anne could respond, a tremendous, heart-stopping cracking sound came from the mountaintop. The great shelf of rock at the peak split off and hurtled down the mountainside. It broke apart as it fell, sending gigantic boulders cascading in every direction. The largest section crashed into the center of the academy, flattening buildings and smashing staircases to pieces. Another large chunk struck the headmistress's tower dead center. The tower crumbled, sending a shower of white stones and brown roof tiles down into the valley.

Anne was stunned. "W-what happened?"

She became vaguely aware that Penelope was pulling her along the bridge. They reached Hiro, who had also been knocked over by the shockwave but had managed not to fall off.

Penelope grabbed Anne by the shoulders and shook her. "Anne, the ropes!"

Anne glanced at the guide ropes. They seemed fine to her. A little frayed maybe. Then she looked to where Penelope was pointing: The ropes at the far end, holding up the suspension bridge at the landing zone, were burning.

"R-run!" yelled Anne.

The three of them made a dash for the tethered tier, holding tight to the guide lines, but they weren't fast enough. The main support ropes snapped. The bridge fell. Anne hung on briefly, but the well-worn guide lines slipped through her fingers. She reached out desperately for Penelope and Hiro, but they, too, lost their hold and tumbled away into the night.

Two thoughts popped into Anne's head as she fell:

First, exactly what spell had Hiro cast?

Second, and perhaps most important, *Ahhhhhh-hhhhhhh!*

Anne's last sight was of an enormous black shape hurtling down at them from the mountainside and a brilliant flash of green.

MODERN ACADEMIES OF THE HIERARCHY: FIVE CENTURIES OF DESTRUCTION AND UTTER MAYHEM CONTAINS THE FOLLOWING PASSAGE:

The Death Mountain Quest Academy has suffered catastrophic destruction no less than seventeen times (each time under a different name, of course). The third-worst incident occurred when all the students in the first-ever Magick 101 class practiced their Minor Exploding Spell in unison. Thereafter all beginner-level magick classes were conducted only in underground bunkers at a minimum distance of one mile from any other academy structures.

The second-worst incident occurred when a supply ship delivering five thousand barrels of lantern oil unexpectedly lost altitude, crashed into a papier-mâché tower, and toppled it into the adjacent Candle Gardens. Following this incident, further use of papier-mâché for major construction projects was heavily frowned upon.

The absolute worst incident occurred when the academy ran out of pudding one day at lunch and the students and faculty mutinied (an event known thereafter as the Great Pudding Riot of Shame).

Mr. Shard

Upon emerging from the fireball, the first thing Anne noticed was the heat—it was absolutely sweltering. She quickly removed her cloak as she took in her surroundings. Anne, Penelope, and Hiro were standing on a large stretch of light brown sand. A cluster of white-domed buildings was nearby, and beyond that the edge of the tier was visible. In the other direction, the lighter sand quickly gave way to a darker, coarser wasteland of rolling dunes. The sun blazed above without so much as a cloud or even another tier in the sky for shade.

Anne held up the gauntlet. "Jeffery?"

Jeffery popped into view. "Is it just me, or did we go from winter to summer in all of about three seconds?"

"What is this place?" asked Anne.

"Allow me to welcome you to the Black Desert tier," said Jeffery. "Over here you have your standard generic village of no particular consequence," he said, pointing a wing toward the white-domed buildings, "and over here your standard unnecessarily ominous-sounding desert." He pointed toward the rolling hills of dark sand.

"How did we get here?"

"Nana," said Jeffery. "She arrived just in time and managed to fireball each of you as you fell."

Anne recalled a green flash of light, but everything had happened so fast, it was still a bit of a blur: the shockwave from Hiro's spell, the destruction of the Death Mountain Quest Academy, nearly falling to her death. . . .

"So where's the tower?" asked Penelope as she removed her cloak.

"Well, the good news is we're on the right tier," said Jeffery.

"And the bad news?" asked Anne.

"Who said there was bad news?"

Anne scanned the horizon. "Jeffery, just tell us where the tower is, please."

Jeffery pointed toward the dunes again. "About fifty miles in that direction."

"You don't count that as bad news?" asked Penelope.

"Not considering I had to recalculate your trajectory on the fly," rumbled a voice behind them.

Anne and Penelope spun around. Nana lay stretched out lazily on the sand.

"Why do you keep sneaking up on us like that?" asked Anne.

Nana yawned. "It amuses me."

Anne noted the sun's position in the sky. "How long did it take for us to travel this time?"

"The standard eight hours again," said Nana. "It's now midmorning."

Anne's shoulders slumped. "That only leaves us a little over two and a half days to finish." She scanned the horizon. "Now that we're not falling anymore, can you send us directly to the tower?"

"Can you pay?" asked Nana.

"Pay?"

"Yes. Pay. As in gold. I receive a flat rate for my work at Death Mountain, and all fireballs to and from the academy for both students and instructors are free. But any other quest-related fireballs are covered by my contract with Fireball Travel Incorporated. Then I only get paid per fireball. And do you know what the commission on zero gold is? Zero."

Anne searched her pack, but other than the rations Jocelyn had given them, it was empty.

"Okay," said Penelope, "how about this: First send us back to the academy, and then send us to the tower from there. Problem solved."

Nana grunted. "You mean send you back to the academy that no longer exists because you blew it up?"

"Us?" said Penelope. "It was your fireballs in the warehouse that destroyed everything."

"Yes, but only after they were set off by *your* wizard," said Nana.

Speaking of their wizard, Anne noticed that Hiro hadn't said anything yet, and although they hadn't known each other long, that struck her as unusual. He was facing away from the group and still had his cloak on. She placed a hand on his shoulder, and he jumped slightly at her touch. When he faced her, his cheeks were moist.

"Hiro, are you okay?" she asked.

He sniffed and hastily wiped his eyes. "I—I'm fine. It's just, I thought I could control it this time."

Anne imagined how their conversation must have sounded, considering all that had happened, and felt a pang of guilt. "Hiro, no one is blaming you."

"Technically, I am," said Nana.

"They *should* blame me." He let out a deep, shuddering breath. "You know how Sassafras said there's always a cost for magick? Well, what you saw...that's my cost. Every time I cast a spell, it has unintended consequences. Sometimes they go out of control, like that Minor Exploding Spell I used. It came out way too powerful. Other times they fizzle out completely. I can never predict what will happen."

"I thought you had only taken the theory classes," said Penelope.

He shook his head. "I got further than theory, but everyone wished I hadn't. Jocelyn knew, but she told me not to worry about it. She said she believed in me and that I would figure out a way to make it work." He bowed his head. "I'm sorry. I should have told you earlier. I'm not fit to be the group wizard. I'm just a disaster waiting to happen." He dug out his wizard token and held it out to Anne. "Please, take it."

Anne took his hand in hers, but she didn't take the token. Instead, she folded his fingers back over the top of it. "Maybe the spell did have unintended consequences, but that doesn't change the fact that we wouldn't have escaped without your help. It also means you're a really powerful wizard, right, to be able to do so much? Either way, you know a lot more than either Penelope or I do about quests. We need you."

Hiro looked up. "Thanks." He sniffed again. "Do you—do you think the instructors got away?"

Anne was worried about that, too. "I honestly don't know," she said gently.

"They're fine," said Nana. "A little banged up, but none the worse for wear. They tend to be a resourceful group—sort of. In fact, the reason I'm here is that Jocelyn asked me to check up on you and make sure you arrived safely."

Hiro sighed with relief at hearing this news.

"Maybe we should go back and help them," said Penelope.

Anne shook her head. "Jocelyn told us to focus on the quest. There's nothing we can do about the academy right now, but there are serious consequences for each of us if we fail. Not to mention that the Matron will still be after us. I think the best thing we can do is to keep moving forward. And for that, we're going to need our wizard. Okay?" She smiled at Hiro.

He smiled back.

Anne turned to Nana. "We haven't said it yet, but thank you so much for saving us. We wouldn't have gotten this far without your help, either. I know it's asking a lot, but I expect you know more about quests than even Hiro does. If there's any way at all you might be able to assist us, we would be grateful."

"Now you're just appealing to my ego," said Nana. "Of which I wholeheartedly approve, by the way." She looked into the sky and sighed. "My mother always said I had too much of a soft spot for humans."

"So is that a yes?" asked Anne hopefully.

Nana nodded. "In principle, yes, but there are two problems to consider. One, officially I work for the academy, not your group, and it's a serious offense for anyone to interfere with an active quest, including dragons. You don't want to attract the attention of the Wizards' Council. They love to stick their noses where they don't belong, and if they think there's been any funny business, they could arbitrarily declare the quest a failure. Two, although I could probably get away with offering you each a standard fireball, remember that they take eight hours, no matter how far you're going. So if your destination is only fifty miles away, you could probably find a faster way to get there and save yourself some time."

"Didn't Jocelyn mention something about premium fireballs?" asked Anne.

"Those you definitely have to pay for."

"Well, assuming we finish the quest, I'm supposed to be inheriting an entire kingdom, right?" said Anne. "We could pay you afterward."

"Not to be unnecessarily discouraging, but your chances of completing this quest aren't exactly high."

Penelope clasped her hands together and dropped dramatically onto one knee. "Pretty please, oh kindest and wisest and most generous of dragons. We're just a group of helpless young orphans, placing ourselves at your mercy."

"Okay, now you're laying it on a bit *too* thick. But only a bit." Nana closed her eyes and mumbled something to herself. "Fine. Out of the kindness of my heart, and also my great sense of nobility, not to mention how much it will add to my ever-growing sense of superiority, I'll extend you the credit for one premium fireball each, to be repaid at the conclusion of the quest. That's the best I can do. You decide when you want to use it."

"What do you think?" Anne asked Penelope and Hiro. "Should we take it now, or try to find some other means of transportation to the tower?"

"Common wisdom would suggest saving the fireballs for when we need them most," said Hiro, sounding a little more like his old self again. "We could check at the village first and see if there's anyone who can take us."

"That gets my vote," said Penelope.

"Are you coming with us?" Anne asked Nana.

"I'm afraid it would look too suspicious." Nana stretched out on the sand. "Besides, the weather at Saint Lupin's was dismal. I could use a good soak in the sun."

"Okay, we'll return when we're done, then."

The three adventurers stuffed their cloaks into their packs and made their way toward the buildings. Eventually, the sand gave way to a cobblestone road that led to an open square in the center of the village. A rectangular piece of wood slightly wider and taller than the average person stood upright in the square, with a rope strung between it and one of the surrounding buildings. An old woman was hanging ribbons from the rope. Her skin looked as tough as leather, no doubt from years spent in the scorching sun. She smiled crookedly, waved to them, and seemed about to say something when Anne waved back.

The old woman stopped smiling. She raised a bony finger and shook it at Anne. "Cursed," she croaked.

Anne lowered her arm. "Um, what?"

The woman trembled all over. "Cursed! A Cursed One walks among us! Beware the one who wears the gauntlet! Beware! Beware!" The woman ran screaming down the street. "Bar the doors! Lock the shutters! Hide the chickens! Do not gaze upon the Cursed One, or it shall be your doom!"

"I'm changing my vote," said Penelope. "Let's just walk to the tower."

Up and down the street, doors and windows slammed shut, and a sense of dread crept over Anne. Then, around the corners of every building soldiers appeared, marching in columns and armed for battle. Her puzzlement changing to panic, Anne turned back the way they had come, only to find that every exit out of the town square was blocked. Anne, Penelope, and Hiro stood back-to-back-to-back as the soldiers fanned out into a ring, surrounding them completely. As they did, a small crowd of curious onlookers also gathered beyond the soldiers.

For one long, tense moment, everyone waited expectantly. Then one section of the ring opened and a man dressed in blue-and-white-striped robes stepped forward and unrolled a sheaf of parchment.

"O Cursed One, hear me now," cried the man, who appeared to be the village herald. "We, the people of the Black Desert village, gather to stand against you and your golden arm of doom. We—"

"Hey, it's not gold," yelled a man in the crowd.

The herald ignored this interruption. "We will, if we must, call upon every man, woman, child, and chicken, so that we might—"

"He said it's not gold," yelled someone else.

"Pipe down," barked the herald. "It's hard enough trying to get into character without you lot constantly interrupting. See, you've made me lose my place." He scanned the parchment again, mumbling as he went. "Cursed One...we the people...golden arm..."

"Look at it, Amar," said a woman to the right. "We're telling you, the gauntlet isn't gold."

The herald put his parchment down in a huff, gave the gauntlet a cursory glance, and looked at Anne. "Are you Jojo the One-Eyed, possessor of the Golden Gauntlet of Destiny?" he asked.

"Um, no," said Anne.

The herald leaned in close. "Are you certain?"

"Quite certain, yes."

His eyes narrowed. "How can we be sure?"

"Well, for one thing, I have both my eyes."

He studied her eyes. "One could be a fake."

Anne shrugged. "I guess you'll just have to take my word for it, then."

The herald harrumphed at this, as though taking someone's word was not the kind of thing any decent person would ask of a proper herald.

"So you're saying you do not seek the door with no tower?" He indicated the piece of wood standing on end behind them, which, now that he mentioned it, did indeed resemble a door. It even had a doorknob.

"Actually, we're looking for a tower with no door," said Anne.

The herald nodded thoughtfully. He took another look at her gauntlet, and then he turned back to the crowd. "All right, people, false alarm," he called. "Wrong quest again. Everybody reset."

The crowd dispersed amid considerable grumbling.

"Sorry about that," said the herald. "We've been expecting a Keeper for days now. It's the first time the town has been selected as a major quest location in well over a century. Naturally folks are a little excited. Old

Mabel's kicked us into action twice already this week. I keep telling her to wear her spectacles, but will she listen to me?" He let out a long sigh. "So, what can we do for you fine folks today?"

"We're looking for transportation to a tower," said Anne. "Just a second. I have a map that shows where it is." She reached into her pack where her cloak was stashed and retrieved the red book, but the title had changed to *The Adventurer's Guide to Letters by Not-So-Famous People*. Anne hastily opened the book only to discover it was now filled with page after page of correspondence by people whose names she sort of recognized but couldn't quite place. "Oh no. The map's gone!"

The herald smiled. "Not to worry. The only tower on this tier is the Infinite Tower, so it's either that or nothing. Unfortunately, you're not likely to find anyone in the village who can take you there right now. We're all tied up with this other quest. But I'm sure you could walk it in a couple of days."

"I don't suppose you have a dragon?" asked Anne, thinking that maybe she could negotiate a deal for another premium fireball. "We're sort of in a hurry."

"One was supposed to arrive last Thursday for the quest, but he got held up at the border by customs officials. Something about illegal dolphin smuggling." The herald rubbed his chin. "If you're *truly* in a bind, though, I do know of someone who might be able to help you. I normally wouldn't suggest him, but..."

"We'll take anything," said Anne.

The herald nodded. "There's a fellow who lives nearby. An archaeologist. Conducts a lot of digs on this tier and has a travel sled and everything. If you head due west out of town, you'll find him three dunes over. Presuming he's even in at the moment. He does travel a lot. Just be aware that Mr. Shard, while brilliant in his own way, is also slightly...eccentric."

Jeffery guided them to the west side of town. They left the white-domed buildings of the village behind and labored over the sloping dunes, the sands shifting under their feet. As promised, at the bottom of the third dune was another domed building. In front of it, a sled of lacquered wood with long metal runners gleamed in the sunlight. The sled was piled high with neatly stacked crates and containers.

As they approached, a tall, thin individual emerged from the building carrying a small wooden box. Although he walked upright, his shoulders were hunched over, and his legs seemed unnaturally short, at least for a person. That he was not in fact human became increasingly evident the nearer they drew. He had a short snout and large rounded ears, and his skin was completely covered in coarse brown fur marked with dark spots, not unlike your typical hyena. Very much unlike your typical hyena, however, he was immaculately dressed, including well-tailored pants and a striped waistcoat over a billowing linen shirt.

The creature gave a large smile, which showed off an impressive collection of sharp teeth. He set the box on the sled and waved them over. "Greetings, greetings, my friends, my neighbors, my casual acquaintances who are good for occasional networking," he said. "Welcome to my humble abode."

He shook their hands enthusiastically, each in turn.

"Excuse me, but are you Mr. Shard?" asked Anne.

"Indeed, I am, young miss," said the creature. "Plutarch H. Shard, at your service." He bowed deeply with a slight flourish of his arm. "And what brings three young travelers such as yourselves to my doorstep? Mere curiosity? Idle inquisitiveness? Or perhaps you've heard I offer the best prices on the antiques market? You strike me, young miss, as a person with discerning taste.

Can I interest you in a one-of-a-kind, never-before-seen magickal amulet?" He spread out his hand. Five painted but otherwise regular-looking rocks lay in his palm. "Two for one, this week only."

"Er, no thanks," said Anne. "We're looking for transportation, actually. Someone in town said you might be able to help us."

A shadow flickered across Shard's face. "Ah, yes. The town. That center of urban pomposity. That would-be city of arrogance. Most of them wouldn't know a good deal if it bit them on the left leg. Then again, who am I to turn down a free meal?" He laughed loudly and his eyes flashed with a predatory gleam. "In any case, unfortunately you've caught me at a bad time. I already have a trip planned and will be leaving shortly."

"Any chance you're heading into the desert?" asked Anne.

Shard stretched out his arms. "It's all desert, young explorer, as far as the eye can see."

"So...is that a yes?"

"Yes. But I'm not headed in your direction."

"We haven't told you where we're going yet."

"True, but I prefer to travel alone. My apologies."

"Please," said Anne. "We're in a hurry and we have

no other way to get there. I'm on a quest." To emphasize the point, she held up the gauntlet.

Shard stepped close and studied the gauntlet intently. "Is that—is that a genuine prophecy medallion?"

"Y-yes," said Anne, slightly taken aback.

Shard stroke his chin. "Fascinating, fascinating. And where exactly was it you said you wished to travel?"

"A place called the Infinite Tower."

Shard threw his head back and let out a high-pitched whoop. "What a coincidence! The Infinite Tower. Exactly where I'm headed. It's fabulous! It's perfect! It's fate! I would be delighted to take you there."

Hiro frowned. "I thought you said you prefer to travel alone."

"I think you must have misunderstood me," said Shard.

"Those were your exact words."

Shard shook his head. "Nonsense. I adore company. I crave it. I sprinkle it like spice on my dinner." He paused. "Actually, forget that last one."

"I should probably mention, we don't have any money to pay you right now," said Anne.

"Not a problem. Help me with my supplies and we'll call it even. Deal?"

Anne looked to both Penelope and Hiro. Penelope nodded eagerly in agreement, and Hiro, somewhat hesitantly, nodded as well.

"We accept," said Anne. She was glad to have found a way to the tower, although she also felt slightly unsettled by Shard's quick change of mind.

Shard bowed again. "Wonderful. Wonderful. Come this way. Perhaps I can interest you in a nice set of antique work gloves? Or in your case, miss, work *glove*." He barked in laughter at his own joke.

They followed him into the building, which turned out to be nothing more than a hollow shell filled with crates and containers. Shard directed Anne, Penelope, and Hiro to pick up specific items and stack them securely on the sled, somehow managing to do none of the actual work himself. When they were finished nearly an hour later, they sat exhausted in the shade of the building.

Shard walked over. "Everything is ready, my friends, my bosom buddies, my newest of new associates. Time to gather the pack. Don't be startled now." He put two fingers to his lips and gave a shrill whistle.

Anne was about to ask what "the pack" was when the sand in front of them erupted in a series of geysers, and Anne, Penelope, and Hiro leapt to their feet, forming a tight circle.

Mr. Shard let out several giggles as the sand raged. "I warned you not to be startled."

When the dust settled, ten large animals stood before them. Each had four legs and a long muzzle and shaggy gray fur, a few shades lighter than the ground from which they had emerged. Their shoulders reached as high as Anne's.

"Are those . . . wolves?" asked Penelope.

"Sand wolves, to be precise," Shard corrected. "Excellent for desert travel. Hard working. Low maintenance. I can offer you first pick from the next litter, if you like. At a price, of course." He grinned widely and batted the eyelashes of his big make-you-feel-like-his-next-meal eyes.

Anne squinted. If she looked at the wolves in just the right way, she could make out the individual grains of sand that made up their fur and bodies, as though they had been born of the desert itself.

Shard walked to the front of the sled, where there were two long high-backed benches under a canopy. He gestured to the second bench. "Come, sit, relax. It will only take me a moment to hitch the wolves, and then we're off."

Anne, Penelope, and Hiro climbed aboard. The floor

in front of them was crammed with smaller boxes and jars filled with brightly colored liquids and leather pouches stuffed with who knows what, but the bench itself offered plenty of room. Holding their packs on their laps, they welcomed the shade of the canopy, even though it could do nothing to block the stifling air.

After he had finished connecting the wolves to the sled, Shard climbed onto the front bench, took the reins, and looked back at his passengers. "Everyone ready?"

The three of them nodded.

Shard cracked the whip, and the wolves surged into motion. The sled accelerated at an alarming rate— alarming in this case being less "I seem to have misplaced my favorite pair of dress socks" and more "I probably should have updated my will." Thankfully, a bar was strategically bolted to the back of the first bench, and they held on to it for dear life. The wolves kicked up a thick column of black sand that was every bit as bad as coal dust—even worse perhaps, in the sense that coal dust wasn't typically coming at you in a constant stream. After coughing and gagging for a few miles, they finally dug out their cloaks and held them over their faces.

For four long hours, they drove up one side of the large black dunes and down the other. There was nothing else to see in any direction. Shard never asked them if they needed to stop or whether they were hungry or thirsty. And the wolves never faltered. They ran on and on and on. Eventually, Shard steered them into a long valley surrounded by black walls of jagged rock that seemed to go on forever and made Anne feel utterly trapped.

Finally, when Anne didn't think she could stand another minute, they left the valley and crested the top of an especially large dune. In the distance, stretching into the sky like a thin black ribbon, was their destination.

The Infinite Tower.

THE PAMPHLET ENTITLED
THE LIMITATIONS OF FOREVER
OFFERS THE FOLLOWING TIP
ON HOW TO PICTURE INFINITY:

Imagine a sandwich. Now imagine a longer sandwich. Now imagine a sandwich even longer than that. Now imagine yourself cutting the sandwich in half. Now imagine giving one of those halves to me. Now imagine each of us eating our half of the sandwich. Now imagine me thanking you for a lovely lunch.

Also, don't bother trying to picture infinity. It's impossible.

The Tower with No Door

The Infinite Tower was, as the cliché went, a sight to behold. The smooth black spire sat atop a low hill and stretched into the sky, rising high above the surrounding dunes and past a few lower-lying clouds. Then it seemed to end abruptly in a jagged break, as though some giant had come along and snapped off the upper portion. The scale of it was overwhelming, and Anne wondered what they would find inside to help them on their quest. Did an infinite tower hold an infinite number of clues?

Shard rubbed his hands together enthusiastically. "Isn't it magnificent? Isn't it awe-inspiring? Isn't it beyond description—except of course for these words that I'm using right now to describe it?"

"Wow," exclaimed Penelope, looking out from under the canopy. "We're definitely not at Saint Lupin's anymore."

"Maybe you could forgo that castle you want and just buy this tower," said Anne. "I'm pretty sure you'd have all the room you need."

"But—it's not infinite," said Hiro.

"What do you mean?" asked Anne.

Hiro pointed to the tower. "The herald called it the Infinite Tower, but it's not infinite. It's not even close. We can see the top of it from here. It's maybe two miles high at the most."

"That's tall enough, isn't it?" said Penelope.

"I was just pointing out that it's inaccurate," mumbled Hiro.

Shard drove the sand wolves down into the valley below the tower, where a campsite was already set up. Three tents had been pitched next to a pool of water surrounded by trees and sheltered by a rock formation. Shard released the sand wolves from the sled, and then he led Anne, Penelope, and Hiro into the largest of the tents. The temperature was several degrees cooler inside, and Anne shivered with delight. She had known it was hot out, but she hadn't appreciated how much until that moment. A large table occupied the center. Spread across it were maps, writing quills, measuring devices, and several stacks of books.

Shard went to the back of the tent and returned with a tray of hard biscuits and strange pieces of orange fruit they had to peel with their fingers. He also brought a large pitcher of water and three glasses. After a hurried meal (curiously, Shard neither ate nor drank anything himself), they helped him unload the sled. Or rather, Shard pointed to the crates and bags and explained where to put them, somehow managing once again to avoid touching a single item of cargo. They put most of the items in the two smaller tents, with the exception of two boxes of books.

"Can we go see the tower now?" asked Anne once they had finished, anxious to solve the first line of the riddle. It was now well into the afternoon, and the clock on their quest was relentlessly ticking away.

"Patience, patience, eager explorer," said Shard. "I must gather a few items first." He rummaged through the boxes and every now and then added another book to the stacks already on the table. Hiro selected a book from one of the piles and began flipping through the pages.

"What's this?" asked Penelope. She was standing next to a large ceramic ball in the corner. A diagonal wooden rod attached to a wooden stand entered through a hole in the bottom of the ball and exited through the top. The surface of the ball was primarily blue with large sections of green and brown. Anne thought it looked like a map, but she'd never seen one like it before.

Shard walked over, placed his hand on top of the ball, and pulled down. The ball spun around the rod. "A trinket, a knickknack, a bauble."

"It's a globe, isn't it?" Hiro said suddenly.

Shard frowned. "A what?"

Hiro pointed to the spinning ball. "Some historians say the Old World used to be shaped like a ball. They called maps of the Old World *globes*."

Shard shrugged. "I have no idea, my learned young friend."

Hiro gave him a curious look and went back to reading the book.

Once Shard finished combing through the boxes, he

directed them each to pick up a stack of books from the table (along with their packs), and then he led them out of the tent. As they trudged up the sandy slope toward the tower, Hiro counted under his breath. When they reached the base, he took a book out of his pocket and flipped through it.

"Did you know your campsite is currently located inside the designated fireball landing zone?" he said.

Shard raised his eyebrows. "I beg your pardon?"

Hiro held up his copy of *Rules for Questing*. "It's all in here." He read from the page, "The area one hundred yards due east of any major quest location shall be designated as the fireball landing zone, to cover an area no less than twenty yards by twenty yards."

"I don't own a dragon," said Shard.

"No, but you see, it isn't only for outgoing fireballs, it's the area for both arrivals and—"

Shard snatched the book out of Hiro's hand, closed it, and dropped it onto the stack of books he was carrying. "I think we've all read enough for now, yes?" he said, his eyes flashing.

Hiro swallowed. "O-okay."

Shard guided them over to the tower. It was

circular and easily a hundred feet in diameter. A platform extended ten feet out from the base around the entire circumference. The tower itself was one smooth unending surface with no visible seams.

"Well, I guess we're not climbing up the outside," said Penelope.

Shard stepped onto the platform and walked over to the tower itself. He tapped the wall, and a rectangular blue grid appeared on it, seemingly out of nowhere. Like magick. The grid contained all the letters of the alphabet along with various arcane symbols Anne couldn't identify. To the right of the grid was a single blue square with a dot in the center.

"What is it?" asked Anne.

Shard leaned over conspiratorially. "I only recently discovered it. I believe it to be the way inside." He tapped on some of the letters. As he touched each one, they appeared again in order in a space above the grid. He spelled out D-O-O-R, and then tapped the blue square. The string of letters flashed once, turned red, and a beep sounded. The word Shard had typed was replaced by two other words.

"'Access denied'?" Anne read.

"That's the only message I've ever received," said

Shard. "But if we combine our efforts, I think we might be able to find the right password."

"The right password for what?"

"To open the door, of course. Logically, there must be one. Simply think of the password as knocking. So go ahead and try anything you can think of. Once you run out of ideas, we'll try random words from these books."

"Okay," said Anne, wondering what words she could possibly know that an archaeologist didn't.

Shard stepped away from the grid and gestured for Anne to go ahead. Figuring there was no reason not to begin with the obvious, Anne tried E-N-T-E-R. ACCESS DENIED flashed again. She tried O-P-E-N, A-C-C-E-S-S, and U-N-L-O-C-K. None of them worked. Anne continued punching in word after word, but without success. She even tried B-L-A-C-K-S-M-I-T-H. After twenty minutes, Penelope took over, and then Hiro after her. Despite their attempts, all anyone received was a beep and the words ACCESS DENIED. The sun beat down mercilessly the entire time.

While Penelope took a second turn, Anne brought out *The Adventurer's Guide*, hoping it might have changed to something more useful, but it was still filled with letters written by not-so-famous people. Hiro offered to skim through it and search for unusual words no one had thought of yet. Anne grabbed a dictionary to do the same thing.

Jeffery appeared over the gauntlet. "Whatcha doin'?"

"Looking for words," said Anne.

He hopped over to the stack of books lying in the sand. "If you let me eat a few of these, I might be able to help."

Anne shook her head. "I can't. They're not my books."

"But I'm starving," he whined, "and you have all of these tasty-looking volumes just sitting here. We're over a day and a half into this quest and I haven't had a single bite. It's animal cruelty."

Anne looked at his colorful feathers. "Are you even a real animal?"

"That's beside the point." He sniffed the blue-covered book on the top of the pile. "I'd settle for part of a book. Even just a short poem."

"Jeffery, I'm sorry, I really am, but we don't have time for this. If you want to help, you can read the books like everyone else. I'll find you something to eat later once we've solved the first line of the riddle. I promise."

"Fine," he said. "See what happens when you really do need me."

And he disappeared.

"Jeffery?" she said, but he didn't reappear. She decided to ignore him for the time being.

Penelope walked over and flopped onto the sand next to Anne. "I'm dying out here."

"Me too," said Anne, shutting the dictionary. "I feel like I've forgotten every word I ever knew."

"Pssst."

Anne looked up. Hiro motioned for her to join him. She scooted over, and he handed her the guidebook.

"Check out this letter," he said.

Anne read the entry he was pointing to.

Dearest Kaarle,

My attempts to gain entry to the structure continue to be unsuccessful. No tool or weapon is able to mark it. No spell or magick is able to penetrate it. Despite my lack of progress, however, I am certain that something lurks inside. I have heard it late at night, and even observed the occasional flash of green light from the top.

I am convinced more than ever that the Old World was indeed originally a sphere, that it was split apart by some catastrophic force (whether natural or unnatural I cannot even begin to speculate), and that the Hierarchy is all that remains. I have several new pieces of evidence to support my hypothesis, but I need to see what's inside this blasted tower before I can publish my findings. As things now stand, I would be laughed out of the Society, and rightly so.

I will find a way inside, no matter what, even if I must spend the rest of my life searching for the answer. Even if what lives in there kills me.

> *With much affection,*
> *P. H. S.*

"Do you think this is about the Infinite Tower?" asked Anne.

"I do," said Hiro. "And look at the signature. I bet it stands for Plutarch H. Shard." He checked behind them to make sure Shard couldn't overhear. Then he said in a low voice, "Shard knows more than he's telling us. He claimed not to know what the globe was, but it's clear from this letter that he does. And what about these comments about something living in the tower? Why didn't he mention anything about that?"

"Maybe he didn't want to frighten us," Anne suggested.

"Maybe." Hiro lowered his voice even further. "But listen to this. Earlier, back in the tent, when I asked him about the globe, I was holding a book on Old World mythology, which has a whole chapter on globe theory. I found it in one of his piles and recognized it from my classes. He saw me holding it, so why would he deny being familiar with it?"

Anne read the letter again. If everything Hiro said was true, it was unsettling.

Hiro started to get up, but Anne motioned for him to stay. "I'll take another turn," she said. "See if you can find out anything else in there."

Anne walked over and tapped the wall. The grid appeared. She raised her right hand to start entering words again, but paused. What if they had been going about it all wrong? They could be there for days on end trying every word imaginable. That seemed to be Shard's plan. But didn't riddles usually provide some key for solving their own puzzle? Then it occurred to her: Shard didn't know about the riddle. The riddle was meant only for their quest.

Anne considered the first line again:

Climb the tower with no door.

The Infinite Tower definitely matched that description, and coupled with the map from the guidebook, Anne felt certain they were in the right place. But what if there was another layer of meaning? Obviously, here was the tower with no door, but was there another way to read the line? Anne pondered the first phrase:

Climb the tower.

Somehow, they had to get to the top of the tower. If there was no way to scale it from the outside, then there must be a way inside.

With no door.

Maybe that phrase didn't only describe the tower. Maybe it was an instruction. Maybe *with* didn't just mean *containing* but also *using*, and the hidden key was the phrase *no door*. With a growing sense of excitement, Anne tapped in the letters N-O-D-O-O-R. At first, nothing happened, but the words ACCESS DENIED didn't appear, either. Then—

"What did you do?" exclaimed Penelope.

Anne stared at the wall but still saw no change. "What?"

Penelope motioned for Anne to step back. "Come over here."

From the edge of the platform, Anne could now see that one section of the hard, smooth wall looked...fluid, like the surface of the Saint Lupin's moat on a windless day.

Shard ran over. He had noticed the change, too. "Fantastically fantastic! Extraordinarily extraordinary! Outstandingly outstanding!"

"How did you do that?" asked Penelope.

Anne explained how she had come up with the password.

Penelope hugged her. "That was brilliant, Anne! Absolutely brilliant!"

"Well done," Hiro agreed, handing the guidebook back to Anne.

Anne stood in front of the shimmering rectangle. "So how does it work? It's not like any door I've ever seen."

Shard picked up a pebble of coarse sand and tossed it. The pebble disappeared into the fluid section of the wall, sending ripples outward from where it struck the surface. The ripples expanded and then stopped, like waves hitting a riverbank, forming a tall retangular outline.

"Well, I'm guessing the sand went somewhere," said Hiro.

"As shall we, dear boy, as shall we," said Shard, clapping Hiro on the back and nearly knocking him off his feet. "Let us collect our things."

While everyone hastily gathered their belongings, Penelope pulled Anne aside. "Are you sure about this?" she whispered.

Anne shrugged. "It's what we came here for. I don't want to turn back from our quest now."

"Not that. I mean, do you really want to go in there with *him*?" Penelope nodded in Shard's direction.

In truth, Anne very much did not want to go anywhere with Shard. If the letter they'd read in *The Adventurer's Guide* was indeed his, then he was hiding things from them. Then again, what choice did they have? Shard now knew the password, too, so they couldn't keep him out. Nor could they delay their quest.

"I'm sure it'll be fine," she said to Penelope, despite her own misgivings. "Everyone ready?" she asked as they rejoined the others. Penelope and Hiro lined up behind her, with Shard bringing up the rear.

Anne took a deep breath and stepped into the doorway.

One by one, the others followed her in.

And one by one, they disappeared.

THE TALE OF THE INFINITE TOWER

Once upon a time there lived a young princess who wished to visit the sky. So she traveled to the Infinite Tower (which was really just a very tall tower, but hey, advertising is everything). Unfortunately, an evil witch lived at the top of the tower, and the witch didn't like visitors, most especially princesses. When the princess drew near, the witch sent down an evil knight to kill her. But the knight fell in love with the princess, and to prevent the witch from harming anyone ever again, he cut the tower in two and sent the top half crumbling to the ground, where it scattered to dust. This actually annoyed the princess, who preferred sensitive knights who wrote in their journals and didn't take out their anger-management issues on poor innocent landmarks.

So the princess bought a circus and traveled the countryside, and the evil knight was never seen or heard from again. To this day, though, there are people who say he lives at the top of the broken tower still.

Inside the Infinite Tower

To the extent that a wall is capable of spitting out a person, the wall spit Anne out. Or, more accurately, spit Anne *in*. She stumbled but managed to stay on her feet. The lighting was extremely dim, and she couldn't make out her surroundings other than sensing that she was inside a large space. She heard several gasps, which suggested the wall had also deposited the others.

"W-where are we?" Hiro said from somewhere to her right.

"My guess would be inside the tower," Anne replied.

Behind her came a tapping sound. "The wall is solid again," Penelope said. "And the grid doesn't appear inside."

"Fear not," exclaimed Shard from somewhere in front of them, "for I shall protect you against whatever nefarious evil might lurk within."

"Great, I feel so much safer now," muttered Penelope.

Thin shafts of light trickled down from somewhere far above. As Anne's eyes adjusted, she could make out the others, if indistinctly, as well as the tower's interior. It was mostly empty. The floor was covered in sand, which in places had drifted into piles, along with large chunks of dark jagged stone. The one prominent feature was a single pillar in the center that extended upward as far as they could see. It would have taken at least eight large people holding hands to reach all the way around it.

The other feature of interest was a staircase. The steps were approximately six feet wide and spiraled upward along the exterior wall. Presumably, the staircase led all the way to the top. Of particular note, it had no railing.

"Spectacular," shouted Shard, his voice echoing in the tower. "Outstanding. Monumental. A true test of skill and bravery. All too fitting for such a hardy group of explorers as we. Incidentally, I've been experiencing some mild back pain, so I wonder if you might help me with my equipment." He dropped a pack into each of their arms, stretched luxuriously, and marched up the stairs (or rather, given his short legs, hopped up the stairs).

Anne sighed and slung Shard's bag over her shoulder.

Hiro crouched next to the first step and moved his hand along it.

"Is there a problem?" asked Anne.

"I'm measuring," he said. "Each step is approximately seven inches high, so that's an elevation of seven feet every twelve steps. One mile contains five thousand two hundred eighty feet, so that means we'll climb a little over nine thousand steps for every mile we go up, or a total of over eighteen thousand steps, presuming I'm right and the tower really is two miles high. If we average, say, twenty-seven hundred steps per hour...uh, this could take a while."

"I could have told you that just by looking up," said Penelope.

"How long?" asked Anne.

"Almost seven hours," said Hiro. "And that's if we can keep going at the same pace. The reality is, we're going to get tired and progressively slower as we go."

"So what?" said Penelope.

"It's late afternoon already. We're not going to make it to the top before nightfall," said Hiro.

Anne placed her foot on the first step. "Then I guess we'd better get going."

Hiro tugged on her sleeve and spoke in a low voice. "That means we're going to have to stop when it's pitch-black and sleep somewhere between here and the top. Thousands of feet above the ground. On an open staircase with no railing. With *him*." Shard had disappeared above, and Hiro pointed in his direction. Even Penelope seemed a little unnerved by the prospect.

Anne took both their hands. "Everything's going to be fine. We'll stick together, okay?"

"Yeah, no wandering *off*," Penelope replied. "Get it?"

Everyone laughed nervously but seemed to relax a little.

"Let's go," Shard called down. "Make hay while the sun shines. Scrape barnacles while the tide's out. Clean a dragon's teeth while he hibernates for the winter—no, wait, dragons don't hibernate. That's bears. Or was I thinking deer mice? You know what? Forget the teeth thing. Just do the first two."

The trio started up the stairs. Anne took the lead

and Penelope brought up the rear. Hiro counted steps softly as they climbed. After a few minutes they caught up with Shard, who had stopped. There was a gap in front of him where about a dozen steps were missing.

"How do we climb without stairs?" asked Hiro.

"Not to worry," said Shard, and he reached inside the pack he'd given Anne and pulled out a twig the size of his index finger.

"What good is that going to do us?" asked Penelope.

"Watch and see," he said.

He laid the twig on the step. While holding it with one hand, he tapped it twice with the other. The twig began to grow, stretching outward and upward, twisting and knotting and even sprouting leaves, until it had spanned the gap. Shard stood, marched up the branch, and hopped off the upper end.

"Perfectly safe," he said.

Anne went first. She set one foot on the branch and then the other, moving steadily forward and upward while using her right hand on the wall for balance. Finally, her feet touched stone again.

"I have a bad feeling about this," moaned Hiro, but despite his apparent fear, he was the next to cross.

Penelope came last, practically running up.

Shard bent down and snapped a new twig off the branch. "See," he said with a wide grin. "Not a problem."

"Is there a cost for using it?" Anne asked, curious. "I mean a magick cost?"

Shard shook his head. "No. This is a completely different branch of magick." He grinned again. "Get it? A different 'branch' of magick." He let out a howl of laughter that sent shivers up Anne's spine. Then he continued up the stairs.

"I hope we don't encounter too many of those gaps," said Penelope.

But they did encounter more. Many more. And although the branch held firm every time, the higher they climbed, the more nerve-racking it became to walk across. Hours later they were all dragging sore feet from one step to the next.

"How far now?" asked Penelope.

"I think…we passed…the fourteen-thousandth step." Hiro was panting and could barely talk.

"I swear, this is the longest two miles of my life."

Hiro shook his head. "It's more than two miles. We aren't going straight up but in a spiral. Each step is roughly a foot long across the top. So eighteen thousand steps is eighteen thousand feet, meaning the actual distance we walk will be closer to three and a half miles, and that's if I'm right about how high the tower is."

"Wonderful. Now this quest is messing with my math," said Penelope.

"Yours and mine both," said Anne.

It grew progressively darker. Anne tried calling on Jeffery, thinking perhaps his glow might help light their way, but she received no response. She tried a few more times, but the little sparrow didn't appear. Was Jeffery still upset about their argument over the books?

"Fine, be that way," she whispered to the gauntlet.

The group kept climbing until they could hardly make out the steps in front of them. Shard called a halt before yet another gap in the staircase, one with at least twenty steps missing, possibly more.

"I think perhaps it's time to stop, yes?" said Shard. "We're pretty much out of daylight, and soon we won't be able to see these gaps. Unless someone else wants to walk first?" No one volunteered.

Anne knew they couldn't afford to lose any more time, but walking in the dark was too dangerous, and they were all so tired they could barely climb another step anyway. The group descended a dozen steps, to get away from the gap, and sat down. Dinner consisted of stale cheese and bread from the rations Jocelyn had given them along with more of Shard's orange fruit. They passed around a canteen of lukewarm water. Shard also offered them some meat from his own supplies, but seeing as it was raw, they declined. Shard tore into the meat and wolfed it down in chunks, snapping and slobbering. Afterward, he licked his fingers loudly and sighed contentedly.

By the time they had finished eating, it was pitch-dark, and they settled in for sleep. The steps weren't wide enough to lie on, so they sat next to the wall, each on a separate step, and leaned against their packs with their cloaks draped over them. Shard settled down several steps below them. Even in the dark, Anne thought she could see the shine of Shard's eyes; he was staring directly at them.

"The very best of nights to you, worthy adventurers," he said. "And the sweetest of dreams."

Anne awoke while it was still dark. She tried to fall back to sleep but couldn't. She was anxious about their quest, and lying only a few feet from an eight-thousand-foot drop didn't help. Also not helping was Shard, whose soft, raspy breaths echoed faintly off the walls. Shard had been kind to them. He had brought them to the tower and been helpful during the climb, especially with his magick branch. Nevertheless, something about him just didn't feel right.

A scraping noise on the step above caused her pulse to quicken.

"Pen, is that you?" whispered Anne.

"Sorry," Penelope whispered back. "It's hard to get comfortable."

"I know what you mean."

A moment of silence passed.

"Sorry I dragged you into all of this," said Anne suddenly. "I thought we were heading off to a wonderful adventure, not getting dropped into the middle of a horrible one."

"Are you kidding me?" said Penelope. "This is the best thing that's ever happened to us. I mean, yeah, okay, so whacking my head on the drawbridge hurt a lot, and the zombie sharks and the iron knights were all kinds of terrifying, and I was unconscious for part of the time, and research is boring and makes me sleepy, and I thought we were finished for sure when those suits of armor attacked us and then that rope bridge broke. And of course, the thought of falling off these steps in our sleep is scary beyond belief, and who knows what we're going to find at the top of this tower, and sure, if we fail miserably, we'll spend our formative years stuck in a dungeon somewhere. But, you know, other than that, I'm having the time of my life."

"When you put it that way, who could resist?" said Anne, not sure whether to laugh or cry.

"Oh, you know what I mean."

Anne grinned. "Actually, I do. Gauntlets and sparrows, prophecy medallions, traveling by fireball, quest academies, cat headmistresses, and to top it all off a fantastically cool guidebook that helps us. When it hasn't been absolutely petrifying, it's actually been a lot of fun."

Another pause.

"Pen?" said Anne.

"Yes?" said Penelope.

"I...I don't think I trust Shard. I think we should leave. Right now. Before he wakes up."

Penelope sat up and grabbed her pack. "You don't have to tell me twice. I'll wake Hiro."

"I'm not asleep," Hiro said in the dark.

"Why, you little eavesdropper," said Penelope.

THWACK.

"Hey, sorry," said Hiro. "I didn't do it on purpose. Your talking woke me up."

"You could have said something," Penelope replied. "And I'm giving you another whack once I can see you properly. I don't think that first one conveyed my complete feelings on the matter."

"Later, Pen," said Anne. "So we're all agreed?"

"Do you really think we can climb all the way back down before Shard finds out?" asked Penelope.

"We're not going down," said Anne at the same time that Hiro said, "We're going up."

"Up?" Penelope squeaked.

Anne shushed her. "This tower is part of the quest. We need to find whatever's up there if we hope to succeed."

"How are we supposed to get across the next gap?" asked Penelope. "And what if there are more gaps?"

Anne hesitated. She knew her answer wouldn't be well received. "Shard's branch," she said finally.

Hiro gasped. "You're going to *steal* it?"

"Are you sure you didn't draw the thief token?" asked Penelope.

"I'm going to *borrow* it. He can always go back and get another twig from the last gap in the steps. Anyway, if we hurry, we might make it to the top and back down again before he even wakes up."

Without further discussion, Anne felt her way down to where Shard's three packs were stacked. She opened the first. It was mostly filled with papers and a few smooth stones, but no wooden objects. She didn't find the twig in the second pack, either, and was just about to give up after searching the third bag thoroughly when she felt something hard along the side. There was an inner pocket that held the twig.

"Got it," she whispered.

The air was chilly, so they donned their cloaks once again and slung their packs over their shoulders. Then Anne squeezed past the other two and slowly felt her way up the steps until she came to the gap. She laid the twig on the ledge and tapped it twice, as Shard had done. The twig vibrated as it grew and extended across the gap. When it stopped vibrating, she assumed it must have reached the other side.

"Follow me," she said, keeping her voice low.

Anne placed one foot tentatively onto the branch. It held. She walked across, keeping one hand on the wall to guide her in the dark. Her brain threw all sorts of terrible images at her—falling, crashing off the wall, striking the bottom—but in truth walking along the branch in the dark was actually easier. Without light, the space below them was merely an undefined pool of blackness. Not exactly comforting, but in some ways less terrifying. Hiro followed behind Anne, with Penelope bringing up the rear. After everyone was safely across, Anne knelt and snapped off a new twig. She pocketed it, and they continued onward. They moved steadily but slowly up the stairs, to minimize their noise and to watch out for more gaps.

They stopped occasionally to listen for any sign that Shard was awake or aware of their absence. They heard nothing. Anne pressed onward, while Penelope and Hiro stayed as close to her as was physically possible without actually stepping on her heels. They weren't sure how long they climbed, but it felt like hours. Then the dim light of predawn came trickling down, and they realized they were near the top. They could see the light coming through jagged holes in the ceiling above.

The staircase ended, leading them into a large room at the top of the tower. The tower's central pillar continued upward in the middle of the room and ended in a jagged break. Rows of smaller pillars filled the rest of the space, although many had been smashed, and large pieces lay everywhere. A cluster of unbroken pillars on one side held up the remains of a roof, but much of the ceiling was open to the sky. The random holes in the floor, some quite large, were no doubt where falling pillars had broken through. The floor was covered in black sand.

As Anne was about to ask the others what they thought had caused all this damage, Jeffery appeared in a burst of light.

"What happened?" he asked.

"What do you mean 'what happened'?" said Anne. "I kept calling for you and you kept ignoring me."

Jeffery shook his head. "I tried to respond, but I couldn't get out. It's like something was blocking me."

"Are you okay?" said Anne, their spat forgotten. "Did you get caught in the loop again?"

He shook his head. "It was different this time. Scarier. Maybe Captain Copperhelm should take a look at me again?"

Anne patted his tiny head. "We'll ask him to check you over just as soon as we get back." She couldn't help wondering if somehow Shard was involved in Jeffery becoming trapped, and she was doubly glad to have left him behind.

"So what now?" asked Penelope.

Anne surveyed the ruins. "I don't know. The first line of the riddle said we had to climb the tower, and we've done that. According to the second line, now we're supposed to find a knight who never lived."

Penelope looked around. "You really think some knight is sitting up here just waiting for a bunch of adventurers to come along and find him?"

"Maybe he doesn't actually live in the tower. Maybe there's something here that will tell us where to find him."

"Is there anything new in *The Adventurer's Guide*?" asked Hiro.

Anne took it out. "No. In fact, now *only* Shard's letter is showing. The rest of the pages have gone blank again." She returned the book to her pocket. "I guess we could split up and look around for clues."

At Anne's direction, Hiro started checking around the staircase, and Penelope headed toward the center of the room. Anne and Jeffery navigated their way along a portion of the exterior wall that was still intact. She scrutinized the pillars closely but found no writing or other symbols. The pillars were as smooth as the rest of the tower. Whatever it was they were supposed to find, she hoped it hadn't been destroyed. Something bad had obviously happened up here, and maybe it was related to the creature mentioned in Shard's—

"Help!" shouted Hiro.

Anne ran back toward the staircase, furious at herself for suggesting the group separate, but she stopped in her tracks before reaching them. Shard was standing there, and he was holding Hiro by the front of his tunic next to one of the holes in the floor.

"I have questions, and you're going to answer them," said Shard. His voice was low and snarling. "Tell me the secret of this tower."

"We don't know the secret," said Anne. "Please let him go."

"I'm through playing games." Shard shook Hiro, who whimpered.

"If you're mad about the branch, I'm the one who took it," said Anne. She removed the twig from her pocket and tossed it over. "There. I'm sorry. Just release him, and I promise we'll help you find whatever it is you're looking for."

"I don't care about some stupid twig," he said. "Tell me the secret."

"I told you, we don't—"

"TELL ME THE SECRET NOW!" he roared, and

he lifted Hiro off the ground as though he were about to throw him.

Suddenly, Shard stumbled forward and Hiro dropped to the floor. At first Anne thought Shard had released Hiro, but then she saw an arm lying on the floor. Shard's arm. She also saw Penelope next to Shard, wooden sword in hand. Penelope looked shocked at the result of her attack, but she quickly recovered.

"Pick on someone your own size," she said.

Then she froze.

They all froze.

The stump of Shard's arm wasn't bleeding. Instead, an oily black smoke poured out of it. Even more worrisome, Shard wasn't screaming in pain over his severed arm. In fact, he hardly seemed bothered at all, like having an arm cut off was simply a thing that sometimes happened.

Hiro scrambled to his feet and joined Penelope. Anne only wished she could do the same, but Shard stood between them.

"What are you?" asked Anne, trying her best to keep her voice from cracking.

Shard's mouth turned upward into a ghoulish grin. His eyes had become glassy and unfocused. He started toward her.

"She knew you would come here," said Shard.

Anne backed away. "Who knew?" she asked, although she had already guessed the answer.

"You think you've escaped her grasp, but you haven't. There's nowhere you can go. She doesn't have to chase you. She's anticipated your every move. You might as well accept defeat now and save her the trouble."

"If the Matron wants me, she's going to have to come and get me herself," Anne said.

Shard gave a high-pitched barking laugh. "Oh, she will, she will. She most certainly will. And think of the reward I'll receive for having captured you."

Anne's heels touched the edge of another hole. She doubted there were any dragons waiting to rescue her from a fall this time.

"Of course," continued Shard, "if you tell me the secret of the tower, I might let you go. She'll still find you, but at least you'll have a few more days, a few more hours, minutes, seconds of your scrawny, pathetic, miserable lives." His breathing became labored, and he dragged his feet across the floor. Smoke continued to pour out of his arm.

A small rainbow-colored streak flew straight at Shard and swooped around his head.

"Leave my Keeper alone, you big bully," yelled Jeffery.

Shard batted the little sparrow away with ease. Anne tried to run, but Shard grabbed her wrist and forced her back toward the hole.

"TELL ME THE SECRET!" he screamed. "TELL ME! TELL ME! TELL ME! TELL—"

Shard's rant was cut short. This wasn't so much because he had run out of things to say but more due to the giant metal hand that had suddenly clamped itself around his neck. The hand was connected to a correspondingly giant metal arm, which in turn was attached to a giant metal…man? He was over ten feet tall, and his gray body was dulled and tarnished with age. In addition to his two regular arms, a third arm protuded from his right shoulder, giving him a hunchbacked appearance.

Shard released Anne and fought to free himself from the hand, and Anne moved away quickly from both her attacker and his attacker. Shard struggled against the giant to no avail.

"Initiating security scan," said the metal man, and a green beam of light streamed from his eyes and swept over Shard. "Security scan complete," he said after the light turned off. "Intruder classification: enemy. Course of action: immediate disposal."

The giant walked over to the outer edge of the tower where the wall had crumbled away. Black, scorched wasteland stretched in all directions. Shard thrashed even harder now, his shirttail whipping in the wind. When they reached the edge, the metal man didn't hesitate. He simply stretched out his arm and opened his hand. Shard dropped over the side of the tower, leaving a trail of billowing black smoke.

"SHE'LL FIND YOU!" he hollered as he fell. "SHE'LL FIND YOU, AND SHE'LL STOP YOU, AND SHE'LL TAKE BACK WHAT IS RIGHTFULLY HERS, AND YOU'LL NEVER EVER WIN AND—"

Soon Shard's words became indiscernible and were eventually swallowed by the wind. Anne didn't know how long it would take him to hit the ground, and they couldn't hear or see what happened anyway, which was fine because Anne didn't want to think about that sort of thing.

The metal man faced Anne. Her knees trembled as she waited for his next action.

"Initiating security scan," he said. The green beam of light swept over her.

"Security scan complete. Intruder classification: friendly. Standing down from security alert."

Anne let out a breath in silent thanks, and relief flooded Penelope's and Hiro's faces as well. She was about to greet the giant metal man, but looking into his face, she found herself at a loss for words.

The metal man's eyes were yellow, just like hers.

"Hello," the metal giant said to them. "I am a PAL series robot. How may I be of assistance?"

AN EXCERPT FROM *THAERESA'S COMPENDIUM OF ROBOTS AND OTHER MYTHICAL CREATURES*:

Of all the creatures of legend, robots are perhaps the most terrifying, with their reinforced steel armor and their laser beam eyes and their extra-capacity memory modules that make them really hard to beat at word puzzles. Parents tell stories about them to frighten their children into eating vegetables and going to bed on time. They lurk in the shadows, prey on our fears, and live in our nightmares.

So lock your doors, pull up the covers, and hang magnets from the rafters, because you never really know. They might be more real than you think.

The Knight Who Never Lived

Anne pushed Shard's words about the Matron and everything that had just transpired out of her head for the moment. She edged her way around the metal man until she reached where Penelope and Hiro were standing. The metal man watched her with apparent interest but made no further moves, hostile or otherwise.

"Are you two okay?" asked Anne.

Hiro rubbed his neck. "A little sore, but I'll be fine." He turned to Penelope. "Thanks for that. You saved my life."

Penelope was clutching her stomach. "I was only trying to make him let you go. I had no idea a wooden sword could do that." She tried to sheathe the sword, but it took her three attempts. "And you know what no one tells you about cutting off limbs?" she continued. "That it's completely gross and makes you want to vomit afterward. Oh, wow, that is not at all what I thought real fighting would be like."

"If it helps, I don't think Shard was human," said Anne.

"It doesn't help. That much was obvious."

"No, I don't mean the hyena thing. I mean the black smoke thing."

"Still not helping."

Anne moved to pat Penelope on the back, but Penelope held up her hand. "Seriously. If anyone so much as touches me right now, Hiro's going to be wearing what little I ate for dinner last night on his shoes. Just give me a minute."

"You were very brave, Pen. I'm so proud of you."

"I'll be proud of me, too, if I can avoid seeing my bread and cheese a second time."

"My shoes would like that as well," said Hiro.

Anne turned back to the metal man. He was holding

out his hand to her. Jeffery's tiny form lay in his palm next to Shard's magick twig. Anne took the twig and put it in her pocket, and then she gently scooped up the sparrow.

The metal man pointed at Jeffery. "Your sparrow has sustained an injury. Do you require assistance? My medical database is currently offline, but I will signal for another unit to come and provide any necessary first-aid treatment." The metal man paused for a few seconds. "No other units are responding to my signal. Please remain calm. I will try again in sixty seconds."

"Thanks, but I don't think that's necessary," said Anne as Jeffery began to stir. "He's just a little stunned, is all." She nudged the tiny sparrow. "Jeffery, can you hear me? Are you okay?"

"I'm not sure," mumbled Jeffery. "I'm seeing weird things, like a big metal guy."

"He's real."

"Oh, okay then, I'm good." He hopped up onto her gauntlet.

"Thank you for protecting me," she said.

"Hey, what kind of sparrow would I be if I didn't have my Keeper's back?"

Anne smiled at Jeffery, and then she regarded the metal man again. She'd spent her entire life around the

213

iron knights, but this was different. Where the knights were uniform in appearance, this newcomer had a more haphazard look, as though its builder had had to make do with whatever materials were available. In fact, it reminded Anne of the pocketknife she'd made, now lost, built from whatever scraps she could find. Also, none of the iron knights had ever spoken or shown any signs of intelligence beyond the ability to recognize and carry out simple commands. And none of them had bright yellow eyes. Was it possible this creature held some link to Anne's real home?

"My name is Anne," she said. "This is Penelope and Hiro. And Jeffery."

The metal man nodded at them. "Hello, Anne, Penelope, Hiro, and Jeffery. My name is Rokk."

"Nice to meet you, Rokk. May we ask what you're doing up here in this tower?"

Rokk looked around. "I am uncertain. I know that I was sent here to guard this place, but some of my memory modules seem to have sustained damage and/or been removed. Thus I am experiencing severe memory gaps. Are any of you by chance a licensed technician?"

"I'm going to go out on a limb and say no, sorry," said Anne.

"That is most unfortunate," said Rokk. "Well, it has been nice chatting with you, Anne, Penelope, Hiro, and Jeffery. I must now return to my patrol." Before Anne could say anything more, Rokk turned and walked off through the rubble, sweeping the pillars with his green beam.

"What is he?" hissed Penelope. "Or it? Or whatever?"

Anne shrugged. "He referred to himself as a rowboat or something, but I have no idea what that's supposed to mean. Maybe it's another riddle?"

"He didn't say *rowboat*, he said *robot*," said Hiro. "It's an Old World term. It refers to a person who isn't really a person. A kind of machine made to look like a person."

"Why make a machine that looks like a person?" said Penelope. "Were they running out of actual people in the Old World or something?"

"They used robots for a variety of tasks," Hiro explained. "Such as personal servants, construction projects, even to fight in wars."

The full impact of these implications hit her, and Anne began to tremble. Is that what she was? A machine? Built to do someone else's bidding?

"Anne, what's wrong?" asked Penelope.

"D-didn't you see his eyes?"

"Yeah. They kind of glow, like there's a little fire lit inside each one."

"They were yellow, Pen. I've been wishing my whole life to find someone who has eyes like mine, and the first person I meet who does turns out not to be a person at all. What does that mean? What am I?"

Penelope took Anne's hand and gave it a squeeze. "Oh, Anne. You're being ridiculous. His eyes are more like lights or something. Yours are definitely of the human variety. Besides, you're not made of metal. You're flesh and blood, just like Hiro and me. I'm one hundred and fifty percent positive you're not a robutt."

"*Robot*," said Hiro. "It's pronounced *ro-bot*."

"But what if I am?" said Anne. "Maybe I'm missing memories, too, and I just don't know it."

Penelope placed both her hands on Anne's shoulders. "Even if you were, it wouldn't change anything. We would still be best friends. And we would still have this quest to complete."

Right, Anne thought. The quest. The reason they had climbed the tower in the first place. The reason they were all together. Anne might actually get the answers she was looking for at the end of this quest, and that was why she could not afford to get sidetracked.

Anne looked over at Rokk. "Do you think he knows anything about the quest?"

Penelope shrugged. "Why don't we ask him?"

Rokk was examining a fallen pillar. As Anne, Penelope, and Hiro walked up from behind, Anne noticed some severely worn letters written across his back. She had to squint to make them out, but they seemed to spell a single seven-letter word:

PALADIN

Anne pointed it out to the others.

Penelope frowned. "I thought he said he was a PAL series robot, not a PALADIN series."

"Maybe he doesn't entirely remember that, either," offered Hiro.

Anne snapped her fingers. "But that's it, don't you see?"

"What's it?" said Penelope.

"A paladin. We've read about them, Pen. They're an elite type of knight, the best of the best. And Hiro, you said robots are machines, which means they aren't really alive, right? So if Rokk is both a paladin and a machine, that makes him the knight who never lived!"

Penelope nodded. "Sounds plausible."

"I think you might be on to something," said Hiro. "Everything fits."

Anne beamed. If Rokk himself was the knight, that meant they had solved the second line of the riddle, and they were halfway through the quest. Actually finishing didn't seem quite so far-fetched anymore. They might really be able to pull this off.

"Okay, okay, so if he's the knight, what do we do now?" asked Penelope.

"The riddle says, 'Ask the knight who never lived,'" said Anne. "So I guess we're supposed to ask him a question."

"Oh, about the key!" said Penelope. "It's the third line of the riddle. I bet he knows something about the key you can't hold."

"That makes sense, too," said Hiro. "Maybe only robots can hold it or something."

Rokk had moved across the room and was shining his green light on the broken pillars. They approached and got his attention.

"Hello again," said Rokk. "I regret I am unable to offer you any refreshments as per my programming. Our

218

supplies ran out ten thousand thirteen years, two days, seven hours, and thirty minutes ago. If you wish, I can take your order now and bring it to you once we have been properly restocked."

Anne cleared her throat. "Rokk, do you know anything about a key?"

Rokk tilted his head. "Key. Definition: an instrument, usually metal, by which the bolt of a lock is turned."

"Uh, yeah, we already knew that," Anne said. "We want to ask you about a specific key. It's called 'the key you cannot hold.'"

"A key you cannot hold logically cannot be held," said Rokk.

"Yes, true," Anne acknowledged. "But we were hoping maybe you could explain that part."

"The input parameters are unsound. Are you also in need of a licensed technician?"

Anne turned back to Penelope and Hiro. "This isn't going well."

"Try *The Adventurer's Guide*," said Penelope. "Maybe it knows what to ask him."

Anne took out the book. The title was the same, and Shard's letter was still the only thing inside. "Maybe it's broken," said Anne.

"Shard's notes," said Hiro suddenly.

"What?" said Anne.

"The guide keeps showing us this one letter from him, but maybe he left other letters, too. Maybe that's what the book is trying to tell us. Shard gathered a lot of information about this tower. The question we need to ask Rokk could be somewhere in all of Shard's notes. We could return to the base and bring Rokk with us."

"It's worth a try," said Anne, shoving the guidebook back into the inner pocket of her cloak. "Jeffery, how much time is left?"

"A little over one day and sixteen hours," said Jeffery.

"And how long did it take us to climb up here, minus the time we stopped?"

"Close to nine hours."

Anne shook her head. "We can't afford that much time. Didn't anyone in the Old World invent something faster than stairs?"

"If you jumped, you could reach the bottom in under a minute," said Rokk.

"We'll call that Plan You Go First," said Penelope.

"Do you have any other, preferably nonlethal, suggestions?" asked Anne.

"You could always use this vertical transport device,"

said Rokk. He walked over to the center pillar and touched it. A crack appeared and a set of double doors slid apart, revealing a small square room.

Penelope stuck her head through the doorway. "You want us to squeeze into this closet?"

"It's okay," said Hiro. "I think it's something called an elevator. They used them in Old World buildings to travel between floors."

"Is it faster than walking?" asked Anne.

Rokk nodded. "This device is capable of returning you safely to the bottom of the tower in 2.78 minutes."

"That's good enough for me," said Hiro, stepping into the room.

Anne turned to Rokk. "Will you come with us?"

"I am not permitted to leave my patrol without a direct order," said Rokk.

Anne was certain Rokk was a piece of the puzzle they needed to solve, but she felt uneasy about telling him what to do. "We're trying to solve a riddle and complete a quest, Rokk, and we could really use your help, but I think it should be your decision."

Rokk paused for such a long time that Anne began to wonder if he had stopped working altogether. "I will accompany you," he said finally.

"Great." Anne held out the gauntlet to Jeffery. "Maybe you'd better hide back in the gauntlet until we're out of the tower."

"Sounds good to me," said Jeffery, and he dove into it with a splash of light.

Anne, Penelope, and Hiro fit into the elevator easily, but Rokk had to crouch and shuffle in sideways, forcing Anne and the others to flatten themselves against the walls to make room.

"I am unable to reach the control panel from my current position," said Rokk. "Pressing the downward triangle symbol on the top left will instruct the vertical transport to descend to the bottom of the tower."

Anne pressed the white triangle and the doors closed. There was a brief jerking motion.

"I think we're moving," said Hiro nervously.

"Do not be alarmed," said Rokk. "We are now descending."

It was an unsettling feeling, as though they were almost falling but not quite. After slightly less than three minutes of this, the room jerked again, throwing Anne off balance. Thankfully, given how cramped the space was, her body had no place to go. The doors slid open again, and they found that they had indeed traveled back to the bottom of the tower. Rokk squeezed out first, and Anne and the others followed.

"How about nobody points out how much easier and faster it would have been to reach the top of the tower if we had known about that elevator thing in the first place," said Penelope.

"Agreed," said Anne and Hiro in unison.

"Affirmative," said Rokk.

They walked over to the wall.

Anne stepped forward. "We tried opening the door again, but couldn't get the grid to—"

"Activate interface," said Rokk, and the grid appeared. He shone his green beam of light on it, and a nearby section of wall became fluid. One after the other, they exited the tower.

The air was considerably warmer outside, although the morning sun was still low enough in the eastern sky that the dunes cast a shadow over their campsite in the valley below.

"Anne, over here," called Penelope.

Anne joined Penelope, who was standing next to a pile of well-tailored clothes, the ones Shard had been wearing. Penelope bent down and picked up the shirt. Coarse, dark sand spilled out the arm and neck holes. Shard himself, or his body, was nowhere to be seen.

"What was he?" asked Penelope, kicking at the sand.

"It's like he was made of sand, too, just like the wolves," said Anne. Despite all the stories she'd read, and all the fantastic creatures they had contained, it unnerved her to think they had spent nearly an entire day with Shard and never realized his true nature.

Something glittered in the pile of sand that had poured out of Shard's clothes. Anne reached down and pulled out a gold chain with a crystal on it. Shard must have been wearing it. It was identical to the one the Matron always wore.

"So where should we start?" asked Penelope.

Anne stuffed the gold chain and crystal into her coat pocket. "Let's check the main tent first. His most important documents are probably in there."

The four of them started down the slope toward Shard's tents—

—and stopped short as a green fireball dropped out of the sky and obliterated the entire campsite. They watched in disbelief as small bits and pieces of burning tent canvas and parchment fluttered down from above.

The burning globe rolled across the sand and came to a rest in front of them.

Jocelyn stumbled from the smoking remains of the large tent, coughing and sputtering. Anne, Penelope, and Hiro yelled in surprise and delight, and they ran down the slope to her. Penelope found a chair, and Anne guided Jocelyn to it. Hiro brought a canteen of water and offered it to her. He also gave her a big hug.

"Sorry I blew up your academy," Hiro said.

Jocelyn patted him on the shoulder. "Not to worry, dear. Sometimes it takes a while to work out all the kinks." She took a drink of the water and surveyed their surroundings. "And speaking of working things out, who went and pitched their tent in a designated fireball landing zone?"

"I tried to tell Shard it was against regulations," said Hiro.

Jocelyn finished the water. "Well, no harm done, I suppose." She straightened her vest and checked that her hair was in place.

"What are you doing here?" asked Anne.

Jocelyn pulled a sheaf of papers out of her bag. "Why, dear, I'm here to give you your first evaluation, of course."

THIS FORM IS FOR STUDENT EVALUATION PURPOSES ONLY. FOR EACH QUESTION, PLEASE CIRCLE THE ANSWER THAT BEST APPLIES.

1. Is the trainee still alive? YES / NO*

2. Has anything exploded? YES / NO

   a. Should anything have exploded? YES / NO / MAYBE

   b. In the event something has exploded, does anyone require the expensive first-aid treatment the academy is contractually obligated to provide? NO / NO

3. Are you requesting a raise? NO / MOST DEFINITELY NOT**

4. Do you know the answer to this question? YES / NO

5. Have you filled out this form properly?

PROBABLY NOT / I LET MY PLATYPUS FILL IT OUT

After you have completed this form, you may deposit it in the council's inbox and be entered into the weekly drawing to win a round-trip, all-expenses-paid vacation to a destination of your choosing. The in-box is located behind the main building. Look for the large metal container labeled INCINERATOR.

---

   * If the answer to this first question is "No," in most cases there is no need to complete the rest of the form (use your discretion).

   ** If you thought it would be funny to scratch in "Yes" here, please note such action will appear on your permanent record.

Sand Wolves and Portals

Jocelyn dusted ash from her cloak as she walked to the large oak table that had, until recently, marked the center of Shard's main tent. All the maps and other documents had been burned up, but the table itself was in more or less working condition, although one side was smoldering rather noticeably.

"You're here to *evaluate* me?" asked Anne. Her relief at seeing Jocelyn alive gave way to terror at the thought of getting marked on her performance thus far. What grade did a person get for finding a robot who threw people off towers? Or for dropping a mountain on your own quest academy?

Jocelyn placed the papers on the table. "Despite the unusual circumstances, you are technically still a student of the academy, and as your designated mentor, I am therefore required to submit quarterly performance evaluations."

"I've been on the quest less than two and a half days," said Anne.

"True, but since your quest only runs four days in total, that equals one evaluation per day. Technically, we're behind."

"But the academy got demolished," said Hiro.

Jocelyn chuckled. "A minor setback, I assure you. It happens all the time, so don't give it another thought. If we suspended operations for every little instance of complete and utter destruction, we'd never get anything done."

Hiro seemed relieved to hear this.

"So everyone is really okay?" asked Anne.

"Yes, yes, all fine," Jocelyn assured them. "Although Captain Copperhelm is somewhat upset about the loss of his Dragons of the Hierarchy collector's edition trading cards. Apparently some of them were quite rare."

Jocelyn set a vial of ink on the end of the table that wasn't smoking. She unstoppered the vial and dipped a quill in the ink. "So, this is the tower, is it?" she said, and started taking notes.

"It's called the Infinite Tower," said Anne.

"Yes, of course." Jocelyn gave the tower a cursory glance. "It's quite impressive—although I've seen higher."

"You have?"

"When you've traveled as much as I have, my dear, you learn not to become overly enchanted with every immeasurable tower you come across."

"*Infinite* Tower," Anne corrected.

"Those, too. So, you managed to enter, did you? Then what?"

"We climbed, like, a bazillion stairs," said Penelope.

"And an archaeologist tried to kill us," said Hiro.

Jocelyn nodded. "They can get like that sometimes." She made a special note in the margin.

"And then we met him," said Anne, pointing to Rokk.

"Him who?" said Jocelyn, turning around.

"Him," said Anne, pointing to Rokk again. "Say hello, Rokk."

"Hello, Rokk," said Rokk.

Jocelyn jumped back. "Goodness me. I thought he was a statue."

"Nope," said Penelope. "He's a robot."

Jocelyn quickly regained her composure. "Robot? You mean to say you found a fully functional Old World robot inside?"

"He was patrolling at the top," said Anne. "We're pretty sure he's the knight who never lived, so we brought him down here to figure out what question we're supposed to ask him. That's when you, well, showed up." Anne pointed to the wreckage of the campsite.

"My name is Rokk," said Rokk.

"And, uh, he might not be *fully* functional," Anne added.

Jocelyn studied Rokk. She walked around him and observed him from different angles. Her quill moved quickly across the piece of paper she was holding, and Anne caught a glimpse of a hastily drawn sketch. "This is an extraordinary find, Anne. Simply extraordinary. What do you intend to do with him?"

"Do with him? What do you mean?"

"He's an Old World artifact. If you discovered him, the rules state that he now belongs to you. Personally, I would suggest that a piece this well-preserved belongs in a museum where other scholars and academics can admire and study him."

Penelope clapped her hands together and squealed. "Our own piece of Old World treasure, Anne, just like we talked about. And we didn't even have to get anything pierced!"

"Um, shouldn't he get to decide for himself what happens to him?" said Anne.

Jocelyn smiled. "Anne, dear, I'm not sure you fully appreciate the opportunity here. So much remains unknown about the Old World, despite all our research and exploration. Something like this could advance our knowledge by decades. Maybe even centuries. Not to mention you yourself would become instantly famous. Why, they might even wave the formal requirements and induct you into the Royal Archaeology Society immediately. In fact, if you like, I have a few connections and could make some discreet inquires on your behalf."

Anne looked at Rokk. He might not be human, but that didn't make him some treasure to be claimed. Yes, he followed orders like the iron knights, but he also seemed at least partially autonomous in a way that they weren't, able to make his own choices. It didn't seem right to put him on display in a museum. Plus, Anne still felt sure he was somehow connected to where she came from.

"Rokk is free to choose for himself," Anne said firmly.

Jocelyn frowned. "As you wish," she said. She didn't seem entirely pleased, but she didn't press the issue further.

A distant howl caused everyone to pause.

"Local wildlife?" asked Jocelyn.

"The archaeologist, Mr. Shard, had some wolves pulling his sled," said Penelope.

Jocelyn scanned the remains of the campsite. "And where is this Mr. Shard fellow now?"

"Erm, Rokk might have thrown him off the top of the tower," said Anne.

Jocelyn looked only somewhat shocked. "I see. Well, I'm sure Rokk had his reasons." She held her quill over the piece of paper. "So, how exactly might you describe these wolves, then?"

"Large," said Penelope.

"Toothy," added Hiro.

"Made out of sand," said Anne.

Jocelyn staggered back and caught herself on the edge of the table. "Sand wolves?"

"Yes. Is that a problem?"

Jocelyn restoppered the ink vial and tossed it, the quill, and the stack of papers back into her pack. "Where's the nearest village?"

"About four hours by wolf sled in that direction," said Penelope, pointing back the way they had come.

"And what about dragons?"

"What about them?" asked Anne.

Jocelyn looked to Hiro. "Mr. Darkflame?"

Hiro stood at attention. "All major quest locations are required to be equipped with at least one fully licensed dragon," he said, as though reciting text.

"We haven't seen any dragons," said Anne. "Other than Nana, that is, but she's waiting back at the village."

Jocelyn tied her satchel closed while muttering to herself. "I keep writing to the Dragon Oversight Committee about the need to check these remote locations, but do they listen? No. Fine. Everyone up to the tower. We'll simply enter the way you did before."

Another, closer howl echoed across the dunes and was met by several yipping replies.

Everyone started up the hill at a run.

"Is this really necessary?" asked Anne. "They seemed friendly enough before."

"Without a master to control them, they are highly unpredictable and given to random attacks," said Jocelyn. "They have no doubt sensed the archaeologist's demise by this point, and trust me when I say that sand wolves are nothing we want to face out here in the open."

Yet another chorus of howls erupted, this time closer still.

They reached the base of the tower, and Anne tapped the wall. The grid appeared, and she tapped in N-O-D-O-O-R. Nothing happened. She tapped it in again, more slowly to make sure every letter was correct. Still nothing.

"I thought you said you had found a way in," asked Jocelyn, an edge to her voice.

"The password is correct, but it isn't working anymore," said Anne.

"Well, if you've moved on to the next part of the quest, it's possible a new password is required," said Jocelyn.

Anne's heart sank. "We haven't figured out the next part of the riddle yet. We were hoping to find a clue in Shard's notes."

"You would think if there was something the riddle wanted you to ask, it would at least do you the courtesy of providing you with the question," said Jocelyn. At the sound of yet another howl, she drew her rapier.

Jocelyn was right, Anne realized. The same thing had been true of the riddle's first line: *Climb the tower with no door.* The sentence could be read in different ways to reveal different meanings, each of which was important: They had to find and climb a tower without a door, and they could only enter the tower using the password *no door.* Solving the riddle's second line wouldn't require random guessing, but figuring out the full interpretation.

Anne considered both parts of the riddle's second line separately.

Ask the knight.

The word *ask* definitely meant they had to ask a question. And she was sure *the knight* could only be Rokk. Why go to the tower if not to find him? Anne continued with the line's second half.

Who never lived.

This accurately described Rokk, what with him being a robot and all, but Anne noticed that the word *who* was also itself a question word.

"That's it," said Anne. "That's the solution."

"What's the solution?" asked Penelope.

"Who never lived," said Anne.

235

Penelope scratched her head. "But we already know that part."

"It doesn't just describe a knight who never lived," explained Anne. "It also means ask him that actual question."

"What question?" said Penelope.

"Who never lived?" Anne repeated.

Hiro snapped his fingers. "I see what you mean. Excellent!"

Penelope looked from one to the other. "Why does it feel like we're talking in circles?"

A chorus of howls arose as ten sand wolves appeared in the valley below and tore up the slope toward them.

Anne tapped Rokk on the arm. "I have a question for you."

"Proceed," said Rokk.

"Who. Never. Lived?" Anne said, making sure to pronounce the words slowly and clearly.

Rokk's eyes flashed. "Processing query. Command input accepted. Attempting to establish remote connection."

"What is he doing?" asked Jocelyn.

"I have no idea," said Anne.

The wolves were about halfway up the slope, howling and growling and snapping their jaws.

"I am unable to establish a link," said Rokk. "Initiating secondary protocol. Activating homing beacon."

Rokk stepped over to the wall and brought up the grid. He tapped on the symbols faster and faster until his mechanical fingers were a blur and the words on the wall scrolled by so fast that Anne couldn't read them. High above them, a beam of blue light shot from the top of the tower into the sky. Clouds immediately gathered overhead and the wind picked up. Blowing sand stung their faces, and they huddled together next to the wall, pulling up their hoods for protection.

"What did you do?" Anne yelled at Rokk over the rising shriek of the wind.

"Please stand by," said Rokk. "A portal has been summoned and will arrive shortly."

"What did he say?" shouted Jocelyn.

Anne shook her head. "Something about a portal, I think."

"A portal? Here?" said Hiro, sounding alarmed.

"Does it have something to do with that?" said Penelope. She pointed up to where a giant mass of clouds was churning into a funnel shape.

Anne didn't know which was scarier: the violent funnel above or the charging sand wolves. Those with weapons drew them, and everyone braced for the wolves' imminent attack.

A green beam of light swept across the wolves, and Rokk stepped out from the group. "Please excuse me while I dispatch these canine intruders."

Rokk ran straight off the tower base and toward the pack. At the same time, the lead wolf launched itself at the robot. Rokk dodged and swept his arm up in a devastating blow that cut the wolf in half. When the two halves landed, however, they rejoined.

"That's going to make it harder," said Hiro.

The next three wolves attacked together. Rokk kicked the first one back into the other two, and they all exploded into clouds of black sand on impact. But as with the first wolf, the sand reformed moments later, and the wolves became whole again.

The last six wolves jumped and converged on Rokk at once. Rokk leapt into the air and twirled his body, flinging them off in all directions.

The wind velocity increased, and the funnel cloud dropped until it hung in the air only ten feet above Anne and the others. It was a roiling mass, snapping and thrashing and crackling with energy and spitting out whiffs of bluish-colored smoke. The sand wolves shied away, and Rokk retreated to the tower.

"I do not believe I will be able to defeat these adversaries using hand-to-hand techniques," he said. "I shall therefore try another tactic."

"I sure hope the new tactic works soon," said Penelope.

"Have I mentioned I'm not really much of a dog person?" said Jocelyn.

The sand wolves spread out, pacing restlessly. While the others held their weapons at the ready, Anne stretched out the gauntlet in the hopes that it might have some control over the wolves, as it had with the iron knights and suits of armor. The wolves seemed unaffected and kept pacing, however, so she balled the gauntlet into a fist instead. At least that would give her a weapon, too, however ineffective it might prove to be.

Everyone tensed.

The wolves sprang at them.

"Commencing transport," said Rokk, and he double-tapped the grid.

The end of the funnel snapped down, slamming into the sand wolves at full force and ripping them to pieces.

They howled and snarled and gnashed their teeth as their bodies disintegrated, leaving nothing but blowing sand.

By contrast, the center of the funnel where Anne and the others were standing was completely calm. As the funnel spun faster and faster around them, Anne felt as though her head were being pulled upward while her feet remained firmly on the ground. Everything in front of her became a dark blur.

Then the funnel snapped back up into the sky, and the group was gone.

THE ADVENTURER'S GUIDE TO PORTALS
OFFERS THE FOLLOWING ADVICE:

Don't use them. Ever.

A MUCH LESS CONCISE DISCUSSION OF
PORTALS CAN BE FOUND IN *THE COMPLETE
ENCYCLOPEDIA OF ALL FORMS OF MAGICKAL
TRANSPORTATION YOU SHOULD NEVER USE*:

Portals are one of the quickest known means of travel. They are also one of the quickest known means of death, second only to getting between a dragon and its meal—although that itself is second to actually being the meal (which, granted, essentially amounts to the same thing).

In theory, portals open a gateway between two geographical locations thereby allowing a person to step from one place directly to another. Practically speaking, they don't do this at all.

In reality, portals rely on a process known as *scrunching*. Through this process the two ends of a portal are brought together—or *scrunched*, as it were—such that, while it is true a person steps from one place to another, they also travel the entirety of the intervening space, albeit instantaneously. For those who find this difficult to conceptualize, simply imagine the body accumulating the effects of an eight-hundred-mile journey in less than a heartbeat. Presuming, of course, that after the journey your heart is still beating.

First-time users of portals should keep in mind two important tips:

1) Always close your eyes.

2) Don't use them. Ever.

The Key You Cannot Hold

The sky was overcast and gray. The rolling hills were gray. The grass was gray. The trees of the forest in the valley below were gray. Even the dirt of the nearby stone path that led down to the forest was gray. All in all, it wasn't the most colorful of places. Anne, Penelope, Hiro, Jocelyn, and Rokk lay on a hillside. Hanging in the air above them were funnel clouds by the hundreds—thousands, even. Most of the funnels were of similar size to the one that had deposited them on the ground, though some were smaller and a few were much, much larger.

As if exhaustion and hunger weren't enough, Anne's body felt as though it had been trod over by an iron knight who had then backed up and stomped on her several more times just for good measure. She also felt a sharp pain in her side, which turned out to be a corner of the guidebook. She pulled it out and looked at the title, which had finally changed again to *The Adventurer's Guide to Very Very Bad Places That Will Kill You Dead I'm Not Kidding You Should Definitely Get Out of Here*. There was only one sentence on the first page. It read: *Seriously, leave now while you still can.* Anne swallowed.

Jeffery popped into view, his bright rainbow feathers a stark contrast to their bleak surroundings. "Hey, is it me, or could this place use a little sunshine?"

"I feel awful," said Hiro, clutching the sides of his head.

Penelope rubbed her belly. "Ugh. It feels like I ate some bad portal or something."

Rokk stood. Jocelyn quickly followed.

"What is the meaning of this?" Jocelyn said, shaking a finger at the giant robot. "Are you a licensed portal operator? Is this a preapproved quest destination? You can't simply go around calling down portals on unsuspecting people and transporting them willy-nilly across the Hierarchy. We have rights, you know. This is clearly a violation of Sections 416, 506, and 902 of the Questing Regulations, not to mention also being quite rude."

"My homing beacon has been activated," said Rokk. "I must return to my point of origin." Without another word he started down the hill toward the gray forest below.

Point of origin. The words echoed in Anne's ears. She wanted to return to her point of origin as well, but she was no longer certain whether this quest was taking her closer or farther away.

"Come back here," Jocelyn shouted. "I demand you return us this instant."

Rokk ignored her and kept walking.

Jocelyn slung her satchel over her shoulder and straightened her clothes. "Well, I'm afraid to say this is going to reflect very poorly on your evaluation," she said to Anne.

"*My* evaluation?" said Anne. "What did I do?"

Jocelyn pointed to the departing robot. "You're the one who got him to activate his...his homing-thingy, aren't you?"

245

"I just asked him the question in the riddle! How was I supposed to know what would happen?"

"Precisely my point. You have no idea where this is."

"I do," said Jeffery, sounding nervous now. "We've landed on a dead tier."

If possible, Jocelyn became even more serious. "Jeffery, are you certain?"

"What's a dead tier?" asked Anne.

"It's what happens when someone fails a prophecy quest," said Hiro. "It destroys all life on whatever tier you're on at the time."

"Not just any prophecy quest," Jocelyn corrected. "Only a Level Twelve quest. And I truly thought that was a myth. No one has even attempted such a high-level quest in centuries, and one hears all manner of rumors about them."

Anne took in the utter starkness of their surroundings and felt her pulse quicken. "Um, so if this is what happens when a Level Twelve quest fails, what happens if a Level Thirteen quest fails?"

No one seemed eager to speculate.

"This is very serious," said Jocelyn. "We need to leave immediately and seek help. Jeffery, can you contact Nana?"

"I can't contact anyone," said Jeffery. "I don't even

know where we are. And I already used my one allotted emergency signal for this quest."

"I don't think we're going to be able to leave here without Rokk," Anne said, and then she pointed to the sky. "Unless you know how to summon a portal."

Penelope tapped Anne on the shoulder. "Speaking of Rokk, shouldn't we be following him?"

Rokk had almost reached the edge of the forest.

"Come on," Anne yelled and ran headlong down the hillside. The others followed, with Jocelyn grumbling about how she would have chosen sturdier footwear had she known she was going to be gallivanting across some unknown tier. They caught up with Rokk just inside the forest.

"Rokk, we need you to recall the portal," said Anne.

"I must return to my point of origin," said Rokk, and he kept walking.

"Rokk, I order you to recall the portal."

Rokk ignored her command just as he had ignored Jocelyn's.

"I don't think I can stop him," Anne said to the others. "But if the quest riddle is what caused him to bring us here, he should be leading us to the next destination point. Maybe he'll listen once we reach there."

"I certainly hope you're right," said Jocelyn.

Anne hoped she was, too.

Rokk maintained a steady pace, forcing the others into a light jog to keep up with his long stride. The path wound through the forest. None of the familiar sounds of nature were present: the buzzing of insects, the chirping of birds, the spontaneous combustion of humpbacked snorflefizzles. The only sound was the crunch of dry, withered leaves underfoot.

Eventually, the trees thinned and gave way to a field of dead gray grass with a windowless two-story building in the center. Its stone walls were pitted and crumbling, giving the impression of great age. The side of the building facing them was dominated by a set of large double doors covered in dead vines. The doors were tall enough that they could accommodate Rokk with room to spare.

Rokk marched over and stood in front of the doors. From somewhere beneath the vines, a green beam of light shot out and swept over him. There was a distant click, and with a deep groan the doors swung outward on their own, snapping the brittle vines with ease. Inside, a wide staircase descended into the darkness.

"Wonderful," said Anne. "More stairs."

"I have a bad feeling about this," said Hiro.

The oversized steps were obviously designed for someone or something much larger than the average person. Rokk descended them with no trouble whatsoever, but the others had to jump their way down each step. Despite their difficulties, they soon reached the bottom (with several thankful murmurs) and followed a short tunnel to yet another door. Rokk opened it, and they entered to find they were standing on a balcony. The building's main level lay thirty feet below, stretching for hundreds of feet in all directions. A grid of tiny lights covered the entire floor, like thousands of evenly spaced fireflies. The vines had invaded here, too; they hung from the walls and ceiling and even wrapped around the balcony railing. At the far end of the room, barely visible in the faint light, was a tall structure of some sort. Across the floor in front of the structure was an indistinct black line.

The group followed Rokk down yet another set of stairs, their footsteps echoing in the cavernous space. Jocelyn kept muttering to herself and writing things in her notebook. When they reached the main floor, they could see that the "fireflies" were actually thousands of tiny spheres sitting atop thin metal rods. The spheres pulsed with a dull amber light.

"What do you suppose those are?" asked Hiro.

"I don't know," said Anne. "But they're numbered." She pointed to one of the spheres, where a five-digit number was inscribed.

Before they reached the far end of the room, the floor dropped away into a seemingly bottomless chasm. On the other side of the chasm was a wide shelf of rock, which contained the structure they had seen from the balcony. It turned out to be a white pillar that extended from the shelf all the way to the ceiling high above. Curiously, it resembled the elevator in the Infinite Tower. A bridge led across the chasm—or at least it would have if not for the ten-foot gap where the center had collapsed. All in all it was the sort of place where words like *foreboding* and *sinister* would feel right at home, and even the phrase *ill-omened* would have been comfortable stopping by for a biscuit and a quick cup of tea.

"Now what?" asked Jocelyn.

"We must cross," said Rokk, pointing across the bridge.

"Yes, but how?"

Anne reached into her pocket and brought out the twig she'd taken from Shard. She cautiously walked onto the bridge and knelt before the gap. Then she placed the twig down and tapped it twice. It grew until it spanned the gap and attached securely to the far side.

The others began to move onto the bridge, but Rokk held out his massive arms, blocking the way. "Please remain here. Only the Keeper and I may proceed across." He pointed to Jeffery. "That includes the GPS."

"This is highly irregular," said Jocelyn.

"It's fine," said Anne. "I'll only be a few feet away. You'll be able to see and hear everything that happens." She nodded to Jeffery, and the little sparrow complied and fluttered over to perch on Penelope's shoulder.

Rokk went first. The branch creaked in protest but held. Once he was across, Anne followed, keeping her eyes on the far side and doing her best to ignore the black emptiness below. Once past the gap, she hurried onto the shelf and joined Rokk. In front of the white pillar was a thin gray box just slightly shorter than Anne herself.

"What now?" asked Anne, wondering if perhaps the key lay inside the box.

Rokk didn't respond. Nor did he lead her over to the box or the pillar. Instead, he lifted his leg into the air and brought his foot down on the end of the bridge. A ringing clang echoed throughout the chamber.

The rest of the group on the other side cried out.

"What are you doing?" yelled Anne.

Rokk still didn't answer. He slammed his foot onto the bridge a second time, and then a third. Each time, the bridge supports shook and groaned under the furious assault. Finally, on the fourth strike, the supports gave way. The portion of the bridge connected to the shelf broke away and crumbled into the chasm, taking Shard's branch and most of the other bridge section along with it. As the branch fell, Anne realized she had forgotten to take a new twig, so she couldn't grow another branch to get back to the other side.

Anne backed away from Rokk. Had something gone wrong with him, or was this part of the quest? He was obviously tied to the quest somehow, or else speaking the line from the riddle to him wouldn't have triggered the response it had. Still, had she been foolish to trust him? Anne kept expecting Rokk to attack her as well, but he stood perfectly immobile.

"Are you all right?" Penelope called across to Anne.

"I'm fine," said Anne. "But what do we do now?"

"That's easy," said a voice behind her. "Now you lose."

Anne turned around.

The white pillar was indeed another elevator, and the doors had opened to reveal…

The Matron.

Anne gulped as the Matron stepped out of the elevator and regarded her with undisguised hatred. The doors to the elevator closed, and something told Anne they wouldn't open again unless the Matron wanted them to. Anne looked desperately at Rokk, hoping the Matron's arrival might trigger his security scan, or whatever he had called it, but he remained impassive, unmoving.

"H-how do you keep finding us?" asked Anne, willing her voice not to crack.

The Matron chuckled. "A perk of the position. Antagonists are permitted up to three dramatic entrances per quest, and I like to get my money's worth. So I'm afraid, my dear, you're going to find that you are always a step or two behind me. That's not your fault, necessarily." Her eyes flicked across the void to Jocelyn. "Someone should have prepared you better."

The Matron walked over to the edge of the shelf and stared at Jocelyn. "Well, well, look who's come to visit. We didn't have time to catch up back at the academy, what with your trying to vanquish me and all, but I'm not surprised to find you in the middle of this."

"Do you know her?" Anne asked Jocelyn.

Jocelyn ignored Anne's question and addressed the Matron. "Let them go, Evelyn. Then you and I can work this out."

The Matron laughed. "Work it out? I'd say it's working out quite well already, thank you. And very much in my favor."

"How do you know her name?" Anne pressed Jocelyn.

The Matron placed a hand over her own mouth in mock surprise. "You didn't tell them of our connection? Well, the lies do keep compounding themselves, don't they?"

"Any connection we have is irrelevant," said Jocelyn.

"So that's how you think of me, is it?" said the Matron. "Irrelevant. Your very own sister."

Anne stared in disbelief. "The Matron...is your sister?"

"I assure you, Anne, that changes nothing," said Jocelyn. "Everything I told you is true."

"So you're still claiming I was chosen for the academy completely at random?" Anne said.

Jocelyn paused. "Everything I told you is true except for that part."

Anne opened and closed her mouth several times, not even sure where to begin. "What have you gotten us into?" she said finally. "Infinite towers? Sand wolves? Robots? Elevators? What kind of professor sends new students out on a Level Thirteen quest?"

"I had no idea it was Level Thirteen, I promise you," Jocelyn said earnestly. "In any case, I never expected you to activate the quest when you did. I came to Saint Lupin's to take you to the academy, remember? I fully intended to train you, to prepare you for all of this before you ever had to face any of it."

"Prepare me for it? When did you plan on even *telling* me about it?"

Jocelyn lowered her eyes. "When the time was right."

The Matron cleared her throat. "Well, as much fun as it is to bring pain and heartache into the lives of others, I'm afraid time really is running out." She turned to Anne. "So, as I like to say, we can do this the easy way or the hard way."

"I'm not helping you," said Anne, crossing her arms in defiance.

The Matron smiled. "The hard way it is, then." She gestured at Rokk with her metal hand.

Rokk sprang into action. Before Anne could so much

as blink, he grabbed her and dragged her toward the gray box.

"Let go!" Anne shouted.

"Leave her alone!" shouted Jeffery.

Anne turned her head toward the sparrow. "Jeffery, stay back!" The last thing she needed was for him to get knocked into some bottomless chasm, lost forever.

As they approached the box, a circular hole opened in the side. Rokk shoved Anne's gauntlet-hand inside. The gauntlet clicked into place and the hole closed around her forearm. Rokk released his hold, but now Anne was stuck fast.

"Let her go!" yelled Penelope.

"Don't let yourself become a clichéd plot device, Rokk," said Hiro.

Penelope nodded. "That's telling him."

No matter how hard Anne tried, she couldn't pull free. Something pricked the end of her index finger, pricked it through the gauntlet, and a high-pitched whirring noise came from the box.

"Ouch," said Anne. "What's it doing?"

"Making sure you have the right blood," said the Matron. "And for your sake, I hope you do." She held up her metal hand and wiggled the fingers as if for emphasis.

Anne stared at the gray box with renewed horror. She struggled even harder to remove her arm, but it was no use. The box held her arm firmly, and the whirring noise continued.

"How does my blood have anything to do with this?" asked Anne.

"I won't bore you with a lesson in Old World history or the field of study known as genetics, but suffice it to say there aren't many people whose blood can do what I expect yours is about to do."

The whirring stopped. The box clicked again and the hole reopened. Anne quickly extracted her arm. Strangely, there was no visible pinhole in the gauntlet to show where an object might have poked through.

With another click, a small golden object appeared in the air above the box, spinning slowly. A key.

The Matron stared at it. "So, hiding here all along," she murmured. "Clever, clever."

The Matron reached for the key, but her hand passed through it, as though the key didn't exist. She made several more attempts, but each time her hand passed through where the key appeared to be.

"What trick is this?" roared the Matron. "Why can't I take it?"

"It is called the 'key you cannot hold,' dear," said Jocelyn dryly.

The Matron pointed to Anne. "You try."

Anne shook her head. "I told you, I'm not helping you."

The Matron gestured with her metal hand again. Rokk grabbed Anne's arm and forced her to touch the key. Her right hand passed through, too.

"Try the other one," said the Matron.

Rokk grabbed Anne's gauntlet-hand and forced it into the key. When the gauntlet touched it, the key disappeared.

"What happened?" said the Matron, scanning the ground. "Where did it go?"

Anne looked, too, but didn't see the key anywhere.

"What did you do with it?" asked the Matron.

"I didn't do anything," said Anne.

The Matron motioned to Rokk. He squeezed Anne's arm tight enough to make her cry out.

"I'm telling you, I don't know what happened to it," said Anne. She gritted her teeth and refused to scream again.

A young woman appeared in front of them. The Matron lowered her metal hand to her side and Rokk

released Anne. That the young woman had material-
ized out of thin air was not the most disturbing part of
her abrupt arrival. She also looked exactly like Anne—
exactly like her, except for her eyes, which were dark
brown.

The young woman bowed slightly and smiled at
Anne. "Greetings, Anvil of Saint Lupin's, Keeper of the
Sparrow. I have been expecting you."

THE TALE OF TWO KINGDOMS

Once upon a time there lived a powerful sorceress. The kingdom she lived in was a very gloomy place where the people were sad and the environment was in pretty bad shape and the property taxes were astronomical. So the sorceress decided to use her magick and create a new kingdom.

She named the new kingdom Khom, because she found it calming, and at first everything was wonderful. But eventually one part of the kingdom rose up and tried to destroy the other. This part she named Torr, because it had torn her beloved kingdom asunder. To prevent further destruction, the sorceress built between the two parts of the kingdom a great wall which she named PEEU, because in her opinion the whole situation really stank.

Then, with nothing much else to do, the sorceress embarked on a string of wild adventures, lived to a ripe old age, and eventually died in outer space.

But the divided kingdom she had created lived on, becoming known as the great Khom-PEEU-Torr.

The Construct

Anne stared at her twin—or near twin. Other than eye color, the most obvious difference between them was how very clean the young woman was, as though she hadn't spent a single second of her life in a mine. There wasn't a speck of coal dust or dirt on her smooth brown skin, and her hair was perfectly combed. Anne felt a bit like she was looking in a mirror that had given her reflection a good bath. The other difference was their clothes: In contrast to Anne's well-worn attire, the young woman wore a simple white tunic with a silver belt, light brown pants, and a long white coat so thin Anne couldn't imagine it provided any protection whatsoever against the elements.

"Who are you?" asked Anne.

"I am the one who never lived," said the young woman. "But you may call me the Construct."

Anne studied her from different angles, stepping from side to side. "How—how come you look like me?"

"I was created to look this way," said the Construct.

Anne frowned. "Created?" She looked to Rokk and back again. "Are you another robot?"

"Not as such," said the Construct, "although we are not completely unrelated. I am a projection of light known as a hologram."

Anne had no idea what that meant, but at the mention of light she did notice the Construct seemed to emit a faint glow.

"How do you know my name?" asked Anne.

"I know many things about you. For instance, I know you are here because of a quest."

"Yes. A Rightful Heir quest."

The Construct shook her head. "For you it is a Rightful

262

Heir quest. But in actual fact it is what is known as a Write Error Check."

"Um, a what?" said Anne.

"The details are unimportant. What matters is that you have acquired the key. In order to finish the quest, you must now use the key to access the computer."

"Computer?" said Anne.

"I've actually heard of that," Hiro interjected. "It's another type of Old World machine."

"That is correct," said the Construct. "A computer was used to create this world. It was built by Dr. Zarala Cole."

"Zarala?" said Anne. "But that's who the dragon symbol on the medallion refers to."

The Construct nodded. "Zarala lived in a world of science and technology, of flying machines and cities of glass and steel. But her world was dying, and she wished to create a world of magick in its place."

"And...this is that world?" asked Anne.

"Yes. But there needed to be a way to fix the computer if something ever went wrong. Hence the Write Error Check."

It was a lot to take in. Anne had never heard about

computers before, or that someone had created the world. She simply assumed the world had always existed. It never occurred to her that someone or something might actually have made it.

"So you're saying there's something wrong with the…the computer thing?" asked Anne.

"Yes," said the Construct. "There is a corruption in the system, and it is beginning to degrade."

"What happens if the Write Error Check doesn't happen?"

"The degradation will continue until the world is destroyed."

"What?" exclaimed Anne. "I thought this quest was about becoming the ruler of some kingdom, of the place I came from. No one told me if I failed the whole world would be in danger." She glanced over at Jocelyn, who avoided her gaze.

"You have the key," said the Construct. "There is still time to prevent disaster."

Anne felt her cheeks grow warm. "Oh, right. Um, about that. We sort of…lost the key."

"Hold up the gauntlet," said the Construct.

Anne did so.

"Now say 'Activate key.' "

"Activate key," said Anne, and her heart leapt for joy as the key appeared over the gauntlet, spinning as it had before. She now had everything she needed to fulfill the riddle's last line and "claim the throne"—whatever that meant.

The Matron suddenly stepped forward. "I'll take that," she said. She grabbed for the key, but her hand passed through it as before.

"Only the gauntlet may hold the key," said the Construct.

Anne reached up with the gauntlet and plucked the key out of the air.

"In that case..." The Matron gestured toward Rokk with her metal hand. Rokk reached for Anne once again, but this time she managed to jump beyond his grasp.

"I'm your friend, Rokk," Anne said to him. "You don't want to do this."

Rokk faltered midstep. He seemed to resist the Matron's power momentarily, but then she thrust out her metal hand and urged him forward again. He took another step toward Anne.

Anne held up her own gauntlet. It slowed Rokk, but it didn't stop him completely.

"Resist her, Rokk," said Anne.

"I...cannot," he said. "Must...obey...her command."

"Resist, Rokk!" Penelope shouted from the other side. "Show her what you're made of."

"You can be more than the sum of your programming!" Hiro yelled.

"Evelyn, stop this at once," said Jocelyn. "You're a better person than this. I know you are."

The Matron only sneered and continued pressing Rokk forward.

Anne retreated along the shelf until she reached the wall and could go no farther. Rokk soon loomed over her. Anne raised her gauntlet-hand and reached out, trembling. She knew she couldn't fight Rokk and win, so she gently rested the palm of the gauntlet on his huge metal hand and spoke softly, encouraging him.

"You can be your own person," she said. "You don't have to do this. You don't have to do what she says. At the top of the tower you chose to come with us, and I know somewhere in there you have the power to choose again. Don't let her take that from you."

Rokk froze with his arm outstretched, quivering.

"What are you waiting for?" shouted the Matron. "Remove that gauntlet."

"I...*can*...resist," said Rokk.

Anne smiled at him. "I believe in you, Rokk."

Rokk slowly lowered his arm and turned to the Matron. "You cannot control me. I will no longer obey your commands."

The Matron gestured at him, but it had no effect. Rokk took a shaky step in her direction. She moved her hand in a different pattern, but he continued toward her. He took another step, and this time the Matron stepped backward herself. With each step, Rokk became more stable, more in control of himself.

The Matron retreated toward the elevator. She passed directly through the Construct, as though the girl wasn't even there. The Construct shimmered but appeared otherwise unaffected. When Rokk reached the Construct, he stepped through her as well. As the Matron passed the gray box, her cane flattened into a sword and she swung it sideways. The blade ripped through the exterior of the box and cut a deep gash. Then she raised her metal hand and the elevator doors opened.

"This isn't over," said the Matron, quickly stepping inside. She swept her hand down and the doors slammed shut just as Rokk reached them.

The Matron's words echoed inside Anne's head as she took a deep, steadying breath. Too many conflicting emotions vied for her attention: Rokk's attack, finding out the real purpose of the quest, discovering she had a twin of sorts.

Rokk returned to Anne. "My apologies," he said. "I did not wish to attack you."

Anne took his huge metal hand in her own. "I know. I'm proud of you."

A shower of sparks erupted from the gash in the gray box and smoke poured out.

"I'm guessing that's not a good sign," said Anne.

"There is not much time," said the Construct. "As I'm sure you have discovered already, the gauntlet grants you limited power over Old World technology, and the key will enhance that power. It will also allow you to access the encrypted coordinates to Zarala's lab, which are contained within the medallion. You must go there and complete the quest. In the lab you will find—"

The gray box exploded. Rokk stepped in front of Anne and took the full force of the blast. When it was over, he stepped back, slightly singed but otherwise unharmed.

Anne coughed from the smoke. "Thanks." She scanned the debris and the surrounding area. "Wait, where did that girl go?"

Rokk pointed to the ruins of the box. "She disappeared when that device exploded."

Did that mean the Construct had been connected to the box somehow? Anne felt a sense of loss. Even if the Construct had only been made of light, she didn't deserve an end like that. There was so much more Anne had wanted to ask, questions she felt certain the Construct could have answered.

Anne looked across the chasm. "How do we get back?"

"I believe I can traverse the distance while carrying you," said Rokk.

"You mean jump?"

Rokk nodded.

"What about the elevator?"

"I calculate an eighty-seven percent likelihood that the Matron will sabotage it."

Anne suspected he was right. Plus, taking the elevator would mean leaving the others behind, and they couldn't do that. Anne climbed into Rokk's arms and held on tight. He backed up to the pillar and surged forward, running. When he reached the edge of the shelf, he launched himself into the air. As they flew across the chasm, Anne closed her eyes and pictured green fields and castles and pirate adventurers and definitely not falling for eternity into endless darkness. Seconds later, Rokk landed solidly on the far side.

Penelope came running and began checking Anne over. "Are you okay? I thought I was going to faint when the Matron appeared. And then all that stuff with Rokk, which"—Penelope looked at the metal man—"you and I are going to have some serious words about, Mister." Penelope turned back to Anne. "And what was up with your glowy identical twin? And what do you think the key does? And where do you think Zarala's lab is?"

Before Anne could even decide which question to answer first, Jocelyn approached and said, "My apologies, Anne. I should have been more forthcoming."

"Can you at least tell me the truth now?" Anne pointed to the gauntlet and medallion. "Why does the Matron want these so badly?"

"I can only conclude that she wishes to be the Keeper of this quest. In fact, I believe she already attempted it using another gauntlet. She herself hinted at the outcome of that attempt."

"You mean her hand?" said Anne.

"Yes," said Jocelyn. "That might also explain what happened to this tier, if this is where she failed. Many generations ago our family was entrusted with protecting this quest. When Evelyn and I came of age, I was given the gauntlet for safekeeping, and she the medallion."

"If the two of you are supposed to be protecting them, why is she trying to take control?"

Jocelyn shook her head. "I don't know. She used to be a sweet person, shy even. But then she changed drastically, and we had a terrible falling out. I haven't visited Saint Lupin's in years, since before you arrived there."

"So why did you come back now?"

"My mother left instructions for me to return on a certain day."

Anne felt her chest tighten. "Did she say why?"

"Yes," said Jocelyn, and she stared directly into Anne's eyes. "So that I would find you."

Anne reeled. Her heart was pounding. She felt like a fly trapped in a spider's web, struggling to break free, sensing the spider approaching but with no idea which direction it was coming from.

There was a dull rumble and the ground shook.

"What was that?" asked Anne.

"I do not believe this tier is entirely stable," said Rokk. "And the destruction of that device might have triggered a security threat response."

Anne was about to ask what exactly he meant by

"security threat response" when Hiro called to her. "Anne, you'd better look at this. Quickly."

Anne and the others hurried over to where he was standing. Hiro pointed to the rods. The spheres on top of the rods were pulsing red, making them semitransparent. Inside each sphere was a cloud of tiny black shapes. The shapes were moving violently, as though trying to get out.

"What are those?" asked Penelope.

"I don't know," said Hiro. "But I don't think we want to stick around to find out."

"But I thought dead tiers were, you know, dead," Penelope said. "Those things don't look dead to me."

Anne held up her gauntlet-hand. "We got what we came for. Everyone head for the surface."

No one argued.

They raced across the room and up the staircase. At the balcony, before she headed down the tunnel, Anne looked back. The spheres were pulsing faster and brighter.

Anne dashed after the others. The enormous stairs were an obstacle for everyone except Rokk. They had to leap up onto each step and clamber over the edge, which quickly became tiring. By helping one another, though, and with Rokk's assistance, they soon reached the top and ran through the main doors and back outside. Jeffery flew circles over them and yelled encouragement the whole time.

Rokk stopped and attempted to close the doors, but they wouldn't budge.

"They have been rendered inoperable," he said.

As they turned for the forest, a distinct buzzing sound echoed from inside the building. Anne thought she saw a shadowy cloud of movement at the bottom of the stairs. She and the others backed away. Something small flew up out of the entrance. It had a long body and two sets of wings.

"What's that?" said Anne.

"It looks like a dragonfly or something," said Penelope.

Several more appeared. The group continued moving toward the tree line, slowly at first, but more quickly as additional insects flew out of the entrance. Then one of the dragonflies buzzed forward and struck Anne, biting her on the arm.

"Ouch!" she yelled.

A few more dove at her and she swatted them away. More dragonflies flew at the others, and soon dozens of dragonflies were swooping and buzzing at everyone. The group swatted at the tiny attackers as fast as they could and stomped on any that got knocked to the ground. Rokk took out several of them at once by clapping his giant hands. As Anne ran and dodged, Jeffery landed on the gauntlet and dropped one of the dead dragonflies into her hand. Its crushed limbs had a metallic glint, and its body was sparking.

"What *are* these things?" she asked.

"They appear to be robotic," said Rokk.

An even louder buzzing drew their attention back to the entrance.

"Uh, I don't think this is all of them," said Jeffery.

More dragonflies poured out of the building. Many, many more. And these were much larger than the first few. They were easily the size of Anne's fist.

"I think perhaps an even hastier retreat is called for," said Jocelyn.

"I agree," said Anne. "Everybody run!"

They turned and fled into the forest, and Jeffery soared into the sky. The buzzing sound increased, and the forest, which had previously been so quiet, was suddenly filled with the sounds of life (except it was the sort of life that signaled approaching death). Anne pounded her way along the path beside the others, and soon her leg muscles, already sore from climbing the Infinite Tower, were burning from the effort. The dragonflies drew closer.

"I'm...not...going to...make it," Hiro wheezed between gasps for breath.

"Me...either," Penelope panted.

Rokk scooped Hiro and Penelope under one arm, and grabbed Anne with a second hand and Jocelyn with the third. He carried them along the path, his powerful strides putting distance between them and the oncoming swarm. When they reached the edge of the forest, Rokk charged out of the trees and up the hillside to the spot where they had first arrived.

Rokk set everyone back on their feet.

"What now?" said Penelope, still panting.

"Rokk, can you return us through the portal?" asked Anne.

"Yes," said Rokk. "But without the tower to amplify the signal, I will require several minutes to summon it."

"I don't think we have several minutes," said Hiro, looking down the slope.

As if to confirm that, Jeffery came zipping out of the forest and up the hill. "They're coming!"

Penelope drew her sword. "I guess we'll just have to hold them off, then."

Jocelyn drew her rapier and stood beside Penelope. Hiro took out his letter opener. Anne had nothing with which to defend herself. All she had was the gauntlet. What had the Construct said, though? The gauntlet had power over Old World technology, and the key made it stronger.

"Wait here, everyone," Anne said.

Anne ran back to the crest of the hill, a plan forming in her mind. Her palms were sweating and her stomach was doing flip-flops. The dragonflies flew out of the forest and swarmed up the slope. As the first ones reached the top, she raised her gauntlet-hand.

The dragonfly robots froze in midair, their wings still humming.

As more and more crested the hill, Anne's gauntlet stopped them as well. Sweat began dripping down her face, and her arm trembled, but she held on nevertheless. Soon the air was filled with thousands of dragonflies, all caught as if stuck to a giant invisible sheet of flypaper.

Finally, no more came. Anne had stopped them all.

"You did it!" Penelope shouted.

"Wonderful," Anne said between clenched teeth. "Too bad...they couldn't...have made it...more of a challenge."

As if in response to Anne's words, a sound like a million dragonflies rearing up and saying "Oh, really?" reverberated in the air. A giant shape rose from the center of the forest, towering over the trees. It had two sets of wings, but it also walked on two hind legs and carried a large club.

Hiro gasped. "What is that?"

"It's like a half-man, half-ogre, half-dragonfly," said Penelope.

"Technically, that's three halves," Hiro pointed out.

"Well, that tells you how scary big it is."

"It appears to be constructed out of the smaller creatures," said Rokk. "They have joined together in order to concentrate their attack."

The massive dragonfly-ogre creature lumbered toward them, knocking aside trees as if they were blades of grass.

Penelope looked at Anne. "Can you stop it?"

Anne shook her head. She could barely maintain her hold on the ones she had already frozen. But if she couldn't stop the dragonfly-ogre, perhaps she could use the ones she did have control over to her advantage. If these creatures were able to join together to form something larger...

Anne thought of a shape, and the previously frozen dragonflies moved in response. They linked with one another in the air until they formed a giant circle several layers thick.

"A shield?" said Penelope.

"Well done," said Jocelyn. "Simply brilliant. Everyone gather underneath and deal with any incoming strays so Anne can concentrate."

The others formed a ring around Anne, and Jeffery swooped above them in circles, while she held the shield in place.

The dragonfly-ogre burst free of the forest and started up the slope. It reached them in three long strides, surrounded by a small cloud of dragonflies that broke off and attacked. Penelope, Hiro, Jocelyn, Rokk, and Jeffery fought them off while Anne positioned the shield to block the giant. The dragonfly-ogre raised its club high into the air and gave a mighty swing. The club thundered against the shield, crushing hundreds of the dragonflies. But the shield held, and so did Anne. She even managed to take control of some of the stray dragonflies and use them to repair the shield. The dragonfly-ogre drew back its massive club to strike again.

"How...much...longer...Rokk?" she panted.

"Sixty seconds," said Rokk.

The club hit the shield with a deafening crash.

This time, Anne's knees buckled. The ground around her was littered with smashed dragonflies. She tried to repair the shield again, but it had become difficult to concentrate. As though sensing her need for help, Penelope came alongside her and held one of her arms, and Hiro held the other.

The club crashed into the shield a third time, scattering it completely. If it hadn't been for her companions, Anne would have been driven to the ground.

"Why...can't you...metal bugs...just DIE!" Anne screamed through gritted teeth.

As soon as the words left her mouth, the gauntlet pulsed blue.

Penelope stepped back. "What's happening?"

Anne stared at the gauntlet in surprise. "I don't know."

The light pulsed quicker and quicker until it was a steady glow. The dragonfly-ogre raised its club above them, preparing to smash the group into oblivion, but before it could strike its final blow, a ball of blue energy exploded from the gauntlet. It washed over Anne and her friends with no effect, but it was devastating to the dragonfly robots. The dragonfly-ogre was shredded to pieces, exploding into tens of thousands of individual creatures that then disintegrated. The blue energy wave rippled across the top of the hill and down the slope, destroying all the remaining dragonflies as it went.

Anne sank down onto her hands and knees. She took in air in great, heaving gulps, as though she'd been holding her breath underwater. A shower of burning dragonfly parts fell from the sky, raining across the hillside.

"Well, that was certainly unpleasant," said Jocelyn, sheathing her rapier.

Hiro crouched beside Anne. "That was amazing," he said.

Anne nodded. "You...weren't so bad...yourself."

"I'm telling you, we're going to have that castle before we know it," said Penelope.

"Yes," said Jocelyn. "I would say bonus points all around."

"Even for sparrows?" asked Jeffery as he alighted on the gauntlet.

Anne laughed. "Yes, especially sparrows."

She surveyed the hillside. Her heart was still racing,

and she found that she was excited and bone tired all at the same time. She had faced the Matron and escaped once again, and even more important, they had acquired the key. They might just finish this quest after all.

"The portal will arrive momentarily," Rokk announced. "Where do you wish to go?"

Anne recalled something the Construct had said. "Jeffery, do you have the coordinates for the final destination from the medallion?"

Jeffery tapped his head. "Right here. They're encrypted, though. Only a dragon can actually understand them."

It figured. Just when she thought they might catch a break.

"Return us to the Black Desert tier," she told Rokk. "We're going to need Nana."

As before, clouds gathered overhead and a funnel cloud extended down to a spot just above them. Anne felt herself stretch. Then the funnel snapped down and back and whisked them away. One nausea-inducing portal ride later, Anne found herself deposited back onto a wide stretch of familiar black sand.

And straight into a pair of hand shackles.

THE FOLLOWING IS A LIST OF THE TOP FIVE OFFENSES FOR WHICH PEOPLE ARE LIKELY TO GET ARRESTED:

1) High treason (to be distinguished from "high tree son"—that is, making your son live at the top of a high tree—which isn't illegal, but also isn't recommended)

2) Forgery (not to be confused with a letter "for Jerry," unless of course it, too, is a forgery)

3) Any utterance whatsoever of the phrase "petrified hippopotamus beak"

4) Unauthorized use of a squirrel in combat

5) Kidnapping your mythology professor (this happens alarmingly often)

17

Prisoners of the Council

Anne stared at the shackles, which had seemingly appeared out of nowhere. The one for her left hand was wide enough to fit over the gauntlet. A woman in armor—the person who had applied the shackles—stood in front of Anne. Penelope, Hiro, and Jocelyn were also shackled and facing their own armor-clad people. They were all standing on the platform at the bottom of the Infinite Tower, and at first Anne couldn't figure out why they were there. Then she realized her mistake. She had meant to return to the Black Desert village, to the spot where Nana was waiting, but Rokk had never been there and so had assumed she meant the tower, the exact spot from which they'd left.

Since their departure, things had changed. Now three sailing ships hung in the air with their anchors lying in the sand, and a cluster of guards were waiting by the remains of the destroyed campsite along with a small purple dragon who kept trying to kiss everyone.

"Whoa, some help over here," shouted a man in armor. He had been trying to place shackles on Rokk, but Rokk had shattered them to pieces. Two dozen additional guards rushed over with heavy chains and, after a considerable struggle, finally managed to pin Rokk's three arms to his sides.

"Don't you hurt him!" yelled Penelope.

"Those ships belong to the Wizards' Council. I recognize the emblem," Hiro whispered to Anne, nodding up at the seven-pointed black star on the mainsail of the nearest ship. "These must be council guards."

"What's going on?" Anne asked the guard in front of her.

"Isn't it obvious?" said the guard. "You're under arrest. Your reign of terror is over."

"Reign of terror?" said Anne.

The guard unrolled a piece of parchment and read aloud from it. "Theft of a magickal gauntlet, theft of a prophecy medallion, activation of the aforementioned prophecy medallion without a proper permit, escaping from an orphanage without a letter of permission, falsifying an academy admission form, lying to an official of the Wizards' Council, choosing the role of blacksmith but not doing any actual blacksmithing, destruction of a quest academy, entering a tower with no door by being a smarty-pants, unauthorized consultations with a mythological mechanical entity whose existence the council refuses to acknowledge despite solid evidence to the contrary, setting up a campsite in a designated fireball landing zone, wanton destruction of the aforementioned campsite, unauthorized use of a portal, and abuse of an undead marine animal." She leaned in close. "Just wait until the animal activists hear about that last one."

"Unhand me," said Jocelyn, struggling with her own guard. "I am not a member of this adventuring party. I am a professor of mythology at the Death Mountain Quest Academy. My credentials are in my coat pocket."

The brawny guard who had shackled Jocelyn reached into her pocket and pulled out a card. He read it over and nodded. "All right, then. If you're not part of the group, why were you with them? It's serious business to interfere with a quest, you know. Even for professors of mythology."

"Of course I know that," said Jocelyn. She met Anne's eyes briefly and then turned back to the guard. "If you must know, these students kidnapped me. They went rogue and destroyed our beautiful academy, and when I confronted them about it, they forced me to go with them. They nearly killed me, truth be told."

Anne's jaw dropped. She couldn't believe Jocelyn would sell them out just to save her own skin. Especially after Anne had just saved her life.

The guard gave Jocelyn a doubting look. "You're asking me to believe that three raw recruits overpowered and kidnapped a full professor?"

Jocelyn pointed over to where the guards had wrestled Rokk into a wooden crate. "Did you see the size of that monster they have with them? Did it not just take two dozen of your well-trained guards to subdue it? I am only one person, you know."

"What is that thing, anyway?" asked the guard.

Jocelyn leaned in close. "I suspect dark magick. If I were you, I'd have one of the council wizards check it over. They tried to pass it off as an ancient robot, if you can believe that nonsense."

The guard shook his head sympathetically. "Probably wanted the Old World treasure reward. It's pathetic what some people will try to pull. Believe me, I've heard it all." He consulted his parchment again. "Still, it mentions your name specifically under the wanton destruction charge."

Jocelyn sighed. "Very well. Check my other pocket."

The guard pulled out a second card and read it aloud. "Official Betrayer?"

"What?" exclaimed Anne.

"Traitor!" yelled Penelope.

"Will this go on our permanent records?" asked Hiro, but his guard shushed him.

"Yes," admitted Jocelyn. "You see, I've been working against this group from the beginning, in league with my sister, the Matron of Saint Lupin's. She's the Official Antagonist for their quest. The truth is, I allowed myself to be kidnapped in order to foil their plans. We would have preferred keeping it a secret until the end, of course, to achieve the highest betrayal score possible, but I don't suppose it matters now that their group is safely in your custody."

The guard nodded. "I understand. Fake kidnapping is a good move, too. Fools them every time. Also, the sister angle is a nice touch. All too often you get siblings working against each other on these types of quests." He slid the two cards back into Jocelyn's pocket. "Very well, then. This all seems to be in order. You're free to go. And sorry about the mix-up," he added, removing her shackles.

Jocelyn rubbed her wrists. "Not at all. You were just doing your job. I'm glad to see the council has finally decided to hire some guards with a bit of common sense."

"Always glad to help, Professor." The guard nodded in Anne's direction. "And we'll be sure to add those kidnapping charges you mentioned to the list."

"They deserve everything that's coming to them," said Jocelyn. "I would also appreciate access to your dragon so that I might return to my colleagues and inform them that the young rascals have been apprehended."

"Certainly. Right this way," said the guard, and he led Jocelyn toward the fireball landing zone.

"But she's lying," said Anne. "She's the one who destroyed the campsite. And we didn't kidnap anybody. She came with us on her own."

"That is just what someone who kidnapped her would say," said her guard.

Anne took a step in Jocelyn's direction, but the guard held her back. "Oh, no," she said. "You're going this way."

The guards marched Anne, Penelope, and Hiro over to a rope ladder. They were forced to climb up to one of the waiting ships with their hands still shackled. Once aboard, other guards escorted them into the belly of the ship, tossed their possessions into a cabinet, and locked the three of them in a small cabin. The room was cramped, with only two beds and barely enough space in the middle for one person to stand. Penelope sat on one bed and Hiro on the other. Anne remained standing. She was too agitated to sit.

Anne stared out between the bars of the porthole. Jocelyn's betrayal had her fuming. She didn't have to give Anne the gauntlet in the first place, so what was her motivation for doing so? And there had been many times when Jocelyn could have stopped Anne, Penelope, and Hiro before this, so why now? Why not back on the dead tier, when her sister was present? Maybe Jocelyn wanted the credit for saving the world all to herself. Maybe she was simply so desperate to save her academy that she would do anything, even stooping to the betrayal of three young adventurers on their first quest.

Anne shook her head to clear it. She couldn't allow

herself to get distracted by any of that now. She had the key. All she needed to do was "claim the throne without a crown" and finish the quest, and then she would have a place to live free from anyone's meddling schemes.

Anne held up the gauntlet. "Jeffery, how much time is left on the quest?"

"Fifteen hours," he chirped as he flashed into view.

Anne's eyes widened. "What? But that's an entire day gone. There's no way we were on that dead tier for that long."

"That was a weird place," Jeffery said. "I think time must work differently there or something. I checked my internal clock as soon as we arrived back, and it's definitely correct. We were there for roughly one hour, which means every hour spent on the dead tier must equal twenty-four regular hours." He disappeared again.

Anne paced back and forth, which was difficult to do in the confined space. "We have to get out of here."

"Too bad they confiscated Hiro's catalog," said Penelope. "He could have blasted the door away, no problem. Well, probably more like he'd blast away half the ship. Right, Hiro?"

"Hmmm?" said Hiro, who had been distracted by his own thoughts and not listening. "Oh, yes, probably."

"What's up with you?" asked Penelope.

Hiro stood in an unexpectedly decisive manner. "I'll create a distraction so the two of you can get away."

"We're not going to leave you behind, Hiro," said Anne.

Penelope laughed. "And besides, what distraction could you possibly cause?"

"Just this," he said, and before Anne or Penelope could react, Hiro took a deep breath and yelled out, "Guard! Guard! Open this door at once!" Penelope tackled him, and Anne tried to clamp a hand over his mouth, but this was hard to do with shackles on. Hiro kept yelling, "Guard! Guard!"

The door opened and a beefy guard crammed into the room, proving once and for all that it wasn't a four-person cabin. Anne and Penelope both fell back onto the bunks. Hiro, however, stayed on his feet.

The guard surveyed the three of them. "Here now, what's all the racket? Who called for the guard?"

"I did," said Hiro, and he stepped forward confidently—or rather, he stomped his foot confidently while standing in one place, since there was no longer space to take an actual step. "Do you have any idea who I am?"

The guard looked him over. "You're a juvenile delinquent, that's who you are. And from what I hear, you're in big trouble. The lot of you. So if you know what's good for you, you'll sit here and keep your traps shut."

"Before you get too blustery, my good man, you might want to have a good look at this." Hiro turned, held up his hair, and showed the guard the back of his neck.

The guard started to laugh, but then he did a double take and paled visibly. "B-but...th-that's..."

"Exactly," said Hiro, turning back. "I want to speak with the sergeant of the guard at once, as is my right."

"I don't...I mean, it's not generally permitted for prisoners to—"

Hiro puffed out his chest. "I am not some common prisoner simply to be tossed into a cell with the rest of the riffraff."

"Hey," said Anne. "Easy on the feelings."

Hiro ignored her and continued. "When my parents hear about this, and rest assured they most certainly will hear about it, I can make you look cooperative or I can paint a very different picture, if you take my meaning."

The guard apparently took his meaning. "Yes. I mean, yes, sir! Right away, sir!" He saluted, backed out of the room, and closed and locked the door once

292

more. The guard's footsteps quickly retreated down the corridor.

Penelope rounded on Hiro. "What in the world was that all about? 'Yes, sir'? 'Right away, sir'? What exactly did you show him?"

"There's no time to explain. When the sergeant of the guard arrives—"

Penelope pulled Hiro into a headlock and peered at the back of his neck. "No time to explain? Listen, buster, you're going to *make* time, is what you're going to do. Or I'm going to wedgie it out of you. Understand?"

Hiro put up a decent struggle, making a valiant attempt to hold Penelope off, but there was no way he would ever win a wrestling match against her.

"Let him go, Pen," said Anne.

"But you saw what happened," Penelope protested.

Anne raised an eyebrow.

"Oh, fine," said Penelope, and she released him.

Hiro stood and straightened his collar. "Thank you."

"Don't think I won't put you straight back in if you don't start talking, though," warned Penelope.

Hiro glanced at them both and lowered his eyes. "I...wasn't entirely honest with you. Back when we first met. And I don't just mean about the spell thing."

Penelope crossed her arms. "You don't say?"

"I didn't lie or anything. I just didn't reveal the whole truth."

He turned and held up his ponytail. On the back of his neck was a small tattoo in dark ink that at first glance looked like a simple circle, but upon further inspection Anne realized it was actually a depiction of a serpent swallowing its own tail.

Hiro let his ponytail drop. "My parents work for a secret branch of the Wizards' Council," he continued. "They have powerful connections, but also many powerful enemies, groups who would like nothing better than to cause harm to them and their family. So you see, my arrival at Death Mountain wasn't just about my magick abilities. Jocelyn agreed to hide me, to keep me safe. Because who would search for a star pupil at some backwater academy, right? The position in the council is hereditary, so in a few years, once I'm old enough and fully trained, I'm supposed to join them and my other siblings in the family business."

"But won't using your influence now expose you?" asked Anne.

Hiro shrugged. "Possibly. But if it helps you finish the quest, it's a risk I'm willing to take. Besides, if I can't get my magick under control, I'm not going to make much of a secret agent, so I figure I might as well make myself useful as best I can."

Penelope flopped back onto the bed. "Aw, I can't pound on him now. He's being all heroic and stuff."

"Believe me, if there was any other way, I would gladly take it," said Hiro. "But we're out of time. Consider it my thanks, for believing in me, and for being my—well, you know, for both of you being..." Hiro blushed.

Anne took Hiro's hand and placed hers on top of it. She motioned to Penelope, who placed her hand on top of both of theirs.

Anne smiled. "Yeah, we know. And we're all in this together, to the end, no matter what. Now tell us the rest of your plan."

They released their hands, and Hiro cleared his throat and continued. "When the sergeant of the guard comes, I'm going to demand an immediate tribunal so that I can hear the charges against me. I will also demand that you two be allowed to accompany me as witnesses. That might prove slightly more difficult, but I think I can get them to agree."

Penelope frowned. "But how—"

"Let him finish," said Anne.

Hiro pressed on. "I've been inside the building on the Wizards' Council tier where they hold the tribunals. The witness room has a large window overlooking a river. I'll be sure to put on a good show, ensuring all eyes are on me and not on a couple of underage witnesses. The river is a bit of a drop—"

"Er, how much is a bit?" asked Anne.

"—but it will take them time to get down there, and you might be able to get away. I can't help you with finding a dragon, but there are plenty around, and having that gauntlet will probably convince at least one of them to help you."

Penelope planted her hands on her hips. "Putting aside for the moment all the bizarre stuff you just said— which is all of it, in case you are wondering—you want us to go through all that in the hopes that we *might* be able to get away?"

"If you have a better plan..." Hiro started to say.

"If I had my sword, I'd get us out of here," said Penelope, and she grabbed a pillow in one hand and jumped up on the bunk. "I'd hold them at bay, and we could make a run for it." She started swinging the pillow over her head, whipping it faster and faster.

The door burst open and a stout guard with sergeant's stripes on her helmet strode in.

"What's this nonsense I hear about a tattoo?" she said—or at least that's what Anne supposed she had been about to say, for somewhere between "this" and "nonsense," Penelope, surprised by the sergeant's entrance, lost her grip on the pillow. The pillow struck the sergeant in the face, and she stumbled back into the corridor, shouting as though she'd been attacked by a wild animal. The three adventurers heard a thump and a crash followed by a distinct THUNK, and they peered out the door to find an unconscious sergeant of the guard slumped on the floor. Apparently, she had stumbled into the opposite wall and been knocked out by a falling unlit torch, which had smacked her in the helmet and rolled away.

"Wow," said Anne. "I never thought of using a pillow as a weapon."

Hiro stared at the sergeant and said, "But...but..."

They retrieved their belongings from the hallway cabinet, pulled on their cloaks, and Penelope yanked the sword out of the sergeant's sheath. "Let's go," she said, and ran down the corridor.

"You're ruining my perfectly good escape plan, you know!" Hiro shouted after her.

As Hiro mumbled about people not being able to follow simple instructions, Anne grabbed his hand and pulled him down the corridor after Penelope. Several sleepy guards stuck their heads out of cabin doors to see what all the commotion was about, but before they could react, the three escapees had already run past. They kept running up two flight of stairs and down the long corridor that led to the deck with the rope ladder. The door opened at the end of the corridor, letting in a stream of sunlight. For a brief second, Anne thought they might actually have a chance.

A guard entered the corridor, but Penelope charged into him and bowled him over. A second guard standing just outside scrambled to draw his sword, but Anne ran through the doorway and jammed her heel into his foot, sending him hopping and cursing across the deck.

Anne pointed to the railing where the rope ladder attached.

"Hiro, go!" she shouted.

Hiro ran over to the ladder and climbed down, out of sight. Anne was about to follow, but she realized they were all of a sudden missing Penelope. She looked back. Penelope was standing in the middle of the deck, facing off against a third guard. Anne didn't doubt Penelope's bravery one bit. Her skill with a real sword, on the other hand, was still very much a question mark.

The guard held back.

"What's the matter?" asked Penelope. "Afraid I'll beat you?"

"How old are you?" asked the guard.

"Thirteen," said Penelope.

The guard backed up. "Hey, I'm not fighting an underage kid. I'll get a citation."

"Come on, coward."

Penelope twirled the sword in one hand and passed it over to the other. Then she attempted a behind-the-back maneuver—

—and suddenly Anne flew through the air and landed heavily on the deck. She tried to rise but collapsed back, unable to catch her breath. When she looked down, she was very surprised to see a sword sticking out of her chest.

*THE ADVENTURER'S GUIDE
TO MORTAL COMBAT* SAYS THE
FOLLOWING ABOUT GETTING STABBED BY
A MEMBER OF YOUR OWN PARTY:

Eh, it happens.

Robot vs. Dragon

For what it was worth, Penelope had been extremely apologetic.

Lucky for Anne, she had tucked *The Adventurer's Guide* back into the inner pocket of her cloak. The sword had pierced the book first, preventing the blade from penetrating farther than it would have otherwise, which was already plenty far in Anne's opinion. The guards had pulled Penelope away from Anne and immediately summoned their purple dragon, who in turn had sent Anne via emergency fireball to the council's main headquarters (which, due to government cutbacks, still took the standard eight hours; on the upside, the healing properties of fireballs meant that much of the damage had already been repaired by the time she arrived, and Anne was left with only a couple of bruised ribs). She'd been taken to the nearest barracks and admitted as a patient to the healing wing, which is where she was now.

The third-story treatment room contained shelves filled with various medicinal herbs and smelly ointments. After the council healers finished wrapping her midsection in bandages, they left her alone, though two guards were posted outside the door. Anne spent most of the next several hours sitting on the bed and staring out the window watching airships arrive and depart at the nearby docks. Every few minutes she asked Jeffery to update her on the time, and she wondered what had happened to Penelope and Hiro after their failed escape attempt. At dinnertime an orderly brought Anne something to eat, but she otherwise didn't see or speak to anyone, except for Jeffery, who mostly paced back and forth along the windowsill.

"Time?" asked Anne, as she regarded the sky now dark and filled with stars. Midnight had to be getting close.

Jeffery patiently replied, "A little over an hour remaining."

Anne shifted on the bunk and Jeffery hopped down onto her leg. "Feeling any better?" he asked.

Anne shook her head. "I'm facing a list of charges as long as my arm and likely life in prison. Not to mention who knows what happens when I officially fail this quest. Honestly, I might be better off dead."

"Hey now, don't talk like that," he said, patting her knee with his wing. "You have a lot to be proud of. Plus, if my Keeper dies, I don't think I receive my end-of-year bonus."

Anne watched a distant tier pass in front of the moon.

"I don't suppose they grade quests on a curve, do they?" she asked.

"Sorry. It's pretty much pass or fail."

Anne saw all her hopes and dreams scatter like stars in the night, never to return. She would never find out where she had really come from. She would never discover the true nature of the gauntlet or of the medallion. As if that didn't make her heart feel heavy enough, even worse was the knowledge that she had let Penelope and Hiro down and would probably never see either of them again.

Someone inserted a key into the lock, and Jeffery

disappeared in a flash of light. A moment later the door opened and Captain Copperhelm entered. The same Copperhelm whose valuable trading card collection had been destroyed when Anne and her party blew up the academy and then crushed it with a mountain. He didn't exactly look happy.

Anne stood up, wincing slightly at her still-tender ribs. "Captain Copperhelm, what are you doing here?"

He crossed his arms. "I hear you got stabbed while trying to escape custody."

Anne felt her checks flush. "Er."

"It was the redhead, wasn't it," he said. It wasn't a question.

Anne nodded.

Copperhelm grunted and shook his head. "That one's got talent, no question. One of the best raw recruits I've seen in a long time. And once she gets some solid training under her belt, she'll be a force to be reckoned with. But until then, she's a menace to society." He pointed to Anne's side. "How are the ribs?"

"Not too bad now. My guidebook got the worst of it." She picked the book up from a nearby nightstand. There was a deep gash through the center of the cover, but the title was still legible. It read: *The Adventurist's Guilt for Pink Assassin Hedgehog Volcano Pants Blah blaH blargh.* Inside, the pages kept flickering from one text to another at random.

"I keep telling them they should give adventuring books iron covers." He studied her, as though he were trying to make up his mind about something. "Well, you're definitely not one to back down from a challenge, I'll give you that much," he said finally.

Anne wasn't sure how to respond. Was he praising her or practicing his eulogy?

"Come with me," he said. "And don't say a word."

"But—"

"I mean it. Not a single word."

"If—"

"That's a word."

"Can I—"

"That's two words."

"But I just wanted to say—"

Captain Copperhelm rounded on her and held up a finger for silence. "You've gotten yourself in quite enough trouble for one quest, wouldn't you agree? Not another word until I tell you."

His eyes brooked no nonsense. Anne closed her mouth and kept it closed. Copperhelm led her past the two guards stationed outside her door and down the corridor to a little waiting area at the end. He signed a form and motioned for her to follow. They continued along another corridor, down three flights of stairs, and finally into the front lobby of the building. Copperhelm walked up to the front desk.

"I'm signing this one out," he said, jabbing a thumb in Anne's direction.

The guard at the desk glanced up. "I thought she was being held pending charges at tomorrow's tribunal."

"She's carrying a high-level prophecy medallion that's about to fail." Copperhelm leaned in close to the counter, as though he were sharing something he shouldn't. "They're going to isolate her on an airship well away from any tiers, just as a safety precaution." He slid a small piece of paper across the desk.

The guard read the paper and nodded. He stamped it and slid it back. Copperhelm took the paper with a word of thanks and motioned for Anne to follow.

"Shouldn't there be more guards escorting us?" asked Anne.

Copperhelm adjusted one of his sword hilts. "Pretty sure I can handle one untrained thirteen-year-old."

Anne felt uneasy. Copperhelm led her out the front doors, down the wide stone steps, and across a small plaza, where, even this late at night, squadrons of council soldiers marched in formation, each led by a wizard in dark robes. The pair followed a wide avenue to an intersection and turned left.

"Isn't the dock the other way?" asked Anne.

"I said no talking," Copperhelm snapped.

They walked on, encountering fewer and fewer soldiers until eventually there were none at all. They cut left into what Anne thought was a narrow street between buildings but which turned out to be a dark alleyway. She could barely make out the shape of the short man ahead of her. Then all of a sudden she was alone.

Anne looked around but saw no sign of her weapons instructor. Somewhere in the distance, a horn sounded, and she heard shouts. Her heart raced. Where exactly had Copperhelm brought her? Were soldiers coming to hunt her down? Didn't Copperhelm say he was getting her off the tier before the medallion failed?

"C-Captain Copperhelm?" she called out.

Copperhelm stuck his head out of a side alley behind her. "What are you waiting for? It's this way."

Anne stared down the side alley. If possible, this one was even darker. How could a ship dock here? Maybe her crimes were even more severe than she thought. Was her "punishment" to never be found again? She contemplated making a run for it, but she had no idea where she was, let alone where she might find safety.

She decided if this was the end, she would face it head on. Let them play their games. She wouldn't run anymore. Anne took a deep breath and rounded the corner, where she immediately tripped over something. When she put out her hands, she felt something large and scaly and recoiled in shock.

"H-hello?" she called out.

A lantern flared to life.

She blinked.

Penelope, Hiro, Jocelyn, and Sassafras (with the platypus sticking out of his sleeve) were waiting in a small courtyard, along with Nana, whose tail Anne had tripped over. Having a twenty-foot-long dragon in the alley made for a tight fit. Penelope threw herself into Anne with a fierce hug.

"What's going on?" Anne asked once they pulled apart.

"It's called a jailbreak," said Copperhelm. "I was under the impression you were familiar with them."

"Professors Daisywheel and Sassafras sprang Hiro and me from the council prison while Captain Copperhelm went and got you," said Penelope.

Anne looked at Jocelyn. "Then that whole business about you being the Official Betrayer..."

Jocelyn smiled. "I always find it handy to keep a few extra cards in my pocket, just in case. And I felt we could do with some assistance. If that nitwit from the council had had the brains to check the file, he would have realized your quest doesn't even have a registered betrayer. But that's what you get when half the guards you hire are complete morons."

"Actually, I think they've dropped back to only thirty percent morons," said Sassafras. "Then it's forty percent imbeciles, twenty-five percent utter fools, and five percent blockheads."

"They're all equally flammable," said Nana.

Anne laughed and cried with relief at the same time. "I really thought I was in big trouble."

"Oh, you're definitely in big trouble, dear," said Jocelyn. "But we can deal with the council later. First things first: You need to finish your quest."

Anne's heart skipped a beat. "You mean there's still time?"

"Provided you can get past an entire battalion of battle wizards, get yourself to some hitherto unknown location in the Hierarchy, find this 'computer' thingy, and upload the key or whatever it is in, oh, about fifty minutes, then, yes, you should have no problem," said Jocelyn.

"Not to mention you have a contractually obligated final Battle to the Death," added Copperhelm. "Skip that and the paperwork is a nightmare."

"Battle to the death!?" said Anne.

"It's just a figure of speech, dear," said Jocelyn. "Except for the literal parts."

"Are you coming?" Anne asked Jocelyn.

Copperhelm shook his head. "Teachers can't. We'll keep the guards distracted long enough for you and your group to get away, but technically it's against the rules for nonparty members to interfere with an active quest."

"Um, aren't you interfering now by helping me escape?"

Copperhelm pulled out a small slip of paper—the same paper he had given the guard at the front desk. It read:

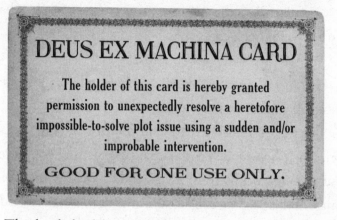

DEUS EX MACHINA CARD

The holder of this card is hereby granted permission to unexpectedly resolve a heretofore impossible-to-solve plot issue using a sudden and/or improbable intervention.

GOOD FOR ONE USE ONLY.

The back had been stamped with the word USED in bold red letters.

Copperhelm grunted. "Never said we couldn't bend the rules a little. Now, do you want to finish this thing or not? Because we're spending an awful lot of time yakking and very little time blowing things up."

Copperhelm and Sassafras exited the way they had entered, while Jocelyn guided Anne, Penelope, and Hiro in the other direction. Nana followed, squeezing herself along the narrow passageway. They walked quietly, and when they reached the mouth of the alley, Jocelyn doused the lantern. The alley opened onto a plaza. There was a seven-story building on the far side and a circular walled-in yard in the center. The fireball landing zone, Anne guessed.

Guards filled the plaza; many were scurrying back and forth, barking orders.

"Where are we?" asked Anne.

Hiro swallowed. "Wizards' Council headquarters. Something tells me they know we've escaped."

"It's riskier and slower to send you from a random location. Nana has a much better chance of getting you to your destination quickly from that yard," Jocelyn explained. "Since in this case we can't assume the destination has a designated landing zone, and since you won't have much time once you do arrive, we have to give you every advantage."

"Aren't you glad you saved those premium top-speed fireballs?" said Nana.

"That still doesn't explain why we came to the council's front door," said Anne.

"It was the nearest yard," Jocelyn explained. "I'm afraid we're out of options. We'll wait here until the others have given their signal."

"What's the signal?" asked Anne.

"The captain didn't say exactly, but I expect we'll know it when we see it."

Not five minutes later, a commotion arose down the

street. Anne risked a peek around the corner. Sailing straight down the main avenue, barely twenty feet off the ground, was one of the council ships. Copperhelm was at the wheel, bellowing at the top of his lungs. Sassafras leaned over the railing and shouted something at a statue in the plaza. The statue exploded in an impressive display of fireworks and sent the guards running in all directions. The falling pieces of marble unexpectedly transformed into yappy poodles that chased after them.

"I'm pretty sure blowing up council property is against regulations," muttered Hiro.

"Come and get us, you scurvy dogs," yelled Copperhelm.

The plan worked. The square emptied as soldiers and wizards alike tried to either board the ship with grappling hooks, dodge Sassafras's spells, or escape the wrath of the growing army of poodles.

Anne stepped forward, but Jocelyn pulled her back. She pointed to the walled-in yard, and Anne noticed something she had missed the first time: A large green dragon with three eyes and three great horns on its head lay sleeping in the middle of the yard, apparently unbothered by the chaos all around it.

"Who's going to take care of the council dragon?" asked Penelope.

"Can't Nana?" said Anne.

Nana swung her long neck around. "Not if Nana is expected to also perform the intricate calculations needed to get you to your destination quickly and also ensure you don't crash into the side of a tier or land in a lake full of acid or something. Encrypted coordinates are tricky business."

"Actually, someone else has already agreed to take care of it," said Jocelyn, and she pointed behind them.

Rokk stepped out of the shadows.

"Rokk!" said Anne, running over and giving him a big hug.

Jocelyn pointed to the sleeping dragon. "Rokk, we need you to clear that landing zone."

Rokk nodded. "I will attempt to have the subject leave voluntarily using alternative dispute resolution techniques."

"That's fine," said Jocelyn. "But if he doesn't volunteer quickly, move him. Once we leave the safety of cover, we're not going to have a lot of time."

"Acknowledged," said Rokk, and he marched out of the alley.

"Kick his big scaly green butt," yelled Penelope.

Rokk strode across the plaza and into the yard. The dragon lifted its horned head, and Rokk raised a hand in a gesture of greeting.

"Hello," he said. "My name is Rokk. I am a PAL series robot. My companions and I are attempting to conduct an illegal escape. Would you be so kind as to remove yourself from the premises?"

Anne winced.

"That's...not going to be good," said Penelope.

The dragon opened its mouth and spewed red flame, which engulfed Rokk. Penelope groaned, and Anne covered her face with her hands, although she peeked between her fingers, because as hard as it was to watch, she couldn't bear not to. The fire barrage went on and on; when it finally stopped, Anne held her breath, waiting for the smoke to clear. Incredibly, Rokk was still standing. He glowed slightly but looked otherwise unharmed. Penelope jumped up and down and clapped Anne on the back.

"I am interpreting your response as a refusal to comply," said Rokk. "I will now have to kick your big scaly green butt."

The dragon reared up, but Rokk stepped in to meet him. He wrapped his three arms around the dragon's long neck and twisted, hurling the beast into the wall of the yard with a thunderous *BOOM!* Rokk immediately charged in, but the dragon lashed out with its tail and knocked the robot off his feet. *THUNK!* Penelope gasped and gripped Anne's arm.

Rokk rolled three times but righted himself in time to deflect an incoming blow from the dragon. The two opponents backed off and circled each other for a moment. They were evenly matched. The dragon had a definite size advantage, but Rokk was able to counter with speed and technique.

The dragon charged.

Rokk caught its front leg and with a great heave of strength sent the dragon up and over the wall and into a small kiosk with a mighty *CRASH!* This brought a cheer from everyone gathered in the alley.

Rokk leapt the wall and pummeled the dragon with his three fists.

The dragon knocked Rokk to the ground with its horns and stomped on him with its massive feet. *CRUNCH! CRUNCH! CRUNCH!* For a brief moment all seemed lost. Then Rokk kicked up and sent the dragon tumbling through the air and back down to the hard stones of the plaza.

WHAM!

As the two titans struggled, Jocelyn placed a hand on Anne's shoulder. "Anne?"

"Yes?" said Anne, unable to tear her eyes from the fight.

"If…if you do encounter my sister again, keep in mind that nothing is written in stone, not even the outcome of a quest. You always have choices, even in an official confrontation. And whatever Evelyn has become…well, please remember that she did dedicate at least part of her life to protecting this quest. I would just ask that you take that into account, should you find yourself with a decision to make."

Anne faced Jocelyn. "I just want to finish the quest. I honestly don't want anyone to get hurt, not even the Matron."

Jocelyn smiled sadly. "Thank you, dear."

A loud *CRACK!* brought their attention back to the confrontation in the landing zone. Rokk had blocked yet another strike from the dragon's tail, and now he punched the dragon in the side with his two right fists and sent it reeling.

"Run, run as fast as you can! You can't catch me. I'm a PAL series robot with hydraulic limbs," Rokk chanted. Then he turned and sped off in the other direction.

The dragon gave chase.

"That's our cue," said Jocelyn, and she led the others out of the alley. Everyone ran straight to the center of the yard.

"Now what?" said Anne.

"Now your sparrow transfers the encrypted coordinates to me, and I do the actual work of sending you to your destination," said Nana.

"Please," said Jeffery, popping into view. "Everyone knows all the real work is done before you ever receive the destination, encrypted or not. If it were left to the dragons, no one would ever get anywhere."

Nana snorted. "This coming from a tiny bird who lives in someone else's smelly old glove."

"Hey, that's tiny *magickal* bird, thank you very much," chirped Jeffery. "And I'll have serious words with anyone who disrespects my gauntlet."

"If you like words so much, I have two for you," said Nana. "The first word is *barbecued* and the second word is *wings*."

"Big talk for an oversized flying lizard with bad breath," said Jeffery.

"Jeffery, be quiet and let Nana concentrate," said Anne.

"Fine," said Jeffery. "But this isn't over, you big lump of charcoal."

Nana snorted but said nothing. Jeffery flew up and landed on top of Nana's head. Nana closed her eyes. Anne looked to both Penelope and Hiro, and they nodded their readiness. The three of them formed a line, with Anne at the front, since she would be the first to travel.

"How long will this take?" Anne whispered to Jocelyn, not wishing to disturb Nana's concentration.

"It's difficult to say," Jocelyn whispered back. "There are many variables to take into account, and the calculations must be absolutely precise. The slightest mistake could result in—"

Nana's eyes snapped open. "Got it."

"Really?" said Anne. "That's great. How soon can you—"

But Anne's question was cut off by the roar of a green fireball.

She was really starting to hate that.

THE ADVENTURER'S GUIDE TO FINAL BATTLES OFFERS THE FOLLOWING PIECE OF WISDOM:

Make sure you win. Or at the very least, make sure you don't lose.

The Throne Without a Crown

As the flames dissipated, Anne was instantly aware of two things: One, she was only a step away from almost certain death, and two, she was alone.

Between the moon and the stars above and the soft illumination of the Big Glowing Field of Magick filtering up from below, she had enough light to see that her feet were precariously perched on a narrow ledge. Penelope and Hiro were nowhere to be seen.

Anne inched backward till she felt the solid wall behind her. She looked around. The rock face rose some twenty feet high. To the left, the ledge continued around a bend and out of sight, and to the right there was a wide gap. It all felt vaguely familiar, and then it struck her. She was back at Saint Lupin's. This was the ledge where she had fallen four and a half days earlier, and from which Jocelyn had rescued her, except now she was on the other side of the gap.

Anne held up her gauntlet-hand. "Jeffery, how much time is left?"

"Twenty-nine minutes," Jeffery chirped as he appeared. "Hey, wow, nice view."

"Why are we back at Saint Lupin's?"

He flapped his wings at her. "Hey, don't look at me. I gave Nana the encrypted coordinates exactly as I received them." He hopped onto the cuff of the gauntlet and kicked the silver medallion. "Stupid prophecy medallion."

"And where are Pen and Hiro?"

Jeffery peered over the ledge. "Well, hopefully not down there."

"Jeffery!"

"What? I mean it. I hope not. That would be horrible. I mean, not just for us, but for them, too. Anyway, they're probably wherever you were supposed to end up. The final destination place."

"But I'm supposed to be there, too!" cried Anne.

"So why did you come here, then?"

Anne slumped against the rock face. "We're doomed."

"Only if you lose. Or violate Section 27 of the quest contract. Or deliberately set a fire in an enclosed space. Your insurance doesn't cover that, and the deductible is outrageous."

It couldn't end like this. Not stranded here on the side of the Saint Lupin's tier, waiting to be rescued (again). Not with Penelope and Hiro who-knows-where, waiting in vain for Anne to arrive with the key so they could finish the quest. Not while the Matron was still out there trying to—

The Matron.

Anne straightened. "We need to get to the Manor."

"And do what?" said Jeffery. "I can't summon Nana, and neither of us knows how to call a portal."

"If my hunch is right, we don't need either. The Matron keeps showing up everywhere we go, right? But we've seen no evidence of her using dragons or portals. If we can discover how she's been traveling all over the Hierarchy, we might be able to use that method ourselves."

Anne scanned the smooth rock face. There was no way she could climb it by herself.

She glanced along the ledge. "Where does this lead to?"

"I don't know. Somewhere in that direction."

Anne rolled her eyes. She started along the ledge, hoping to find a place where she could climb. The ledge narrowed in places, but thankfully no other sections were missing. After several minutes of hurried shuffling, she came to a tunnel.

Anne peered down the dark passageway. "Where do you think this goes?"

"Beats me," said Jeffery.

Perhaps the tunnel led to the surface, or perhaps it led nowhere. For all Anne knew, the ledge circled the side of the tier with no way up. As she stood in the opening trying to decide what to do, a light breeze emerged from it and tickled her arm.

That was it.

Air flowing through the tunnel meant there must be another opening, and with any luck it would lead her topside.

She entered.

Jeffery's bright, multicolored glow helped Anne navigate the dark passage. The floors and walls were smooth and straight, with no doorways or offshoots as far as Anne could see. The only notable feature was that it sloped steadily—not upward toward the surface, as she had hoped, but downward. She increased her pace, her footsteps echoing down the long corridor and, even with Jeffery's glow, keeping her right hand on the wall as a guide.

After several minutes of near running, she began to despair that she had made a terrible mistake, and that possibly her hunch about the Matron having another means of travel was wrong, too, when her foot kicked a small stone. Then another. And another. Rubble was strewn across the floor, and soon her hand hit empty space. A rupture in the wall. Someone (or something) had broken through, and another tunnel led away to the side.

"What's this?" asked Anne.

"Looks like a mine shaft," said Jeffery.

She peered inside. "Do you think it leads to the surface?"

"I could go check."

The mines were a labyrinth, and Anne had no time for wrong turns. She stepped into the opening, but she couldn't sense any flow of air. That probably meant the way was blocked. But the only blocked mine shaft she knew about was...

Shaft Eleven! Where she'd hidden from what she thought was a roaming dragon. If this was indeed that shaft, it suggested the Matron had been down here before. In fact, maybe she was still coming down here. Maybe the mine shaft wasn't as "caved in" as everyone had been led to believe. After all, the only evidence was a boarded-up entrance and a threat of punishment for anyone who went near it. If the Matron really did have a secret means of traveling all over the Hierarchy, what better place to hide it than down here, where no one else would ever stumble across it? With renewed purpose, Anne returned to the main tunnel, raced forward...

And hit a dead end two minutes later.

A black wall.

The air was still flowing, but it seemed to be flowing directly into the wall itself. Anne suppressed a cry of frustration. Her mistake had quite likely cost her the quest. She pounded a fist on the wall—

—and leapt away as a blue grid appeared.

Just like at the Infinite Tower.

She reached out tentatively and ran her hand along

the surface. It felt like the same material as the Infinite Tower. Acting on instinct, she typed the letters N-O-D-O-O-R into the grid. The words ACCESS GRANTED flashed, and the wall became fluid.

Anne had no idea where this would take her, but she didn't hesitate.

She plunged into the entrance.

Anne entered a large, circular room. The floor, walls, and ceiling were mostly tiled in white except for three evenly spaced sections of smooth black stone, including the one through which she had just entered, and a large circle of glass in the center of the floor. The space felt like a tomb that had lain sealed and undisturbed for hundreds, perhaps even thousands, of years.

Seven smooth white pillars formed a semicircle around the glass section. They were about as wide as an iron knight and rose from the floor at an angle. Light filtered up through the glass, illuminating the room. Anne moved to the edge of the glass and cautiously looked down. Currents of magick roiled and crashed together in the BGFM, sending up brightly colored flares. She was standing at the bottom of the Saint Lupin's tier.

"Jeffery, what is this place?" Anne asked.

No response. In fact, only at that moment did she realize he was no longer with her.

"Activate GPS," she said, but nothing happened.

Anne concluded he must be blocked from coming out of the gauntlet again, like when they were at the Infinite Tower. Or more specifically, when they were *inside* the tower, now that she thought about it. Perhaps it had to do with being inside certain spaces. If so, and if this room was one of those spaces, then she was truly on her own.

Pressing onward, Anne walked over and examined the pillars more closely. Were these elevators? Did they connect to the Manor? As she neared the first pillar, she noticed something she hadn't seen from the entrance. Words were engraved at the base:

PROJECT
C.R.O.W.N.

Below the words was a small rectangular hole.

A keyhole.

Heart racing, Anne held up the gauntlet and braced herself. "Activate key."

The key appeared in the air, and she grabbed it with the gauntlet. Holding the key firmly, she bent down and inserted it into the keyhole. It turned with a soft click. Seams suddenly appeared along the surface of the white pillar, forming the outline of a hatch, which opened and swung upward. The interior of the pillar was hollow, an inner chamber lined with cushions that formed a couch or bed of sorts.

"Congratulations."

Anne spun around. The Matron stood in front of the shimmering black door. The one that Anne had opened and used. She had let the Matron inside.

"Don't feel too bad," said the Matron, seeming to read Anne's thoughts. "If you hadn't let me in, I'd eventually have found my own way."

"But—but what are you doing here?" Anne asked. "I thought you would be at the final destination."

"This *is* the final destination."

It made no sense. Anne had come down here to find the Matron's device for traveling. How could this room be the final destination, unless—

"I'm the heir to Saint Lupin's," Anne said suddenly, and in saying it, she knew it to be true. This must be Zarala's lab that the Construct had mentioned. More than that: If

Saint Lupin's really was the final destination of the quest, this was Anne's true home. She studied the room anew, trying to soak in every detail while a million questions flooded her head. Had she been down here before? Had she touched these pillars? Had she watched the BGFM through the glass floor? And what had happened to her family? How had she ended up at the orphanage?

"You're not the heir yet," said the Matron. "Only the one who completes the quest can become the true heir."

Anne was hit with a sudden realization. "You never really cared about the gauntlet or the medallion, did you? All you ever wanted was access to this place."

"Smart girl. Not smart enough, of course, but this is only your first quest. What a pity that it's going to be your last as well. Personally, I think you would have done well as a Keeper. But please, don't let me stop you," she said, gesturing to the pillars. "I believe you were in the process of opening these chambers."

"I'm not helping you."

The Matron's cane flattened once again into a thin blade, and she pointed it at Anne. "Oh, but I insist. And if you test me, this time I really will cut off that gauntlet of yours and simply use the key myself."

Anne didn't know if that would work, but she decided not to find out. For the moment, she chose to cooperate, which would at least buy her time to try to figure out a way to stop the Matron or to escape. Anne moved to the next pillar and inserted the key. Another hatch opened, revealing a similar chamber lined with cushions. She worked her way along the row of pillars until all seven had been unlocked. Then the Matron motioned Anne to step away with a wave of her blade.

The Matron chuckled. "Ah, simplicity itself." She turned to Anne. "Surely you've figured it out, no? The meaning of the last line of the riddle."

Anne hadn't, in fact. She had guessed that perhaps, since *she* didn't have a crown, maybe that's what would allow her to claim the throne. She brought the line to mind again.

Claim the throne without a crown.

She stared at each chamber in turn. They were identical, down to the cushion-lined interiors. Down to the engraved words at their base. Except she now realized she had missed one important detail. She hadn't paid close attention when she was unlocking them. A small crown symbol had appeared over the words of each chamber—each one, that is, except for the center pillar. That had to be it.

The correct answer must have shown on Anne's face, because the Matron smiled. "Figured it out, have we?"

Anne leapt for the center chamber as the Matron also sprang forward. Before Anne could even place her hand on the side, the Matron swung her sword. Anne blocked the blade with her gauntlet, but the force of the blow sent her stumbling back. When Anne recovered, the Matron stood between her and the chamber.

"Let me finish," said Anne. "You can have Saint Lupin's, if that's what you want, but I need to get into that chamber and finish this quest or else a lot of very bad things are going to happen."

"That's the part you don't seem to understand," said the Matron. "I'm not here to *prevent* very bad things from happening. I'm here to ensure that they do."

The Matron swung her sword at the pillar, and Anne watched with dread as the blade ripped a gash down the side, producing a shower of sparks and exposing bundles of metal wires underneath the smooth exterior. Anne ran forward, knowing she stood no chance against the Matron but knowing equally that she had to at least try.

She grabbed the Matron's arm, but the Matron flung her away and sent her crashing into one of the other chambers. Anne fell to the floor, momentarily dazed. The Matron continued to attack the center pillar, swing after swing, each blow tearing through the outer shell and creating deep, gaping wounds.

Anne jumped to her feet and launched herself forward yet again, this time seizing the sword hilt. The Matron hurled Anne away forcefully, but this time Anne managed to pull the sword from her grip. Anne landed hard beside the end chamber, and the sword clattered onto the glass circle in the floor. She tried to rise, but she fell back, struggling for breath.

The Matron didn't bother to retrieve the sword, but simply tore at the pillar with her metal hand, reaching into the gashes she had already made and yanking out the wires inside.

"She failed," snarled the Matron. "All her elaborate plans to destroy us, all her brilliant scheming, and she still failed. Now she'll never be able to—"

A brilliant flash seared Anne's eyes.

The concussion of the exploding chamber reverberated in the closed space.

The glass floor shattered.

The Matron was thrown backward and tumbled through the open space where the glass had been.

Anne was protected from the blast by the other chambers, all of which were damaged to some degree. She crawled through the debris from the destroyed chamber and over to the edge where the glass floor used to be. The Matron dangled several feet below; her metal hand was entangled in some still-attached wires extending from the center pillar. They were the only thing keeping her from an unthinkable fall. The Matron's face had also been severely burned. Anne thought of all the terrible things the woman had done, all the punishments for minor infractions, all the endless chores and shifts in the coal mine, all the freezing nights with few blankets and no heat. Perhaps this fate was her just deserts.

Then Anne recalled Jocelyn's words, about always having a choice, and after a moment of reflection she sighed and reached over the edge.

"Take my hand," she said.

The Matron coughed. "You could never lift me, child."

Anne extended her gauntlet-hand farther. "Take it."

The Matron smiled a wickedly evil grin. "I told

you…" she said with effort, her words slurring. "I told you that you have no idea what's really going on."

The Matron brought up her other hand, and Anne caught the flash of metal as a thin blade arced through the air. The sword. Anne flinched, but the Matron didn't strike her. She struck the place where her own metal hand attached to her arm and sliced it off. Now free of the entangling wires, the Matron dropped away from the tier. Anne's eyes widened in shock—not at what the Matron had done to herself, but rather at what it had revealed.

Thick black smoke poured from the Matron's severed arm.

The same as Shard.

Anne watched the Matron fall toward the BGFM until there was nothing to see except the wispy trail of black smoke. Only an intensifying heat brought her back to her circumstances. Anne looked behind her. One of the other chambers had erupted into flames, and smoke was rapidly filling the room. Keeping low, Anne scuttled back over to the entrance only to discover that the door had become solid again. She tapped the wall, but the grid didn't appear.

"Hey, did you not hear the part about fires and

enclosed spaces!" said Jeffery, who suddenly appeared in a flash of light. He wasn't solid as per usual, but instead had a transparent, almost ghostly appearance. He also kept flickering erratically.

"Jeffery, where have you been?" asked Anne. "And what's wrong with you?"

"Something was blocking me again. Now it's not. Or at least, not completely."

Anne glanced back at the shattered section of the floor. Back at the tower, Jeffery had only reappeared once they'd reached the top, which was mostly open to the air. If the room itself was the thing blocking him, perhaps the hole in the floor allowed him to appear again.

Anne scanned the room. "We need to get out of here."

"Try one of the other doors."

Anne crouched and ran over to the next section of black wall, which was closer to the burning chamber. The heat was suffocating. She tapped the wall, but nothing happened with that one, either.

"What's wrong?" she said. "Why isn't it working?"

Jeffery shook his head. "Try the last one!"

Before Anne even made it to the third black section of wall, another chamber exploded. The concussion shook the room and sent her tumbling to the floor, and she was hit by burning debris, which she hastily brushed from her cloak. Now two more chambers were on fire.

Anne crawled to the third section of black wall and tapped repeatedly. Nothing happened. She collapsed against the wall in a coughing fit, bracing herself with her gauntlet-hand. As the gauntlet touched the black surface, the wall responded by scanning Anne with a green beam of light. As soon as the beam touched the medallion, the entire section of wall disappeared, revealing a dark space beyond. Anne half-fell, half-crawled through the new doorway and into the pitch-black room. She took a deep breath of the cooler, cleaner air that welcomed her. Smoke poured in from behind, but she had no idea how to reclose the door.

"See if you can find an exit," Anne said to Jeffery.

Jeffery flew ahead of her into the room. The only light was that filtering in through the open doorway, making it difficult to see. Anne felt her way along, banging into crates and tripping over random objects scattered on the floor.

"Over here," called Jeffery from somewhere ahead.

She followed his glow to a stack of crates.

"You need to see what's back here," he said.

"Jeffery, we have to get out of here! If this quest fails,

everything on the tier I'm on might die. So I have to get off the surface..."

Anne left the rest unspoken. She now realized what she had to do. The only way to save Saint Lupin's, to save her home, was to go back to the first room and jump through the shattered floor before the quest deadline expired. At least that way she wouldn't be on any tier when the quest officially ended.

She turned back toward the burning room.

"Trust me," said Jeffery, and something in his voice convinced her to stop and risk a look.

She squeezed herself between the wall and the crates. In a small alcove, hidden by the crates, another pillar rose from the floor. This pillar wasn't smooth and sleek and white like the ones in the first room. This pillar was rough and gray, and it looked as though it had been built out of scraps. Wires dangled out of missing panels. Jeffery landed on the floor next to the pillar and pointed to the engraving at the bottom.

"Look," he said.

The engraving didn't read PROJECT C.R.O.W.N.

It read PROJECT A.N.V.I.L.

It was the final piece of the puzzle, the true throne without a crown.

"Jeffery, how much time is left?" asked Anne.

"Two minutes."

Anne frantically searched the base for a keyhole. Once she located it, she activated the key in the gauntlet and inserted it. The hatch opened. As with the other chambers, the interior was lined with cushions, albeit ones that were worn and dirty. Anne climbed inside. At first nothing happened. Then the hatch shut on its own with a soft click. Instead of being pitch-dark, as she had expected, she found she could still see through the walls to the room beyond. From this side, the hatch was transparent.

"What now?" asked Jeffery.

Anne felt around the space.

"What's this down by my left side?" she asked. "I can't get a good look at it."

Jeffery hopped over. "It looks like some sort of slot."

"Big enough for a gauntlet?"

"Maybe."

Anne hesitated briefly, recalling the gray box on the dead tier, but now wasn't the time to be timid. She jammed her gauntlet-hand into the hole. It clicked into place.

Nothing happened.

Jeffery danced from one foot to the other. "There's less than thirty seconds left."

Anne closed her eyes and thought of the last line of the riddle one more time.

Claim the throne without a crown.

"Twenty seconds."

Claim the throne.

"Ten."

Claim—

"I claim the throne!" Anne shouted.

The interior of the chamber sprang to life. All around them tiny lights turned on, some blinking, others glowing steadily. Words and symbols scrolled across the opening, most too fast for Anne to read. She caught fleeting glimpses of strange phrases like *decryption key* and *upload commencing,* but little else. A whirring noise came from somewhere above her head, and the air inside the chamber cleared of smoke.

A blue square flashed on the window in front of her. She quickly tapped it.

More words appeared:

COMPUTER ACCESS GRANTED.
WRITE ERROR CHECK PROGRAM SUCCESSFULLY UPLOADED.
RIGHTFUL HEIR QUEST COMPLETED.

The last line kept flashing.

There was another click, and Anne found she could remove the gauntlet from the slot. The silver medallion was gone. And the gauntlet felt looser on her hand.

Anne sighed as a flood of emotion washed over her. She turned to Jeffery and smiled. "We did it," she said simply. She rested her head back against the cushions. Despite the odds, despite the many obstacles and the opponents she and her friends had faced, she had finished the quest. She had become the heir, and in a Level Thirteen quest, at that. This was going to take a while to sink in.

"That's it?" said Jeffery. He hopped onto her shoulder and read the flashing words. "It's a bit anticlimactic, if you ask me."

"I'll take it," said Anne.

"What, no lively music? No medals? No dancing flamingos?"

"Well, if you really—"

An explosion rocked the chamber, and the lights and the words disappeared.

"I take it back," said Jeffery in a rush. "I'm fine with a nice boring ending. We can skip the flamingos."

Suddenly, flames were licking the outside of the pillar,

and the temperature in the chamber rose rapidly. Then the hatch was ripped away—or was it blown away?—and smoke poured in. Anne couldn't breathe, and as she coughed, smoke filled her lungs; she became wracked with convulsions. Tears blurred her eyes, and her mouth and throat burned from the scorching air. Dark edges crept into her vision from all sides, but she thought she saw a dark figure looming over the chamber like a phantom floating above her.

Then there was only blackness.

DUE TO THE UNPREDICTABLE NATURE
OF QUEST OUTCOMES, *THE ADVENTURER'S
GUIDE TO HAPPY ENDINGS* OFFERS THE
FOLLOWING DISCLAIMERS:

1) A happy ending cannot be guaranteed.

2) In the interest of fairness, an unhappy ending likewise cannot be guaranteed.

3) The aforementioned lack of guarantees themselves cannot be guaranteed.

4) Fireball Travel Incorporated has redefined *guaranteed* to mean "eaten by a sand wolf."

The Rightful Heir

Anne opened her eyes.

And immediately let out a yelp.

She was lying in a bed—her old bed in her room at Saint Lupin's, or so it looked at first glance. Except the sheets were brand-new and clean and soft, and sitting next to her, staring directly into her face, was a cat. Not just any cat, Anne realized, as her initial shock wore off, but the headmistress of the quest academy: Her Royal Highness Princess Fluffington Whiskers of the Mousetrapper Clan. The orange cat seemed unperturbed by

Anne's reaction. She blinked slowly, curled into a ball, and promptly fell asleep.

Something else was different, too. The gauntlet! Anne was no longer wearing it. She was about to leap from the bed and begin a frantic search when she saw it lying on her nightstand. Even it looked a little cleaner. She looked at her left hand. Given the dramatic way in which the gauntlet had attached itself, she hadn't known what she'd find when it came off (if it ever did come off, that is), so she was greatly relieved to see that her hand was completely normal and unharmed.

Footsteps echoed in the hallway outside, and a moment later the door opened. Jocelyn stood holding a tray of food.

"Finally awake, I see," she said.

Jocelyn walked into the room and set the tray next to the gauntlet. "Wonderful. One of the council healers fireballed by earlier and said she expects you to make a full recovery."

Anne noticed that Jocelyn's eyes seemed slightly puffier than usual and that her voice wasn't quite as bright and chipper.

Anne sat up and looked around the room. "How did I get here?"

"As soon as Nana sent you off at the council yard she realized something was amiss with the coordinates she had received. It turns out they were not coordinates for a specific place, but rather a formula for returning any given traveler to their place of origin. Of course, in your case that worked out and sent you where you needed to be. It took Nana a while to trace where the fireball had actually taken you, though, and by the time Ms. Shatter-blade, Mr. Darkflame, and the rest of us arrived, events had already progressed considerably. Luckily, Rokk was able to pull you out before the lab became completely engulfed in flames."

"Did much survive?"

Jocelyn shook her head. "I'm afraid not. A team of archaeologists has arrived from the council and are sifting through the debris now, but I'm afraid the fire did quite a thorough job."

Anne sighed. That room had held the promise of so many answers. But they were all destroyed, thanks to—

"I'm sorry about your sister," said Anne. "I really did try to save her. I don't know if this helps, but I...I think something might have been controlling her." Anne described their encounter and what the Matron had done at the end, and she also shared everything Shard had said and done and explained about the black smoke in both instances. "There was definitely some connection between the two of them, but I don't know what any of it really means."

Jocelyn turned away momentarily, dabbed her face with a handkerchief, and then turned back. "I felt something terrible must have happened, for her to have changed so much. It doesn't provide all the answers, but it at least gives me a place to start looking, so I thank you for sharing that with me. And it serves as yet another example of your generous spirit." She smiled. "Speaking of which, I must say, I have taught many talented students over the years, but you have distinguished yourself among them. Rarely have I witnessed someone demonstrate such fierce determination, leadership, and self-sacrifice, and at such a young age. I realize we've only known each other a short time, but for what it's worth, I want you to know that I am very proud of you."

Anne warmed at her words. Princess Whiskers snuggled against Anne's leg and purred.

"So, um, what brings the cat here?" asked Anne.

"Why, she's here to officially congratulate you on a job well done. And to present you with this, of course."

Jocelyn picked up a piece of cheap-looking parchment from the tray and handed it to Anne. It was a certificate announcing her successful completion of the Rightful Heir quest. The letters were printed in peeling gold ink. "Framing costs extra."

Anne read the certificate with a big smile on her face. She knew it was just a simple piece of parchment, yet it stood for so much.

Jocelyn handed her another piece of paper. "And here is my final evaluation report."

Anne read this over, too, and her smile faltered slightly. "How come under Goals and Motivations I only received 'satisfactory'?"

"A perfectly acceptable mark for a first quest. Especially a Level Thirteen."

"But I had all kinds of goals and motivations!" Anne ticked them off on her fingers as she listed them. "Escape Saint Lupin's, attend a quest academy, find my real home, avoid life in prison, solve the quest riddle, avoid death, save the world, inherit a kingdom."

"But that's rather the point, isn't it, dear? So many competing threads, each vying for attention. It's all a bit much, to be quite honest. There's a certain elegance to simplicity. Not to worry, though. I'm sure you'll stream-line it better on your next quest. And look, I gave you top marks for blacksmithing."

"But I didn't do any of that. Like, not in the entire quest."

Jocelyn shrugged. "No one really reads these evaluations anyway."

Anne set the two documents aside. "So what now?"

"Well, you're the Rightful Heir. Such a position carries many responsibilities."

Anne had been so busy trying to get through the quest in one piece, she hadn't stopped to consider the significance of actually finishing it (beyond avoiding several horrible and even deadly fates). "Responsibilities?"

Jocelyn swept her arms wide, as if to take in all of their surroundings. "Saint Lupin's isn't going to run itself, dear."

Anne sat bolt upright. "What? You mean I'm actually in charge? What am I going to do with an entire orphanage?"

"Well, I need to speak with you about that. It's a fair question: What *are* you going to do with an orphanage all to yourself? I mean, one person, running an entire kingdom? I expect it would become quite burdensome. Not to mention all the paperwork and taxes and...well, who wants to deal with all that alone?"

"Why do I get the feeling you have something in mind?"

Jocelyn cleared her throat. "Funny you should ask! You see, with the destruction of the academy, we happen to be in need of a new location. Large campus. Buildings suitable for various purposes. Preferably an outdoorsy type of setting. In short, something more or less identical to Saint Lupin's would be ideal, if you take my meaning. Not to mention that when you filled out your application form for the academy, there may have been some minor subclauses regarding liabilities." She looked around the room with interest, as though she were planning its redecoration.

Anne nearly jumped out of bed. "Oh! That would be fantastic! I could give it to you. I mean, it's not exactly a wealthy kingdom or anything."

Jocelyn gently pushed Anne's shoulders till she was lying down, and then she pulled the covers back over her. "That's extremely generous of you, dear, but I was thinking more along the lines of a lease. Legally, you will remain the Rightful Heir. We would simply become your long-term tenants."

"What will happen to the other orphans?"

"Why, they'll become your new classmates, of course. As I said at the beginning, the more the merrier.

And you can rest assured, we'll all take excellent care of the place."

Anne looked at her suspiciously. "You mean take care of it…as in cleaning?"

"Certainly, certainly," said Jocelyn. Anne caught a twinkle in her eye. "Of course, as one of our registered students, you would naturally be assigned your share of the chores."

Anne thought about it, and the more she thought about it, the funnier it struck her. She burst into a fit of laughter.

"I'm not sure I see what's so funny about chores," said Jocelyn.

"It's not that," said Anne with a gasp. "It's about Penelope and me. We're right back where we started. We had such big plans for going on some grand adventure, and we did go on one, but it led us right back here. So much for escaping."

Jocelyn smiled. "I suppose there is a certain humor in it. And speaking of being back, I have a visitor for you." She raised two fingers to her lips and gave a sharp whistle.

A black streak shot through the doorway and leapt up onto the bed, sending Princess Whiskers howling and hissing onto the windowsill.

"Dog!" said Anne as he licked her face profusely.

"One fire lizard, returned safely as promised," said Jocelyn.

"Thank you," said Anne, and she laid back contentedly on the soft pillow as Dog snuggled up to her. "Is that everything?"

"Everything for now," said Jocelyn. "Before I go, however, I must also inform you that Lord Greystone arrived not too long ago and has requested a meeting with the Rightful Heir of Saint Lupin's. I was going to put him off and tell him you weren't yet recovered enough to attend to guests, but you can only avoid him for so long. If you're up to it, it's probably best to get it over with now."

Anne nodded. "That's fine. Today, I can handle Greystone. Today, I think I could handle just about anything. Where is he?"

Jocelyn looked at her meaningfully, and suddenly Anne knew exactly where he was.

The Matron's office was precisely as Anne had left it. The large oak desk, the X on the floor, the chair no one ever sat in. As the tier rotated east, the early-morning sunlight created a kaleidoscope of colors across the glass domes.

Anne entered without knocking.

Neeva, Lord Greystone's crow, watched her from one of the windowsills, but she ignored it. Greystone himself stood in front of the shelves, hands clasped behind his back. He seemed to be studying the inscriptions.

"This is quite a medallion collection you've inherited," he said without turning. "I daresay you'll be the envy of the Hierarchy. Some of these go back thousands of years. There's even a few here I've never heard of, and that's saying something."

"And I suppose congratulations are in order," he said, facing Anne. "Jocelyn informs me you finished your first quest with distinction."

"Are you actually congratulating me, or just pointing it out?" asked Anne, keeping her tone neutral.

"Well, if nothing else, I'm impressed you were able to keep it from me. Hiding in plain sight. That's a bold move."

Anne shrugged. "I didn't really have much choice."

Greystone smiled. "You know, I've decided I like you. You have true heart. The sort of heart that will eventually get you killed, no question, but I admire it nonetheless. It's rarer than you think. Rarer than most of these medallions, I daresay."

Greystone walked behind the Matron's desk, and Anne saw that she had stopped on the X on the floor, probably out of sheer habit. It was only as she stood there that she also noticed a stack of documents on the desk. The pile wasn't straight and neat like the Matron kept her papers. Rather, it had the appearance of having been hastily gathered, as though someone had rifled through the desk drawers and grabbed whatever they could in a short time.

"Speaking of rare objects," said Greystone, "let me also acknowledge your acquisition of that gauntlet. I did a little research after our last meeting. A remarkable feat, no question."

"What do you mean?"

"Come now. That gauntlet isn't just rare, it's beyond rare—one of a kind, in fact, if my sources are correct, and they usually are. It certainly didn't come from one of the council academies. I would ask you where Lady Jocelyn obtained it, but something tells me you would be reluctant to divulge that little secret."

"Jocelyn already told you it's a castoff."

His eyes bored into hers, searching for any hint of deception. "I see. Well, while I'm disinclined to believe that, we'll play it her way for now. Strange, though, don't you think, that you should happen to receive that gauntlet when you did. And that you should have obtained that particular medallion at the same moment. If I didn't know better, I'd say someone had been planning these events for a long time. The precision is remarkable, especially given where you yourself came from."

Anne perked up at this.

"I thought I came from here," she admitted. "Isn't that what the quest proved?"

He stared at her for a moment and then laughed. Not a light mocking laugh like before, but a deep genuine laugh, which frankly made her even more nervous. "Oh, how rich," he said, wiping a tear from his eye. "You really don't know, do you? I admit I missed it myself at first. The eyes should have been an immediate giveaway. But for you yourself not to... Well, if that Matron of yours didn't tell you, far be it from me to ruin the surprise. I must take my leave now, but suffice it to say I expect we'll be seeing each other again, sooner rather than later, I think. I shall look forward it."

Greystone gathered up the loose pile of papers, the crow jumped over to his shoulder, and he walked out from behind the desk.

"Those documents belong to me now," said Anne.

Greystone stopped.

Even though they were several feet apart, he never-theless seemed to tower over her. "By all means, try to take them if you wish."

Anne knew there was no way she could stop him, but she met his gaze without wavering.

"That's what I thought," he said. "Enjoy your cel-ebrations. While you can." He smirked at her one last time and turned to leave. As he turned, Anne caught a glint of something under his collar. Something hanging from a gold chain. Something crystal.

Greystone exited the room.

Anne stood there for a long time, her heart thumping loudly.

Anne and her friends stood by the gate, watching as moving crate after moving crate arrived by fireball from the remains of the old academy: Sassafras's spell books, Copperhelm's weapons, and well over a hundred crates filled with Jocelyn's collection of artifacts. A whole squadron of Fireball Travel Incorporated dragons must have been on the job. It was surprising how many things could survive having a mountain fall on top of them.

Anne told Penelope and Hiro about her encounter with the Matron down in the lab. All three speculated endlessly on what her final words might have meant. She also told them about her meeting with Lord Greystone and showed them the crystal that had belonged to Shard and mentioned the one that the Matron wore. Everyone agreed there must be some connection, but no one knew quite what to make of it.

"So what happened after Nana discovered she couldn't send you after me?" asked Anne.

"Penelope was fantastic," said Hiro. "She put one of the council officers in a headlock and wouldn't let him out until he told his entire squadron to surrender."

Penelope smiled. "Don't sell yourself short. Mr. Wizard here cast a Minor Sticky Tree Sap spell from the catalog, and it exploded big-time and stuck half the battalion to the plaza. They're probably still digging them out."

"And is everything else okay?" Anne asked Hiro. "Everyone's secrets are still safe?"

Hiro smiled and nodded.

"Yeah, some mysterious agent guy from the council dropped by and told us everything is fine," said Penelope. "We're sworn to secrecy, though."

"I also received a note from my parents," said Hiro,

pulling a card out of his pocket and reading from it. "They said they appreciate you accepting me into your adventuring group despite a high-percentage chance I could blow us all up, and they hope your association with me won't mark you both for a swift death at the hands of our family's many, many enemies."

Anne and Penelope gulped.

Hiro tucked the card back into his pocket. "I wouldn't read too much into that last part, by the way. My mother tends to be rather blunt. Mostly that's just her way of saying hello."

They watched as another fireball landed.

"So why aren't we in prison?" asked Anne. "What happened to all the charges?"

"In recognition of your saving the world from certain doom and everything, and also to avoid the embarrassment of being outsmarted by three thirteen-year-olds, the council issued a retroactive permit for the medallion," said Hiro. "The quest is now completely legitimate. Or was. Or whatever."

"Great, after the fact," muttered Anne.

Penelope rubbed her hands together. "When's our next adventure?"

Anne shivered at the thought. "If anyone comes

across another medallion before we're done with our training, keep it as far away from me as possible."

"Anne," said Penelope, "the Matron's old office is full of them, remember? You're surrounded."

She was right. Anne decided the first thing she would do would be to put every last medallion into storage. And also the gauntlet. No more impromptu adventures for her.

"So, what do we do now?" asked Penelope.

Anne shrugged. "This is the new campus. Once everyone gets settled in, we'll probably start classes."

"Aren't you forgetting about the renovations?" asked Hiro.

"What about them?" asked Anne.

"For this to become the new academy, a lot of work needs to be done in order to bring it up to code. The kitchen needs a complete overhaul. There's no hot water in any of the bathrooms. The height of the outer walls was fine under the old building code, but the new code requires at least another two feet. Over a dozen illegal mine shafts need blocking up. And don't even get me started on the zombie sharks."

"You've been here less than a day," said Penelope. "How could you possibly know all of that already?"

Hiro shrugged. "Jocelyn asked me to do a survey of the grounds to see what needed addressing. Speaking of which, I'm supposed to deliver my full list to her now. See you at lunch."

Hiro headed off in the direction of the Manor.

Anne and Penelope continued to watch the fireballs arrive. It was, admittedly, rather memorizing.

"So," said Anne after a while.

"So?" said Penelope.

"Not quite the castle you had envisioned."

Penelope shrugged. "It'll do for now."

"Thanks for sticking with me, Pen."

"Are you kidding me?" said Penelope. "I'm the one who should be thanking you for making me part of your group." She grinned mischievously. "Although I still say I could have tossed you aboard that ship."

"A theory we're definitely not going to test, and shall henceforth refer to as Plan Don't Even Think About It," said Anne.

Penelope stretched. "You know, I think I'm really going to like it here. It feels like a completely different place."

Despite any number of as-yet-unanswered questions, Anne knew exactly what she meant.

"Yoo-hoo, students," Jocelyn called from across the yard. "Time to get ready for the victory celebration! I have a list of chores for each of you."

Penelope slapped Anne on the shoulder. "Of course, some things never change, eh?"

Well past midnight, after the celebrating was over, everyone headed off to bed. Penelope and Anne returned to their room, and Penelope immediately fell fast asleep under a double pile of thick blankets, snoring not-so-softly.

Anne lay in her own bed, wide awake. The events of the past five and a half days flashed through her mind in a collage of sound and color: the gauntlet, the silver medallion, travel by fireball, the quest academy, Shard, sand wolves, the Infinite Tower, Rokk the robot, portals, the Construct, the computer, the Wizards' Council, and the Matron, not to mention Lord Greystone's final words to her and his crystal pendant. And yet over and over, Anne returned to a single question: What exactly was her connection to Saint Lupin's? She had been so certain her yellow eyes would provide the link to wherever it was she came from, but now she wasn't so sure.

At the very least, it was clearly more complex than she had originally assumed.

Anne gazed at the gauntlet on the nightstand. Pale moonlight glinted off the metal strips.

"Jeffery?" she whispered.

Jeffery appeared in a flash of light. "Hey," he whispered back.

She smiled in the glow of his bright rainbow-colored feathers. "I wasn't sure if you'd still be here."

He tapped the gauntlet with his foot. "Well, technically, I'm always here. But yeah, once a quest is over, the GPS is supposed to shut off, too. Which is good, because I'm really sleepy. But I figured I'd hang around a little longer to say good-bye."

"When will I see you again?"

"When you activate a new quest."

"But that could take years."

"I'll still be here." He peered at her. "Why? Was there something you needed?"

Anne shook her head. "I just wanted to say thank you. We couldn't have done it without you."

"It's all part of the job." He gave her a salute with his tiny wing and disappeared, and she knew he was gone for good this time, or at least for this quest.

Anne snuggled deep under her own thick quilts, resting her head on the soft feather pillow. She didn't know what lay ahead exactly, but she was determined to prepare herself as best she could. She might not have gotten all the answers she wanted, but at least now she had a means of searching for them.

She was, after all, a Keeper of the Sparrow.

THE
(PROBABLY
NOT QUITE)
END

A Kind of Epilogue

And so Anne became the Rightful Heir, and the Kingdom of Saint Lupin's became the official home of the newly minted Saint Lupin's Quest Academy. Princess Whiskers took over the Matron's office and spent most of her time either sleeping on her cushion or batting around the prophecy medallions, while Dog resumed his place in the basket in the corner. However, since Nana also insisted on continuing to sleep in the office, everyone who entered the room had to climb over her tail, and eventually they elected to hold all staff meetings in the bathroom down the hallway.

Rokk moved into the bell tower and rang the bell every hour on the hour. His timekeeping was accurate to one one-millionth of a second.

When Hiro wasn't busy making lists of things that needed fixing (mostly of things he himself had blown up), he spent much of his time helping Sassafras search for his lost slippers or chasing stray poodles. Captain Copperhelm trained Penelope in advanced sword fighting techniques—that is, until she accidentally stabbed him in the buttocks. And Anne helped Jocelyn prepare the new campus. They hired top instructors from all over the Hierarchy, installed hot showers in the bathrooms, and sent the iron knights to work in the coal mines.

In the end, they also kept the zombie sharks.

Just in case.

Oh, and the red-covered guidebook with the gash in it, tucked carefully under Anne's mattress, finally managed a title that made sense. It read: *The Adventurer's Guide to Magickal Book Repair (Please!)*

OSWALD: OPEN FOLDER/PROJECT ANVIL

M70: FOLDER OPENED.

OSWALD: STATUS UPDATE

M70: "RIGHTFUL HEIR QUEST" COMPLETED. LEVEL
ONE DIAGNOSTIC RESULTS: A WRITE ERROR HAS BEEN
DETECTED.

OSWALD: ISOLATE BAD SECTOR

M70: UNABLE TO COMPLY.

OSWALD: INITIATE FULL FORMAT

M70: UNABLE TO COMPLY. YOUR ACCESS LEVEL DOES NOT
ALLOW YOU TO DESTROY/RECREATE/RESET THE WORLD.

OSWALD: RUN LEVEL TWO DIAGNOSTIC

M70: COMMAND ACCEPTED. INITIATING DIAGNOSTIC. NOW
LOADING "DRAGON SLAYER QUEST."

The Secret Epilogue

N ot long after these events, in the lower levels of the Hierarchy, on a tier as yet unseen by modern eyes, in a castle untouched for many thousands of years, across a screen coated in dust so thick it would take you several minutes of solid scrubbing and maybe even a small hammer and chisel to get it really nice and clean, appeared the following:

LOGIN NAME: OSWALD

PASSWORD: *****

M70: WELCOME BACK USER OSWALD. IT HAS BEEN THREE MILLION SIX HUNDRED FIFTY-SEVEN THOUSAND ONE HUN- DRED SEVENTY-EIGHT DAYS SINCE YOUR LAST LOGIN.

FIRST-YEAR READING LIST FOR WOULD-BE ADVENTURERS

(If you haven't run away screaming after reading the list, you might have a chance.)

—◆◇◆◇◆◇◆—

QUESTING 101

- *The Adventurer's Guide to Adventurer's Guides: The Best Guide for Determining the Best Guide for You*
- *The Keeper's Handbook*, 23rd Edition
- *Nez and the Art of Gauntlet Maintenance*
- *Introduction to Sparrow Psychology*
- *Five Hundred Impractical Outfits for Adventurers*
- *Dead Keepers of the Hierarchy and How They Met Their Ultimate Demise*

HISTORY OF ADVENTURING 101

- *A Complete History of the Hierarchy (Minus the Boring Parts)*
- *A Complete History of Adventuring: Fact vs. Fiction vs. Hearsay vs. Stuff Your Uncle Once Told You When You Were a Kid vs. Things People Sometimes Mumble in Their Sleep*
- *The Book of General Knowledge Not Generally Known*

COMBAT 101

- *Your Sword: More Than Just a Pointy Stick to Annoy Your Friends With*
- *The Pacifist's Guide to Basic Combat*
- *The Fine Art of Pillow Fighting*
- *Squirrels: Friend or Weapon?*

MAGICK 101

- *An Introduction to Magick and Why You Should Probably Never Use It*
- *Magick: A User's Guide (Bandages Included)*
- *Magick Without a Hitch: How to Determine Your Cost for Magick Without Losing Your Hair (Unless, of Course, Your Cost for Magick IS Losing Your Hair, in Which Case Sorry but We Can't Help You)*
- *The Rules of Magick for Mannequins*

DRAGONS 101

- *Travel by Fireball: Innovation of the Century or Just One More Stupid Way to Get Yourself Killed*
- *Red Means Dead*
- *Why Humans Make Good Toothpicks*
- *What to Do When a Dragon Sits on You (and Other Helpful Tips)*

ACKNOWLEDGMENTS

First and foremost, my thanks to my family: to my wife, Wendy, for her support, counsel, cheerleading, and occasional nudging, and for being the person who makes me laugh more than anyone else in the whole world; to Josh, Greg, and Zach, for reading (or listening to me read) many drafts of this book and still laughing at all the right parts; to Phil, for reading and critiquing way more drafts than any reasonable person should ever be asked to read (including the first draft, which no one should ever be asked to read) and giving invaluable feedback; to Lisa and Mom for their ongoing enthusiasm and encouragement; and in memory of Dad, who I think would have found it funny, especially travel by fireball.

Thanks to my wonderful agent, Elizabeth Kaplan, for her sharp wit and steady guidance, and for believing in the book in the first place and continuing to work tirelessly on my behalf. May all your flowers bloom in season.

Many thanks as well to my eagle-eyed editor, Lisa Yoskowitz, for her brilliant insights and unwavering passion for Anne and her story, to Mariano Epelbaum for his fantastic artwork, and to the entire team at Little,

Brown Books for Young Readers, including (but not limited to) Kheryn Callender, Maggie Edkins, Jen Graham, Jeff Campbell, Saraciea Fennell, Jessica Shoffel, Melanie Chang, and Megan Tingley, who helped transform this author's words into the book you now hold in your hands.

My thanks to the following readers and fellow writers who read some version of the story, whether in whole or in part, and provided me with such insightful and thoughtful comments: Betsy Aldredge, Tim Beers, Aimee Blume, Juliana L. Brandt, Ken Byars, Sarah Byrne, Laura Capasso, Senner Dan, Julie Dao, Arielle Datz, Kit Davis, Cale Dietrich, Sandy Fetchko, Tatum Flynn, Jane Forni, Keith Grant, Robert M. Graves, Mary Hallberg, Jeanne Haskin, Rita de Heer, Naomi Hughes, Michelle Hulse, Kathryn Jankowski, Kimberly Johnson, Michael Keyton, Kim Long, Casey Lyall, Rebekah Maxner, Danayi Munyati, Katrina Oppermann, Dragon Paradise, L. K. Pinaire, Sarah Schauerte, Caitlin Sinead, Phillip Spencer, Kimberly Vanderhorst, Sue Wachtman, Max Wirestone, and Kim J. Zimring. My thanks as well to everyone in the Best Word writers' group for being a great support and cheering me on.

A huge thank-you also to the following younger readers: Heidi, Robyn, and Sarah.

And finally, my thanks to the squirrel who bit me when I was ten years old. Your contribution to this book should be self-evident.

KEEP READING FOR A SNEAK PEEK AT ANNE, PENELOPE, AND HIRO'S NEXT ADVENTURE!

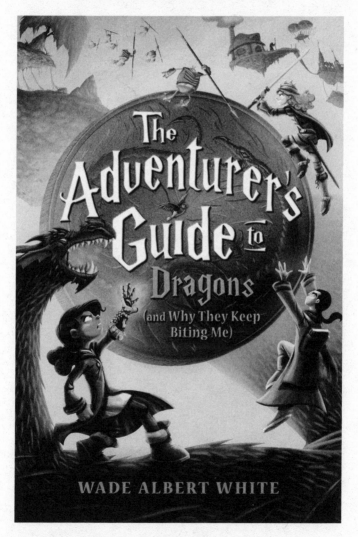

The Sapphire Palace

Anne was leaving Saint Lupin's.

The annual Quest Academy Awards were being held that evening in the Hierarchy's capital, and Anne and the other members of her adventuring group had learned they were nominated in the category of Best Illegal Quest That Nearly Destroyed the Entire World. The category wasn't as prestigious as Longest Duel with a Rabid Pumpernickel, but it was certainly preferable to Most Spectacular Protagonist Death, since you actually had to die in order to be eligible—meaning they buried the award with you (or whatever was left of you). Award nominees enjoyed a fancy lunch at the royal palace, got front-row seats to the awards ceremony, and were invited to a host of after-parties where people sat around on uncomfortable chairs, held drinks decorated with little umbrellas, and pretended to like one another. It was quite an honor.

There was only one problem: Anne didn't want to go.

Or more accurately, she didn't want to go if it meant wearing her new formal academy dress uniform.

Anne winced as a needle jabbed into her thumb.

"My apologies, dear," said the woman standing next to her. Her name was Jocelyn, and she was for all intents and purposes the headmistress of Saint Lupin's Quest Academy (if you overlooked the fact that, according to the official paperwork, the actual headmistress was an orange-and-white cat named Her Royal Highness Princess Fluffington Whiskers of the Mousetrapper Clan, who was currently sleeping atop a cushion on the desk next to them). Jocelyn had dark brown skin, a head of voluminous, meticulously styled black hair, and twinkling brown eyes.

Anne always noticed people's eyes, mostly in hopes of someday finding others with yellow eyes just like her own.

They were in the academy's main office, an octagonal

room lined with wall-to-wall shelves and three large stained-glass windows. Anne was standing on a stool, trying to remain as still as possible, while Jocelyn fussed and fidgeted with her new formal uniform, which had only arrived that morning. Anne watched as a tiny bead of red formed on her dark brown skin where Jocelyn had poked her. She pressed a finger over it to stop the bleeding. Apparently, a quest academy could be a dangerous place even if you were just getting dressed.

Jocelyn regathered the loose material of Anne's cloak and continued jabbing at it with her needle. "I cannot believe they got your size wrong," Jocelyn said for the umpteenth time. "I sent them everyone's exact measurements. All the others fit just fine."

Given that the uniforms had arrived in a box marked HORRIBLE HENRY'S TERRIBLE UNIFORM SHOP: THE PLACE TO BUY YOUR UNIFORM WHEN YOUR BIG DAY HAS ARRIVED AND ALL OTHER OPTIONS HAVE RUN OUT, Anne was surprised anyone's had fit properly. But they had, and so her best friends, Penelope Shatterblade and Hiro Darkflame— who were the only other students at the academy besides Anne—had gone ahead to the capital while she remained behind getting hers altered.

After a few more swipes of the needle, Jocelyn tied

off a final knot and stood back. She smoothed out the wrinkles of her own bright yellow jacket, which had pearl buttons down the front and coordinated well with her light brown pants and dark red leather riding boots. As always, Jocelyn looked every bit the professional adventurer, albeit one who spent more time in the library doing research or in a well-padded gymnasium practicing her sword fighting than going on actual adventures where one might come into contact with dirt or grime or unpleasantness of any kind.

Jocelyn studied her handiwork. "I never claimed to be much of a seamstress, so hopefully that will suffice."

Anne looked down. The cloak was a sickly green and featured a wide, floppy collar and three oversized pockets. It was also several inches too long. The material bunched at her sides, and multiple threads crisscrossed one another in a haphazard pattern. The rest of the uniform consisted of a pair of stark white pants that attracted dirt like a magnet, a blinding orange tunic, and a pair of stiff leather boots that were already causing Anne's feet to blister. In addition, she also wore her most prized possession: a single brown leather glove covered in strips of overlapping metal, with a circular inset on the underside of the wide extended cuff. This was her questing gauntlet.

"So," said Jocelyn, "what do you think?"

"Er," said Anne.

"Still too loose?"

"No, that's not the problem."

Jocelyn picked up a wide-brimmed hat that featured a black veil and a large peacock feather sticking out of the top. "Shall we try the headpiece?"

Anne grimaced.

Jocelyn caught her expression. "Did I forget one of the pins?"

"No," said Anne. "It's just…"

"Yes, dear?"

"It's just…the uniform…it's…"

Jocelyn nodded encouragingly. "Yes?"

Anne sighed. "It's ugly."

At first Anne thought Jocelyn would scold her for being ungrateful. Instead, Jocelyn burst into laughter. "Oh, my dear, you're absolutely right. The whole thing is a disaster, in every way possible. The design is an affront to fashion, and the colors are giving me a headache. And even Dog would do a better job with the alterations." At the mention of his name, Dog, the small black fire lizard napping in a basket in the corner of the room, briefly raised his head. Seeing nothing of interest, he dropped immediately back to sleep.

Jocelyn tossed the hat back on the desk. "Headgear is optional. Unfortunately, there's nothing to be done about the rest. And anyway, this ridiculous outfit is not what's important. It's you, the newly minted Rightful Heir of Saint Lupin's. That's who people will be eager to meet."

"Does that mean I can wear one of my regular outfits instead?" asked Anne.

"No," said Jocelyn.

"But you just said—"

"Dress uniforms are required at such functions. Anything else would go against proper etiquette."

"Do we always have to follow proper etiquette?"

Jocelyn raised an eyebrow, and Anne sighed inwardly. Jocelyn would give up breathing air before she would give up proper etiquette.

A distant chime sounded from elsewhere in the building, and Jocelyn looked out the window. "My goodness, is it noon already?" she said. "We need to be on our way." Jocelyn belted a rapier around her waist.

Anne walked over to an eight-foot-tall suit of armor

near the door—an iron knight, one of three that belonged to the academy, or rather to Anne, since she had inherited them along with the rest of Saint Lupin's upon the completion of her first quest. They obeyed her commands, provided she was wearing the gauntlet. Curiously, they each also had a small white stone in the middle of their helmets that glowed red whenever they grew agitated. The knight by the door held a plain wooden box.

Anne paused.

"Is something wrong?" asked Jocelyn.

"Are we sure it's safe?" asked Anne. "For me to travel around wearing the gauntlet, I mean."

"Why wouldn't it be?"

Anne shifted uncomfortably. "Because the last time I put it on, it activated a Level Thirteen quest that nearly killed me and my friends and the entire world along with it."

"Hence your award nomination," said Jocelyn with a note of pride. She placed an arm around Anne and gave her shoulder a reassuring squeeze. "That gauntlet marks you for what you are, my dear: You're Anvil of Saint Lupin's, Keeper of the Sparrow."

Anne cringed at the mention of her real name. She'd been an orphan from birth, and she had always assumed whoever had named her hadn't given it much thought. All of that had changed two months ago when she discovered that beneath the academy grounds were the remains of an Old World laboratory, and inside that lab were the remains of a chamber that was inscribed with the phrase PROJECT A.N.V.I.L. Exactly what the project was and what it had to do with Anne was still a mystery, not the least because the lab had been completely destroyed in a fire, leaving no clues. In fact, pretty much everything about Anne was a mystery.

"Besides," Jocelyn continued, "it will be in its box most of the time, and in any case you've been wearing it here for the past hour surrounded by all of these." She gestured to the thousands of medallions lining the shelves of the office. Each medallion sat on a piece of padded felt underneath its own glass dome, and each contained within it a quest that could be activated by inserting the medallion into the slot of a questing gauntlet. Anne remembered only too well what had happened two months previous, when she had put on that gauntlet in this very office, only to have a tiny silver medallion fly through the air and attach itself to the slot—an unheard-of occurrence, according to Jocelyn. Typically, medallions did not insert themselves.

Anne smiled. "Thanks. I definitely want to wear it. It's just..."

Jocelyn smiled back. "Perfectly understandable, dear."

Anne gestured to the iron knight, and it followed her and Jocelyn down the long hallway, through the main lobby, and out the front doors. The grounds were empty. Although anyone could go on a quest, the academy typically accepted only students aged thirteen or older. Any orphans younger than that who had lived there while it was still an orphanage (which aside from Anne and Penelope were all of them) had been found suitable homes. The trio proceeded over the drawbridge (which spanned the moat filled with zombie sharks) and up the hill to a small observatory.

As they walked along, Anne spotted several massive islands floating in the distant sky. These were known as tiers, and the entire world, including Saint Lupin's, was made up of them. The tiers orbited a giant sphere known as the Big Glowing Field of Magick, or BGFM, and together they formed what was known as the Hierarchy.

Next to the observatory was a circle of flat stones, and lying in the grass next to the circle was a twenty-foot-long dragon with black scales, tiny wings, and a spiked tail. At the sound of approaching footsteps, the dragon opened a single emerald-green eye.

"Hi, Nana," said Anne.

"Took you long enough," Nana replied in her low, rumbling growl.

"Anne's uniform required a few last-minute adjustments," Jocelyn explained.

Nana studied the cloak. "Are you sure it doesn't require a few more?"

"Now, now. That'll be quite enough of that," said Jocelyn. "Just transport us to the capital, if you please. We're late enough as it is. And make sure you follow along immediately. Showing up without a dragon would make us the laughingstock of the entire ceremony."

"Am I getting paid overtime for this?" asked Nana.

"The honor of being nominated is payment enough."

Nana snorted. "That's what I figured."

Anne removed her gauntlet and placed it in the box being carried by the iron knight. She tucked the box under her arm, and then she and Jocelyn walked to the center of the stone circle.

Nana reared back. "Two fireballs to the capital city, coming right up—from one highly intelligent, constantly overworked, and severely underpaid dragon."

Jocelyn opened her mouth, presumably to scold Nana again, but the dragon was faster and spewed out a ball of green flame.

Light & Lens Photography

WADE ALBERT WHITE

was born in Canada, has spent an hour and a half in Hawaii, and once dug a well in West Kalimantan, because it seemed as good a place as any. In addition to writing, he teaches part-time, dabbles in animation and filmmaking, and is a stay-at-home dad. Wade lives in Nova Scotia with his wife, three sons, and their cat. He invites you to visit him online at wadealbertwhite.com.

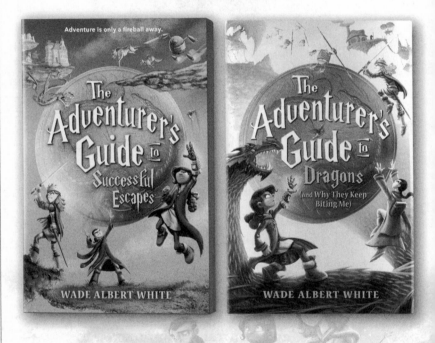